RUIN ME

BECKETT BROTHERS

BOOK 3

L A GALLAGHER

For the readers who prefer their heroes dark, their flags red–and fully erected. 😉

Chapter One

AVERY

Shagging the best man is practically a rite of passage, for a bridesmaid, right? Especially when said best man is tall, dark, and painfully handsome. Raw masculinity radiates from every square inch of Killian Beckett's suited, sculpted, six-foot-four frame. The broody bastard is blessed with a jaw sharp enough to cut steel, lips that I can't help wondering what would feel like *all* over my body, and huge onyx-like eyes that could melt the pants off every woman within a ten-mile radius.

Oh, who am I kidding?

A million-mile radius.

The man is a fucking ride.

Unfortunately, said best man may look hotter than a beach bonfire in Barbados, but he has the personality of a polar ice cap, and just so happens to be the most detached and emotionless creature to grace—and I use that word reluctantly—this earth.

Killian stands stoically beneath the lavish floral arch overlooking St. Flamand's Beach, the turquoise water twinkling in the distance. He watches as his brother, James, exchanges moving, poignant vows with my best friend, Scarlett, without so much as a single flicker of emotion.

What is wrong with him?

I'm not even sure I believe in the concept of marriage, but I can barely see through the tears I'm blinking back. These two gorgeous, love-struck creatures, gazing into each other's starry eyes before us, would make anyone think twice.

'You may kiss the bride,' the registrar says in a thick French accent.

James wastes no time claiming his wife's lips in a way that has every single woman in the vicinity swooning—including me.

It's official—I need to get laid.

A hundred and fifty guests burst into a raucous round of applause. Whistles, cheers and wails pierce the air a split second before the super-hot rock band, Driftwood & Dawn, break into their own acoustic version of 'Ho Hey' by The Lumineers.

James's lips are still firmly locked on his bride's. His large, tanned hands drift over her waist. Three years, and two baby girls later, and they're still kissing like they're horny love-struck teenagers. A pang of longing shoots through my soul.

'Easy,' Killian drawls in a deep, velvety baritone that slides over my spine and seeps into my skin. 'There are kids present.' He nods towards his two nieces, Harper and Halle, in the front row. In matching ivory silk flower girl dresses, they're equally as stunning as their parents as they struggle to break free from the strong grip of their grandparents, Vivienne and Alexander Beckett.

The crowd laughs and James drags himself away from Scarlett with a wolfish grin. He takes her hand in his and raises it into the air, brandishing it triumphantly, blowing their daughters several kisses before guiding Scarlett back down the plush ivory carpet the hotel laid out for them.

No expense has been spared for the wedding of the year. Thousands of white orchids cascade over the custom-built marble pergola, their petals dancing in the warm Caribbean breeze. Chairs draped in baby pink silk ribbons line either side of the aisle, creating an ethereal effect against an opulent white wooden deck. Rose gold lanterns hang from shepherd's hooks, their crystals catching the late afternoon sun. Security personnel in perfectly tailored suits dot the perimeter, earpieces glinting in the sun. Killian's men, no doubt. Killian owns Beckett Security—the most successful security company in Europe. Suited men scrutinise everything and everyone with that same intense focus their boss is famous for. Though with the combined net worth of the Beckett brothers in attendance, I suppose one can't be too careful. Each brother has carved out their own billion-dollar empire under the family umbrella—hotels, security, property, nightclubs.

Killian steps forward and stares at me, his deep dark orbs penetrate mine and it's like he can see all the way down to my soul—and he finds it utterly infuriating. His tailored tuxedo bunches over his huge bicep as he thrusts out a muscular arm. I stare at it for a long beat before realising I'm supposed to take it. As I slip my arm through his, he flinches. I take a deep breath and the scent of his rich, woody cologne swirls between us. A thick current of electricity pulses in my panties.

Yep—I definitely need to get laid if I'm swooning over this emotionless Neanderthalic baboon.

I'm a glamour model—a profession significantly less glamorous than the glossy images suggest. My life mainly consists of early call times, uncomfortable poses, and endless hours under scrutiny. My relentless schedule leaves precious little time for dating, much to my chagrin. However, next month I have a potentially life-altering meeting with ELEGANCE,

America's premier women's magazine, known for featuring women of substance alongside style. The opportunity represents more than just another photoshoot—it's a potential bridge between my psychology doctorate and public platform, ideally opening doors to ventures that engage both my intellect and my admittedly photogenic attributes. Landing this contract would transform my chaotic schedule of scattered shoots across Europe into a focused, lucrative partnership offering ten times the exposure with a fraction of the travel—finally giving me breathing room for something resembling a personal life. And maybe, just maybe, some time to date.

We fall into a slow step side by side, following the bride and groom down the aisle. I plaster a giant smile on my face as we wave at the guests. Killian grimaces, offering the odd grunt or nod of acknowledgement.

'Have you prepared your speech?' I whisper from the side of my lips, waving at Ivy, our new friend, and future wife of Caelon Beckett, Killian's other older brother. Ivy looks stunning in an off the shoulder apricot silk gown that cascades to the ground like a waterfall. For a while there, Caelon could give Killian a run for his money in the cold stakes, but since Ivy stormed into his life and into his heart, he's back to his usual charming self.

A brief flicker of a frown furrows Killian's brows before he composes himself. 'Do I look like a man who would come unprepared?'

'I don't want to think about what you look like when you come anywhere.' I arch a single eyebrow.

Liar.

What I wouldn't give to see Mr Control Freak lose every single one of his senses because he was feral with desire—but I'll die before admitting that out loud. I'd bet everything I own that the man is an animal when he eventually does let go.

It's always the quiet ones. I like my men the same way I like my martinis—dirty. And everything about Killian Beckett promises primal, filthy sex.

Killian gives a subtle shake of his head, but he doesn't bite.

Guess I'll have to try a bit harder. Goading him has become my favourite pastime since we got here three days ago.

'There's prepared, and then there's prepared,' I murmur, blowing a kiss to Caelon's daughter, Orla, before leaning closer to the hunk of steel beside me. 'Did you bang one off in the shower this morning in case you got lucky tonight? Or is some poor unfortunate woman about to be treated to all three seconds of pleasure?'

I glance up to see his jaw tighten. A vein pulses in his temple.

Bingo.

Wicked delight dances in my chest.

'You needn't worry about it either way, *Eye-full Avery*,' he mutters dryly.

'That was one tiny mistake!' I grab his bicep and pinch it as hard as I can.

It wasn't my fault Anton Roche, Paris's sleaziest paparazzo, caught me in a compromising position as I exited a limo at Paris Fashion week. Rage rips through me every time I think about it. I have no problem whipping my breasts out for the camera. Hell, I've made an entire career out of it, but some things should be sacred. Having half my vag printed in the trashiest tabloids with the slogan *"Wardrobe Whoops— Avery gives Paris Fashion Week an "Eye-full,"* was a disgusting violation.

Thank fuck for laser hair removal.

Killian scoffs. 'It was yet another ploy for attention. You just can't get enough of the stuff.'

'Actually, it wasn't. That was one of the worst weeks of my life, not that you care.'

Killian says nothing, as usual, but something—I have no idea what—registers in his pupils.

We slow to a stop as we reach the end of the aisle. Cameras flash blindingly all around us as the photographer, Thorne Blackwood, snaps Scarlett and James from every angle.

Thorne is Dublin's most sought after photographer. We've worked together several times since Zack Kiel, my over-bearing agent, walked into the Luxor Lounge the week before my graduation and offered me a life-changing modelling contract. Thorne specialises in glamour shoots, probably because he's a creepy horn-dog, but there's no denying he's a seriously talented creepy horn-dog.

James had to pull every string going, and pay triple his daily rate to get him to agree to fly out here for this, but only the best will do and, like him or not, Thorne is the best photographer I've ever worked with. The fact he's had a ques-tionable peak in his pants each time he's photographed me is something I'd rather forget. And if James so much as suspects a twitch in Thorne's nether regions while he's photographing Scarlett, it will be the last twitch he ever gets. The Beckett brothers are notoriously possessive of their women, a trait which should raise serious concern yet oddly, I find hot as fuck.

'Avery.' Thorne's beady eyes light as they rake over my blush pink bridesmaid dress. It accentuates every curve I possess—and I have plenty. He beckons me over as Scarlett and James turn to their guests, swamped with congratulatory hugs and kisses.

I attempt to tug my arm free from Killian's, but he squeezes it tighter beneath his bicep, pinning me in position by his side. I glance up at him quizzically. His attention is firmly focused on Thorne. Specifically on the tiny tent in Thorne's crotch. Beige linen trousers are doing less than fuck-all to hide his excitement.

Shit.

Killian is a military trained killer. Plus, he has an army of other trained killers at his disposal. He says little, but he misses nothing.

Thorne has no idea of the level of danger he's in.

'Great to see you!' I lie, waving at Thorne and tugging Killian sideways.

'Just gonna grab a glass of champagne,' I motion to the crystal fountain, 'then we'll be right back.'

'Good. I'm going to need *lots* of photos of the bridesmaid.' Thorne's gaze drops to my breasts. 'And maybe tomorrow I could take a few of you on the beach.'

Killian drops my arm abruptly, pouncing forward grace-fully and silently to tower over Thorne before he can consider he might have overstepped.

'You have a fucking job to do. Go fucking do it, before I'm forced to do mine. And you don't want to know what I do for a living,' Killian hisses.

Wow. Mr Control Freak isn't quite as emotionless and detached as he appears. There's something seriously fucking hot about a hard man, and I'm not referring to the man who's sporting a baby-sized boner.

Thorne takes a step back and scowls at Killian before spinning on his heel. He starts frantically snapping shots of James and Scarlett, who are now surrounded by giddy guests.

'Does he always sport a micro boner when he's working?' Killian snatches my arm up again, tucks it beneath his, and frog marches me away. If it weren't in the direction of the champagne fountain, I might object, but I need a drink.

'Yep.' I watch as Killian snatches up a crystal champagne flute and holds it beneath the stream of fizzing bubbles.

'The guy's a creep.' He hands me the drink, his black eyes narrow as his line of sight trails back to Thorne.

'He is, but he's harmless.' I shrug, bringing the glass to my lips.

'Unfortunately for him, I'm not.' Killian touches his ever present earpiece. 'Eyes on the photographer at all times.'

I roll my eyes. 'I'm pretty sure the best man isn't supposed to be working today.'

'I excel at multitasking.' Our eyes lock, and my mind plummets straight to the gutter.

I don't even like this man and for some reason, I'm wondering if he'd circle my clit with his fingers while he fucks me.

Jesus fucking Christ.

I'm as bad as Thorne.

Thankfully, I don't have a baby-sized boner tenting my pants to reflect it.

Despite the sun beating down on my bare arms, my skin prickles with a weird sensation—like someone's staring at me. I glance around, scanning the guests. Clearly I've been watching too many true crimes documentaries because no one is paying me any attention. No one except Killian, that is.

I down the glass of champagne and hold it beneath the fountain for a refill. Man, I need to get one of these things for my kitchen.

'One more, then that's your lot until dinner,' Killian warns cooly. He stares pointedly at the drink in my hand.

'Who the fuck are you? My father?' I scowl. Of all the handsome, hot billionaires at this wedding, and I get lumped with the dryest shite around.

'Thankfully, no. But I am the man who has to dance with you in front of all of these guests later.' He sweeps a hand around the elegantly dressed crowd. 'Unfortunately.'

Ouch.

I don't know what I ever did to Killian Beckett, but the man hates me.

Well, hate might be a strong word for an emotionless fucker, but he clearly doesn't like me.

'You have such a charming way with words.' I snort, sink my second glass of champagne, then reach for another refill. Defiance races through my blood.

'Wait until you hear my speech.' He deadpans, snatching a tumbler of whiskey from a passing waitress.

'Don't forget to mention how pretty the bridesmaid looks.' I poke him in the chest with my index finger.

He flinches. 'You want me to lie in front of all these people?'

'Twat.' I huff out a breath.

'Right, let's get these fucking photos over with.' He adjusts his silk bow tie.

'I'm going to need another drink before I can fake a smile standing next to you.' I'm not even joking.

'Avery,' his voice drops to a dangerously low level.

Fuck him.

'Yes, Dad?' I smile sarcastically and help myself to another top up.

'Don't call me that,' he growls.

'Why not?' Every minute hair on my body stands to attention as electricity crackles over my skin. I'm disgusted with how viscerally my vagina reacts to this ignorant fucker.

He snatches the champagne glass from my hands and stares at me with enough heat to melt the diamonds dripping from my neck. 'Because the last woman who called me Daddy ended up getting spanked so hard she couldn't sit down for a week. Now move.'

Fuck.

KILLIAN

When James asked me to be his best man, I thought he was joking. Sadly, the joke is on me. Now I'm paired up with the chaotic, loud, attention-seeking Avery Williams. And unfortunately for me, her mouth is as big as her beautiful tits. It's taking every bit of willpower I possess not to stare. Especially when I know what she's hiding under that figure-hugging taffeta dress. There isn't a man on this planet who hasn't seen a photo of Avery topless and for some reason that irritates the shit out of me almost as much as she does.

She's beyond irritating—but there's no denying she's stunning.

Although, she's about to be stunningly drunk if she doesn't stop chugging back the champagne like a student at a free bar.

I watch from my position beside James at the confetti-covered bridal table as she weaves gracefully through the guests, pausing to chat, or air kiss on the way to the bar. The sun set over the sea several hours ago and I just have one more best-man duty to do before I'm off the hook.

The meal is over.

I survived the speeches, thank fuck.

I couldn't bring myself to say Avery looked pretty.

It would have been a lie.

She looks fucking phenomenal.

I couldn't bring myself to say that either. Instead, I settled for the word beautiful, and looked at everyone except her when the words left my lips.

'Great speech,' James says from my left. He claps a huge hand on my back and I battle a grimace. PDAs aren't my thing. In fact, I can hardly tolerate being touched at all. 'Thanks for being my best man,' James continues, his voice thick with emotion as he reaches for his whiskey. My two older brothers have turned soft since they fell in love. 'You were the best brother for the job.'

'It's an honour.' I'd do anything for my brothers. Even kill for them.

'You were the best choice.' James brings his glass to his lips without taking his eyes from Scarlett as she hands their daughter Halle to our sister, Zara. 'Rian's too fucking wild. Caelon has his head so far up Ivy's ass I can see his shit-eating grin every time she opens her mouth. And Sean, well, he's just Sean, isn't he?'

Sean's a mystery to all of us. There's barely a year between us, but he's the brother I know least. He goes out drinking with Rian a lot, but he doesn't indulge in women the same way Rian does. I sometimes wonder if he has different tastes completely.

'Ready to do this?' James looks at the band. They're setting up on the white wood dancefloor overlooking the beach. Fairy lights adorn every available surface, along with ivory lanterns and huge flickering church candles.

'One dance and my best man duties are complete.' The prospect of holding Avery in my arms churns in my stomach, not because I'm repulsed by her—quite the opposite in fact—

but she's everything I avoid in my life. Avery lives for the limelight. I live for the quiet solace of the shadows.

'You never know, you might enjoy yourself.' James quirks a thick eyebrow as he rises from the table. 'Either way, Avery won't be short of willing men to dance with.'

Heat sparks in my chest, but my lips remain firmly pressed together.

'I'm going to join my wife,' he says with a slight smugness. 'See you on the dance floor.'

The guests flock from the white linen tables towards the dancefloor. The sound of laughter carries on the soft, warm breeze. I reach for my drink, down the whiskey, then reach for James's unfinished one and neck that too. If I have any hope of surviving Avery's huge pert breasts pressed against my chest, I'm going to need it. That freak of a photographer might not be the only one with a boner, and unlike his one-man tent, there'd be no missing my industrial sized marquee.

Time to get this over with. I stand, rolling up the sleeves of my crisp white shirt. I lost my suit jacket and bow tie as soon as the photos were over.

The band's grungy looking drummer, Raven McCormac, is cosying up to Avery as I reach the bar. He touches her arm, whispers something in her ear, and she leans into him and laughs.

'Shouldn't you be out there setting up?' I bark.

'Shouldn't you be crunching bones for a toothpick?' Avery rolls her eyes but steps away from the little drummer boy. Her cheeks are flushed with a tinge of pink. Is it the heat? The alcohol? Or arousal? Does she actually like the dirty-looking douche beside her?

Her topaz eyes fall to my forearms, roam over my chest, then back up to meet my eye. I force a neutral expression. What is it about this woman that gets under my fucking skin?

'Move,' I snap and Raven glares at me before stalking back towards the band.

'How am I meant to get laid when you're terrorising my potential suitors?' Avery runs a finger over the stem of her champagne glass and my dick twitches in my pants.

'Use your imagination. Or your right hand.' *That's something I'd pay to see.* 'Now, let's dance.'

'Keen aren't you?' Avery drains her drink again. Is it her fifth? Sixth? I've lost count.

She slips her arm through mine again and I bristle at the contact. Without the security of my suit jacket, her bare flesh brushes against mine. Flames lick my skin, shooting in every direction. Not helpful. How can it be possible to dislike someone so much, and still want to fuck them into next week?

'Keen to get this over with.'

The first chords of Jason Mraz's 'I'm Yours' float through the air as we stride towards the action. A myriad of stars punctuate the sky overhead and the full moon casts a luminosity over the shimmering water. Even I have to admit it's like a fucking fairytale.

We linger by the edge of the crowd as the lead singer calls Mr and Mrs Beckett to the dancefloor for their first dance. My chest tightens as I watch my brother twirl his wife around the floor like he hasn't got a care in the world. I'm happy for him. Really, I am. Doesn't mean I have to blubber up like Avery beside me.

'It's just so beautiful,' she whispers.

So are you. But I learnt the hard way beautiful things can be the deadliest.

The quicker this wedding is over and there's some distance between us again, the better. She stirs things in me that I'd prefer to remain unstirred. It's confronting.

Applause fills the air as the song draws to an end and the

next one begins. Our turn. The first line of James Arthur's 'Say You Won't Let Go' drifts into my ears, something mushy about meeting in the dark. I get a flashback of the first time I met Avery. She was dancing at the Luxor Lounge, wearing nothing but a decadent lace triangle between her legs. It was dark then too, but I saw enough to know she was trouble. The subtle flicks of her hair. The way her tongue darted over her lips. The way she demanded my attention, and the attention of every other man in the room, was downright despicable.

It wasn't her I despised though, not really—I despised myself for wanting her. For being as weak as every other man in the room. I was weak once before and it cost more than I can ever repay. I craved Avery the same way I craved Sarah; the first and only woman I ever loved. And that ended disastrously. I vowed to never be in that position again.

I assumed Avery would stop dancing when she graduated from Trinity. Assumed she'd stop tormenting me with those tits.

I assumed wrongly.

Now they're in every lads' magazine. Every lingerie campaign. And she's all over the TV, radio and internet. There's no escaping her.

'Killian,' her smooth, silky voice jolts me back to the present. 'We need to move.'

Scarlett's beckoning us onto the dancefloor, clutching the bottom of her long white dress in one hand. Her giant diamond rings glint like a beacon on the other.

I inhale a lungful of air and blow it out slowly as I follow Avery on to the dancefloor. It's just a dance. It doesn't mean anything. I've survived a hell of a lot worse.

Scarlett envelops her friend in a huge, teary hug, buying me a few more minutes before Avery's body will inevitably be pressed against mine.

The sound of Rian's ear splitting wolf whistle pierces the air and I wince. Avery turns to face me, staring at me for a long beat like her psychology doctorate didn't entirely go to waste.

Fuck that.

Does she think she can analyse me?

She'd have more luck cracking The Da Vinci Code.

Even I can't work me out. I relinquished the need to try years ago.

I extend a hand, trying to keep our torso's apart, but no, she doesn't get the memo. Her slim hand sinks into mine the same second as her huge breasts rest on my chest.

Fuck.

Her fingers linger on my shoulder. Mine tingle as they gravitate to the womanly curve of her hip. The pebbled outline of her nipples burn against my shirt and sear my skin. Blood rushes to my cock. The intoxicating scent of her peony perfume seeps into my nose.

Tractors.

Football.

Politics.

Brain give me something—anything—to think about other than those fucking taut twin bullets pressing against my pecs. The soft sound of her rhyming off the lyrics is a dangerous melody in my ear. She's trying to kill me. Her voice is like warm, drizzling honey.

It's the longest song in history. Four thousand hours pass with us swaying around the dancefloor, me and my dick aware of every damned inch of her. When the song finally draws to an end, I drop her hand like it's a hot potato and stalk towards the bar.

Thank fuck that's over. I'll avoid her for the next five days, until it's time to go back to Dublin, back to the security of my penthouse, back to work, and back to routine.

The evening passes in a blur. I catch up with cousins I haven't seen in years, watch my parents sway around the dancefloor like they're the damn newlyweds, and sink two more whiskeys.

Rian joins me for a while before hitting on the hotel manager, Alexia Farnborough—a razor-sharp Brit with honey-blonde hair cut in a severe bob that somehow manages to be both intimidating and alluring. I watch, shaking my head as she follows him back to his quarters. My little brother is physically unable to keep his dick in his pants.

Guests begin to retire to their suites, while others kick off their designer shoes and dance barefoot in the sand. Some drink like the bar won't be open tomorrow.

Avery does a combination of the latter two.

Sitting at a high-backed stool by the bar, I watch intently as she sways her hips in time to a reggae beat. Her eyes are closed, she's surrendered her soul to the song, and she's dancing like no one's watching. Although I'm pretty sure every red-blooded male in the vicinity is captivated and drooling. It's only when she stumbles that I notice just how drunk she is.

I leap to my feet, but that slimy prick Thorne beats me over to her. 'Avery, love, I'll walk you back to your room.'

'That won't be necessary.' The words have barely left my lips when three of my security team appear, looking menacing in their dark suits and ear pieces. Thorne slopes away like a rat back into his hole.

'Maybe I should go to bed?' Avery slurs, wobbling on her feet again. 'I do feel a bit woozy, but I'm having *so* much fun.'

I catch her arm and steady her. 'Party's almost over anyway, princess.' Exasperation tinges my tone. What kind of state is this to get herself into? Has she no regard for her own well-being or safety?

'Want us to escort her back to her suite?' Blake Sterling,

my second in command, asks. He's built like a brick shithouse with the temper of a two-year-old. He didn't earn his nickname, Psycho Sterling, for nothing.

'No, I've got her.'

Avery is almost asleep standing. I've never seen her so docile.

I scan the rapidly dispersing crowd. The band are packing up their equipment. 'Take me to bed, Killian,' Avery sighs dreamily.

In my darkest fantasies, I've imagined those words from her lips, but never like this.

Her head rolls onto my chest and she snuggles in closer. How much did she fucking drink?

I sweep her up into my arms like a rag doll, carrying her the short walk to her suite. She's in room 101, overlooking the beach. I know which room everyone is in—for security reasons. I have a master key which opens all of them—also for security reasons. I reach into my back pocket and fish it out.

The second the door swings open, every hair on my body pricks to attention.

Something's wrong.

Someone's been in here.

Don't ask how I know, but I do. I have an innate instinct for danger and right now it's screaming at me.

I touch my earpiece. 'Sterling, room 101. NOW.'

Nudging the door open wider, I flick a switch on the inside wall and brilliant, harsh light floods the room.

My blood turns to ice the moment I see it—a black calla lily placed with surgical precision in the centre of her white silk sheets.

There's a handwritten note tucked beneath it.

Four simple words set my world on fire.

I'm coming for you.

Chapter Three

AVERY

I roll my face into the plumpest, plushest pillow known to man and groan. My head is fucking splitting. I'm fairly sure there's drool on my chin. The last thing I remember is... dancing to a cover of 'Mr Brightside' barefoot with Scarlett and her new sister-in-law, Zara.

I don't even remember getting back to my room.

Damn champagne. Will I ever learn?

I'm going to need carbs. Lots of them. I'm on holiday, after all.

I stretch my arms above my head, prise my sleepy eyes open, then jolt to a sitting position.

What the fuck?

Killian Beckett is in my bedroom, manspreading across a velvet tub chair with a chrome laptop balancing on his lap like he owns the fucking place. He's wearing a grim expression, along with yesterday's suit pants and shirt. Rolled-up sleeves reveal strong, tanned forearms with enough veins to make a map out of.

I grab the blinding white duvet and yank it up over my chest. 'What the fuck are you doing in my room?' I glance down to check if I'm wearing any lingerie. I wasn't wearing a bra to start with. The low back of the bridesmaid dress didn't allow it, but my thong is still securely in position.

'Actually, you're in *my* room.' He sweeps a hand around his meagre belongings; a dark green bottle of cologne, an electric razor, discarded Tom Ford shoes, and worryingly, a sleek steel coloured handgun. 'Your blatant lack of regard for your own welfare is shocking.'

'English, please.' My head continues its incessant pounding.

'You got so drunk you passed out on my chest. I had to carry you back to your room.' His voice is rough, gritty, so fucking *male*.

I squeeze my eyelids shut, trying to remember. Maybe it's a blessing that I can't.

'Did we...?' I open one eyelid and peek at the man in front of me.

'No,' he scowls, rubbing a hand over his strong, square jawline. I've said it before and I'll say it again, the man is a broody bastard, but he's one hell of a beautiful broody bastard. 'Call me old-fashioned, but when I fuck a woman, I prefer her to be conscious.'

It's on the tip of my tongue to say I'm conscious now, but disapproval radiates from him. Maybe if I call him Daddy, he'd bend me over his knee like the last woman? Fuck, I don't know who she is, but right now, I wish I was her.

'That's not the worst of it, Avery.' His jaw ticks.

Oh no.

Fuck my life.

Did I serenade him?

Dance for him?

Strip for him?

'It isn't?' I massage my temple with my fingers.

'Do you know anything about a black calla lily?' His pupils bore into mine unwaveringly.

'I had one left in my dressing room at a shoot a couple of weeks ago.' I sit up straighter and swallow hard. My mouth is drier than the Sahara. 'And actually, there was one on my doorstep before that.'

'Were there notes?' he snaps, raking his fingers over his scalp.

'Yeah, the first one said something like, *A rare beauty, just like you.* The second said *See you soon.*' I thought it was a bit odd, but men send me gifts every day.' A sinking sense of alarm snakes into my stomach. 'How did you know?'

'You have a stalker,' he spits. So much for him being emotionless. He's vibrating with rage. 'You didn't think to mention that?'

I wet my lips. 'I get gifts like that all the time. It comes with the territory. My dressing room is always filled with flowers, chocolates, champagne. Lingerie even. It's no big deal.'

He bangs his fist down hard on the arm of the chair and I jump. 'Goddammit, Avery. Stop being so naïve and so fucking careless. You need to take this seriously. A stranger broke into your room last night and left a single black calla lily on your bed, along with this.' He holds up a handwritten note, and my blood turns to ice in my veins.

'What the...?'

'Blake had it dusted for prints while you were asleep. There's nothing obviously. And there was no trace of any prints or DNA in your room. Which means this guy is a professional.'

I swallow hard as the harsh reality of the situation begins to sink in. 'I don't understand. Is it someone I know? Someone who was invited to the wedding?'

'I ran a background check on all one hundred and fifty

guests on the list, plus every employee this hotel has ever had. Bar finding a few questionable porn subscriptions, nothing else stuck out. But this is a public island. I can't run checks on every single person who sets foot on it. This person, whoever he is, must have the resources and finances to be a serious threat, Avery.'

His words wash over me like a cold wave, soaking into every inch of my skin. 'I don't understand. *"I'm coming for you."* Why?'

He exhales a long, slow breath. 'There's no explanation for why people do what they do. There are some seriously deranged fuckers out there. Impotent fuckers. Crazy fuckers. Egotistical fuckers. They get something in their head and boom—there's no reasoning with them. We need to get this guy.' He eyes me over the top of his laptop. 'Before he gets you.'

I inhale sharply. 'I should go home.' Clearly, I'm not safe here. I look down, wondering how to get out of this bed without showing Killian exactly what my mamma gave me. Then again, he's seen it all before at the Luxor Lounge anyway. Not to mention that 'Eye-ful' vag shot.

'You're not going anywhere. Not without me, anyway,' he mutters grimly.

My head whips up. 'What are you talking about?'

'You need security,' he says, like it's a matter of fact.

'You mean like a bodyguard?' My jaw swings open.

'Yep.' He slams the laptop shut. 'It looks like you and I are going to be stuck with each other. Until we catch this creep anyway. It shouldn't take long. I'm very good at what I do.'

'*You*.' I point my index finger at him. 'You're going to be *my* bodyguard?'

'Believe me, babysitting you is the last fucking thing I want to do for however long it takes to catch this fucker.'

'Is that really necessary?'

'Avery, you can't take care of yourself on a good day, let alone when there's some fucking weirdo out there leaving flowers that symbolise death on your bed.'

I hadn't given much thought to the significance of the type of flower, but he's right.

Still, the prospect of having Killian hovering beside me all day every day is not one I can stand. Especially not when I can't stop imagining him hovering *over* me—but for very different reasons. Even if he is an emotionless control freak.

'Does it have to be you? Haven't you got a million other more important clients? You're a billionaire, from a family of billionaires; you don't even need to work, so why don't you delegate this job to one of your many minions? I'll pay one of them to take care of me.'

His ebony eyes narrow. 'You're not paying anyone.'

'Of course I am.' I might not be a billionaire, but I make plenty of money myself. The last thing I want is to owe him any favours—unless they're sexual ones, of course. I could get over the fact he's a broody bastard if I was lying under him.

Avery.

I smack my palm against my forehead.

'You're not.' His tone leaves no room to argue. 'This one is on me.'

'Why?' I swallow down my surprise.

'Because this crazy cunt gate-crashed my brother's wedding to harass one of his guests, which makes it personal. Besides, I'm the best at what I do. And Scarlett will kill me with her bare hands if anything happened to you and I could have prevented it.'

'So, what...? You're going to come everywhere with me until we catch this crazy fucker?' I push my hair back from my face, flicking it over my shoulder. Killian observes my every movement.

'No, *you're* going to come everywhere with *me* until I catch this crazy fucker.'

'Ha, no chance.' I yank back the covers, exposing my breasts and slide towards the edge of the bed in search of my dress. My mother raised me to be body confident. I'm grateful for my assets, and I'm also aware that they're on borrowed time. Which is another reason I'm praying ELEGANCE sign me.

'For fuck's sake.' Killian makes a show of looking away. Prude. 'Avery, you need to take this seriously.'

'I am! But I have back-to-back photoshoots for weeks, nightclub appearances, and charity lunches to attend. And I'm due in San Francisco in a few weeks for a meeting that I've been manifesting for years.'

Killian's eyes fixate on my face, no matter how badly I will him to peep at my body.

Look down and show me you're human. Look down and show me you find me attractive. Look down and fucking show me this fucked up attraction I feel for you isn't entirely one-sided.

'You manifested it, huh?' He drawls, his tone dripping with sarcasm.

'Gabby Bernstein's manifestation meditation every damn day for the last two years.' I shrug, reaching for my brides-maid dress, which lies in a crumpled heap on the floor. Did he take it off me? Oh God. I wish I'd been conscious to see that. Did he look at me then? Or do I truly repulse him like he makes out I do?

'You have clean clothes in the en suite. Don't use all the hot water. When you're done, we'll compile a list of everyone you may have met, or offended lately. I need your schedule for the next three months, plus the previous year. I need a full relationship history. That includes one-night stands.'

'You want me to tell you the names of every single man I've had sex with?' My cheeks colour at the prospect.

'Names, dates, addresses.' Killian's gaze remains firmly fixed on my face. 'Look, Avery, I don't want to have to listen to every sordid detail of your sex life, but unfortunately, it's necessary. This person has intimate knowledge of your whereabouts. It could be someone you already know.'

'Fuck.'

'I've hacked your social media accounts. Don't even think about posting a video, a picture, or even a damn fucking meme.'

'You hacked my Instagram?' I wail.

'For your protection. My team are running your direct messages through our proprietary threat-assessment algorithm—it uses linguistic pattern recognition to identify genuine threats among the thousands of messages, then cross-references the flagged accounts against known stalker behaviour patterns.' He bristles. 'I also installed a software on your phone to block it from being tracked, but don't even think about opening a social media app, let alone commenting on one of those damn British Royals that you're obsessed over.'

'You know about that?' My eyes widen. I suppose I could have worse obsessions than stalking the princesses of England. Their resplendent style and impeccable fashion choice make me positively salivate. Add in the fucked up family dynamics and royal weddings and I lap it up like ice cream. The youngest princess, Princess Layla Sinclair is a total rebel. In another life, we could have been sisters. Elegance radiates from her, but so does defiance. I bet she gives the Queen hell behind closed doors. Now that's one Netflix documentary I'd pay to watch.

Killian hunkers forwards, resting his elbows on his thick muscular thighs. 'I need you to think carefully. Is there anyone that you got a bad vibe from? Anyone who may have reason to want to hurt you?'

'Ha! You know who's smack-bang at the top of that list?' I shake the creases out of the dress and toss it onto the bed.

'Thorne?' Killian clears his throat. 'That creepy fucker was smack-bang at the top of my list too, but my guys had eyes on him all day. Unless he had an accomplice...'

'Not Thorne! He wouldn't hurt a fly.' I roll my eyes.

'Who then?' Killian's gaze doesn't waver, no matter how much I will him to look at my body.

'You.' I rest my hand on my hip and stare defiantly at him.

In typical Killian fashion, he doesn't bite. 'Sweetheart, if I wanted you dead, you'd be six-feet under already. Somewhere no one would ever find you.'

'Dead?' Panic pierces my tone.

Killian lets out a low, incredulous laugh, 'What? You think "I'm coming for you" means "I'm coming with fairy cakes and champagne for a fucking tea party"?'

'I didn't think about it at all, to be honest.' I pinch the bridge of my nose.

'That's the problem, right there.' He points an accusatory finger at me. 'You. Don't. Think. You party, pose and drink.'

Harsh, but I suppose it's not entirely untrue.

'I get paid hefty amounts of money to pose.' I huff.

Killian's stare could level a building. 'Get in the shower. We've got work to do. The quicker we catch this fucker, the quicker we can go on our merry *separate* ways.'

Sarcastic bastard.

It's going to be a long few days.

It will be days, right?

I can barely suffer Killian Control-Freak Beckett for hours. If it comes to weeks, it will be him that's in danger—from me. There's a good chance I'll smother the hot moody bastard while he's sleeping—with my vagina.

Chapter Four

KILLIAN

'Is that a gun in your swimming shorts or are you just happy to see me?' Avery fires an antagonising wink my way from the sun lounger beside me. She's on her third cocktail. Like I said —reckless, attention-seeking, and incapable of staying out of trouble.

And worse again—she looks fucking delectable in fire engine red bikini bottoms.

Yeah, you heard.

Bottoms.

My newest charge is sitting two feet away from me with her spectacular tits out for all to see. Thank fuck for the Ray-Bans. At least this afternoon, unlike this morning, I can steal the occasional glimpse.

'It's a gun.' Although there is another weapon digging into my shorts too. And even with her oversized Chanel sunglasses on, it's impossible to miss her eyes drifting towards it.

'Shame. For a second there, I thought you might have *something* going for you.'

'Like I said yesterday, you'll never have to worry about it.' I reach for the bottle of water on the table beside me and take a few mouthfuls. What I wouldn't do for a Beckett's Gold, but I'm taking this threat seriously, even if Avery isn't.

The beach is blissfully quiet; most of the wedding guests are up at the main pool where James and Scarlett are hosting their post-wedding barbecue. The Caribbean Sea stretches endlessly in front of us, a sheet of rippling turquoise that catches the afternoon sun like scattered diamonds. I catalogue every detail—force of habit. My security team maintains their positions—Sterling by the beach bar, Thomson near the water sports hut, Walsh scanning the treeline. I've had them re-run background checks on every single wedding guest, and every staff member turning over everything from social media profiles to tax records. Nothing flagged. Nothing suspicious. Name by name, photo by photo, we dug deep—criminal records, financial histories, travel patterns. Which means either our stalker isn't here, or he's a better actor than anyone in attendance.

'Why can't we go to the barbecue?' Avery whines.

'Because there's a crazy bastard hell-bent on tormenting you.'

'Pretty sure there's one sitting right next to me too,' she mutters, tossing her thick golden hair over her shoulder. Her face lights when she spots a passing waiter. 'Excuse me?'

He turns with a smile that morphs into a mass of shock when he registers Avery and her transcendent tits. His face might be funny if I didn't want to punch it. His jaw drops so fast it may need to be surgically reattached. And for reasons that I do not want to analyse, him drooling over her annoys the fuck out of me

'Can I get two more dirty martinis, please?' She flashes him a megawatt smile. Her tinkling laughter echoes through the air. 'And have you got any mint chocolate ice cream? I don't normally eat sweet stuff but, feck it, I'm on holiday.'

His eyes fixate on Avery's bare breasts for a long moment before they snap to her face.

I stare at him stonily.

It's day one, and this is already officially the worst job I've ever had.

Not only am I battling a permanent erection, but I've had to grill Avery for details of every man she's ever had sex with, been on a date with, or refused a date with, and run checks on them too, and I have no idea why every single part of it enrages me.

Yes, she's attractive.

Yes, I fancy the fuck out of her.

But do I want any part of her drama in my life? Unequivocally not.

Yet I now find myself with a long list of men I want to eradicate from the planet.

The waiter finally manages to pull his tongue back into his mouth. 'Yes, Ma'am. Certainly.' He angles towards me. 'Sir, can I get you anything?'

'Is a different client too much to ask for?'

'Sorry?' A look of confusion flits across his face.

'Never mind,' I shoo him away and he retreats towards the white wooden beach bar.

'Did you just make a joke?' Avery screeches, shoving her sunglasses on top of her head. She twists to stare at me like I've got ten heads and six cocks.

'I was deadly serious.' I look at my watch pointedly. It's barely three o'clock. 'Do you really need two more cocktails?'

'Do I really need you, Killian?' She wrinkles her nose in disgust.

'Unfortunately for both of us, yes—you do.'

She exhales a dramatic sigh and flops back on to the plush, plump mattress. 'Kill me now.'

'Careful what you wish for, sweetheart.'

The flash of a camera in the distance catches my attention. If it's that prick Thorne making good on his promise to photograph Avery on the beach, I will bury him ten-feet under the sand. His background checks might have come back clear, but I haven't ruled him out—not by a long shot.

I touch my earpiece. 'Incoming. Six o'clock. Looked like the flash of a camera.'

Sterling's rough Belfast accent blasts through the tiny piece in my ear. 'It's Rian.'

I twist my torso to see my youngest brother strolling towards us with a shit-eating grin on his face and his mobile phone in his hand. If he's filming Avery without her clothes on, I will legitimately kill him. My parents won't be happy about it, but needs must.

'Well, well, well, what do we have here?' He whips his sunglasses off shamelessly in order to get a better look.

'Rian!' Avery beams up at him like it's normal that she's only wearing a tiny pair of crimson bikini bottoms.

Then again, she's a glamour model—it probably *is* normal for her.

And technically, I'm sitting here in a pair of shorts and no top, so why shouldn't she? It's what people do on holiday—in addition to drinking martinis and eating mint chocolate ice cream apparently.

I'm torn between being impressed with her obvious body confidence and being unscrupulously horrified by it. Again—I categorically refuse to analyse why.

'The best man and the bridesmaid, huh?' Rian's pupils dart between us with delight. 'So cliché!'

'It's not like that,' I mutter. I told James everything this morning, and we both agreed the less people who know about

Avery's stalker situation, the better. As far as anyone else is concerned, we're just hanging out.

'Yeah? Well, I heard that Avery moved into your room last night.' Rian takes a seat at the bottom of Avery's sun lounger and she slides her long, toned legs up to make room for him.

'She was drunk. I was making sure she didn't choke on her own vomit.' I nod towards her again. 'And the way she's sinking martinis, tonight will be the same.'

'Lighten up! This is supposed to be a celebration.' Avery shimmies her shoulders, drawing my gaze downwards. Fuck, she really is the most stunning creature I've ever seen–and the biggest attention seeker of all time. She reaches for the SPF bottle beside her, squirts a huge dollop of oil into her palm and precedes to rub it into her shoulders.

Nothing shocks me. Not anymore. I've seen too much. But as my latest charge works oil lower over her pert, gravity defying tits, my mouth pops open and my dick strains against my shorts like a feral beast.

She's trying to kill me—death by dick combustion.

'Damn, girl.' Rian whistles lowly. Her lips lift in a smirk. She's torturing both of us, and she fucking knows it. The woman lives for attention.

'Need a hand?' Rian offers with a twinkle in his eye.

I'm going to kill him.

If he so much as places a finger on her, he'll lose it.

A low noise rumbles in my throat. I mask it with a cough.

'I'm good, thanks.' The soft warm breeze carries Avery's tinkling laughter, the scent of coconut oil, and peony perfume. It's going to be a long day.

'You ever heard the saying "Three's a crowd" little brother?' I shoot Rian a look that would make a lesser man squirm.

He guffaws. Actually guffaws, then slaps his thigh. 'I knew there was something going on with you two!' His pupils flit between us gleefully.

'If she was mine, do you think I'd let you share her sun lounger and drool all over her tits?' I hiss. 'If you must know, we were in the middle of a conversation.'

Rian swats a hand in front of his face. 'You haven't held a proper conversation in years. We're lucky if we get a few sentences out of you.'

Avery's head whips up. 'Lucky? I'd call that a blessing, given every word he utters is an insult or a complaint.' Her palm glides over her nipples with the oil.

Holy fuck.

I need Rian to leave.

Now.

'How's Alexia this morning?' I demand, pointedly.

'As ever, you don't miss a fucking thing, do you?' Rian's lips crack open, revealing perfect white teeth.

'It comes with the job description.'

The waiter returns, balancing a tray with two martinis in one hand and the mint chocolate ice cream in the other. He nearly trips over his tongue as Avery continues to rub oil over her smooth, flawless skin.

'I'll take that.' I snatch one of the martinis from the tray and knock it back. It tastes like shit, but one thing's become abhorrently clear—if I'm going to survive this afternoon, I'm going to need alcohol.

'Better bring two more,' Rian says.

'Don't. He's not staying.' I slam the glass back on the tray and hand the waiter a fifty-euro tip before dismissing him. I turn to my brother, 'If you took a photo of Avery for your wank bank, get rid of it, before I get rid of you—permanently.'

'What do you take me for? Some sort of pervert?' Rian's palm flies to his chest, resting over his heart. 'I was taking a picture of the beach for...' His face falters for a second. 'A friend.'

'You fucking better have been.' I motion for him to hand his phone over.

'Are you defending my honour?' Surprise spikes Avery's tone.

'I'm defending your right to privacy. Not that you seem to care much for it.' I gesture in the direction of her nearly nakedness.

Her comment yesterday about the 'Eyeful' vagina shot struck a chord with me. I assumed it was a publicity stunt. Bad publicity is better than no publicity, or whatever. But the hurt on her face was real. The way her voice cracked when she spoke about it was real. Which is why the pap responsible, Anton Roche, is currently in one of my warehouses in the Wicklow mountains waiting for me to return. Until then, three of my men will entertain him. The bastard had a history of assault allegations that never stuck. Three prior charges, three times he walked. The last one was on a minor. He won't walk this time. In fact, he'll never walk again.

'He's just trying to protect you.' Rian stands, plucks his phone from his pocket and shows us the photo he took. It's all blue sea and white sand. 'I know Killian looks like an emotionless fucker, but my big brother is the most loyal man on this planet.' Rian looks at Avery. 'If you're in his inner circle, he will kill or die for you.'

I shake my head. I don't need a fucking wingman. What I need is for my brother to piss off so I can get back to work scanning the perimeter.

Avery studies me thoughtfully for a few seconds. Her blue eyes blaze with open curiosity again. Like I'm a code she can't quite crack. Bad enough I have to put up with her beautiful body, but I point blank refuse to spend the foreseeable future being watched and scrutinised like a Freudian experiment.

Rian backs across the sand in the direction of the main hotel, 'And one more thing, Avery...' I roll my eyes, waiting for whatever punchline he's about to deliver. Probably his phone number.

'If you haven't shagged him yet, you should. Becketts are blessed, if you know what I mean.' He winks and grabs his crotch. 'And if he won't prove it to you, I will. Enjoy the cock...tail.' Rian snorts as he saunters away.

For once, Avery is speechless.

Chapter Five

AVERY

We spend the rest of the day on the beach, soaking up the sun.

Well, I soak up the sun, while Killian taps his phone furiously, while simultaneously looking good enough to eat. It's the first time I've seen him with no shirt on and fucking hell, he might be a miserable bastard, but the man is seriously ripped. His torso is taut and tanned. Smooth pecs beg to be touched, preferably with my tongue. A dark smattering of hair snakes from his stomach all the way down inside the waistband of his black shorts. And don't get me started on the masculine ink scrawled over his broad shoulders and neck.

Mouthwatering.

'I'm starving.' And not necessarily for food. I'm horny as fuck, thanks to the cocktails, Rian's comments about Killian's apparently massive cock, and the fact that we've been nearly naked together all day. This forced proximity is doing things to my ovaries. I know it's only day one, but maybe I have Stockholm Syndrome? I mean, technically, Killian isn't my captor, but he's hijacked my holiday nevertheless.

I reach for my dress. With the sun kissing my skin and the martinis releasing the tension in my shoulders, it's hard to believe the lily and note were ever anything other than a stupid prank.

'We'll get room service.' Killian stands, surveying the beach.

'You've got to be joking.' I swivel to look at him. 'I didn't come to St. Barths to hide in a suite all week. I already missed the damned barbecue. I want to get out and soak up the atmosphere before I get back to dreary Dublin.'

'We aren't going out.' Killian's tone is final.

'You might not be, but I am.'

'This whole thing is a joke to you, isn't it?' Killian steps in front of me like he's ready to physically restrain me if need be. An image of him tying me to the bedpost forms in my mind, resulting in a sharp jolt of lust striking between my legs.

I've always been attracted to Killian Beckett. Even way back at the Luxor Lounge when I was a pole dancer, I tried to get his attention. But he remains as infuriatingly stoic now as he was then. Maybe that's part of the reason I dislike him so much—because I can't have him. Despite him being a cold, uncharismatic control freak, I can't stop salivating over every hard line and curve of his frankly flawless masculine body.

It's so fucking obvious that something happened to him, probably while he was away on one of his military tours. And despite his strong, stoic front, I'm almost certain there's a man in there who craves attention and affection as much as the rest of us. And for some really fucked up reason, I've spent years fantasising about being the woman who gives it to him. The woman who cracks his outer wall and gets the raw, unfiltered version of him. I'm more convinced than ever that there's a beast beneath that cold façade just waiting to break free.

It doesn't take a psychology doctorate to understand the appeal of wanting the unavailable. It's human nature. Which is why it's impossibly hard to fight.

Killian sighs and pulls his t-shirt over his head. 'Fine, we'll get a table set up here on the beach, away from the main restaurant.'

'That sounds romantic.' There I go again. I can't help goading him. I tug my yellow sundress over my head and wiggle into it before stepping closer to him, close enough that my chest rests on his. Tingles soar over my skin in every direction as the scent of his rich, enticing cologne seeps into my lungs. Man, that scent could get a woman off alone.

'I was aiming for remote rather than romantic,' he bristles, taking a step back. 'Sterling and the others will set up a perimeter. We'll be watched at all times.'

'Good job I'm not shy then.' I arch an eyebrow.

'I noticed,' he mutters.

'Did you?' My heart skips a beat as I close the distance between us again.

He tenses. A muscle ticks in his jaw. 'Pretty fucking impossible not to.'

So, Killian Beckett *is* human, after all.

Before I can probe further, he says, 'We'll go to Scarlett and James's suite for a drink beforehand. I'm sure you missed her today.'

My mouth pops open. Is it possible that beneath that sharp exterior, Killian has a soft side? Hard to believe when he treats me like I'm either a petulant child, or worse again, ignores me completely.

'That sounds...nice.' I bite back my surprise. 'Does she know about the... situation?' I texted her earlier, feigning the worst hangover known to womankind in case she was looking for me at the barbecue. But with a hundred and fifty other guests to get round, we'd have had zero time together anyway.

'No. James didn't want to put a dampener on their big day. And the less people that know about this, the better.'

'Agreed. But how are we going to explain this?' I motion between us.

'We won't have to. Scarlett's too high on life to question anything. Besides, they leave for their honeymoon in a few days.'

James has booked a yacht to take them around the Caribbean islands for a month. I have no doubt she'll come back pregnant with baby number three.

'Perfect.' I link my arm through his and start towards the main hotel. He tenses again, but he doesn't brush me off.

Is he softening towards me?

Or is it all part of the 'hanging out' together act, pretending like he's not my human shield?

His bicep strains against his shirt. It's too tempting not to touch. The cocktails gave me enough courage to brush a finger over it.

'Avery,' his low, deep voice is weighted with warning.

'What?' I feign innocence. 'People are supposed to think we're friends, right?'

'Friends don't go around feeling each other up,' he says darkly.

'Maybe they should.' I shrug. 'A little casual sex might help to pass the time until we catch this calla lily-loving psycho.'

'There's nothing casual about the way I fuck.' His raspy tone sends shivers over my spine.

What a fucking visual.

'And how am I supposed to catch him, if I'm balls deep inside of you? Bodyguard rule number one—never *ever* sleep with your charge. Not that I would anyway,' he adds hastily.

I deliberately brush my breast against his arm. 'I think I could wear you down in time.'

'That's the problem, Avery.' He shakes his head, disapproval emanating from him once again. 'That's the fucking problem.'

What the actual?

Psychology doctorate or not, I have no idea how to work that one out...

Killian's men check the suite before we enter, then give us the nod to go in. The air con blasts through the brilliant white open plan area. In addition to the queen-sized four-poster bed and the white leather tub chair Killian was sitting in this morning, there's a lavish, turquoise, suede couch and a long glass coffee table. Sliding glass doors open up onto a large private decking area overlooking the ocean. It's stunning.

'My men got the rest of your stuff from your suite. Your clothes are hanging in the closet beside mine,' Killian mutters, shoving his Ray-Bans on top of his head. His eyes are utterly arresting—almost ebony, with torrid flecks of gold. I could drown in their depth. 'I'll wait on the decking while you shower and get changed.' He reaches for a bottle of beer from the minibar.

'Or you could join me?' The words are out of my mouth before I can even work out if I mean them or if I'm just trying to shock a reaction out of him—again.

Yes, I'm ridiculously attracted to him, but I don't actually like him.

Then again, I don't have to—not for what I have in mind.

Killian stares at me stonily for a few seconds before turning towards the patio doors.

Am I that repulsive to him?

No, I don't think so.

'I think I could wear you down in time.'

'That's the problem, Avery. That's the fucking problem.'

I love a challenge. Killian is undoubtably that.

Things are finally getting interesting.

I shower—alone—then spend an age applying enough make-up to make it look like I'm barely wearing any. I pick out a simple, short black dress with spaghetti straps and a low cut back, then slather a load of Jo Malone body butter onto my arms and legs before slipping into a pair of diamanté flipflops. I run the brush through my hair a hundred times; it's an odd habit I picked up when I worked at the Luxor Lounge. The repetition of it soothed my initial nerves. I wasn't always this body confident.

By the time I make my way outside, Killian is sitting on the white wicker couch staring out over the ocean. What I wouldn't give to know what's going on in his mind. His head turns as I enter the lounge area. The sunglasses are firmly back in position, hiding his eyes, but he seems to be staring at me for a beat longer than usual.

I grab a bottle of water from the minibar and step out into the balmy evening. The cresting sun casts a luminosity over his sharp cheekbones.

'I'm ready.'

'So I see.' He peels the label from his beer bottle. A sign of sexual frustration, apparently. 'You look… nice.'

I feign surprise, clutching my chest. 'Was that an actual compliment?'

'Don't get used to them.' He takes a deep swig from the beer bottle. 'It's just nice not to actively have to avert my eyes from you.'

'You don't *have* to actively avert your eyes from me.' I sink into the couch beside him.

'Actually, I do.' He stands abruptly. 'Sterling and Walsh are outside the front door. Thomson's gone down to organise a table for us. I'm going to shower.'

I watch as he strides inside the suite. His glutes could be

sculpted from marble. Saliva floods my tongue. In a couple of minutes, he'll be naked. The thought sets a fresh blast of sex hormones surging through my blood. I should tip this bottle of water over my head, not drink it.

Though, I doubt even that would help the fire raging through my body.

Chapter Six

KILLIAN

Taking Avery to see Scarlett was as much for Scarlett's benefit as it was for Avery's. I don't warm to many people, but my new sister-in-law is an absolute doll. I'd do anything for her, the same way I'd do anything for all of my family.

As I watch the two women hug like they haven't seen each other for years instead of hours, James enquires on my progress.

'Nothing.' I admit. Which is worrying on so many levels.

I assumed we'd have found this weirdo by now. My agency is the most successful in Europe because we're the best at what we do. My men are all lethally trained with unique skills in hacking, digital forensics, and cyber infiltration. I've got experts who can crack military-grade encryption in hours, trace untraceable IPs, and retrieve data from devices that have been wiped clean. Some can hack and manipulate CCTV networks, while others specialise in breaking through the most sophisticated firewalls ever created. Everyone is trained in social engineering and digital footprint analysis. When someone tries to hide in the dark corners of the internet, we find them. We're the ones who see everything but can't be seen. Which is why the fact that this stalker has managed to stay hidden makes my blood run cold.

James's eyebrows shoot up in surprise.

'No trace. There's no camera directly facing Avery's suite. We've run thorough background checks on all the guests.'

'What about the hotel staff?' James glances at his wife.

'We checked every single past and present employee of the hotel, even though the likelihood of their involvement is slim to none, as this isn't the first "gift" of this nature.' I scrub a hand over my jawline. 'I grilled Avery this morning about ex-boyfriends, ex-lovers'—I swallow hard—'rivals, and regulars from the Luxor Lounge that she used to dance for. I can't find anything.'

A darkness clouds James's face. 'What about Cole?'

Christopher Cole is one of several of our family's sworn enemies. He used to own the gentlemen's club where Scarlett and Avery previously pole danced, The Luxor Lounge. The term gentlemen is a stretch though. The place was crawling with wealthy dirtbags, the biggest of all being Cole. He wanted Scarlett for himself, and when he lost her to James, he ordered a hit on her. The hitman couldn't get near Scarlett, or James, and my late sister-in-law, Isabella—Caelon's wife and the mother of his children—was caught in the crossfire.

I'm monitoring Cole's accounts, his family, his known associates, and every digital footprint he's made since disappearing into the wind. Money leaves trails, and Cole has plenty of it hidden away in offshore accounts. My team is watching his known properties, tracking his passport aliases, and monitoring anyone who's ever owed him a favour. We've got eyes in every major port and airport, facial recognition scanning CCTV feeds across Europe. A man like Christopher Cole can't resist flaunting his wealth forever—he'll surface eventually. But something about these black lilies doesn't feel like his style. Cole is flashy, arrogant

—he'd want us to know it was him. These threats feel more... intimate. More personal. And that worries me even more. Plus, why would he target Avery? It was Scarlett he wanted.

'It's not him.' I shake my head. 'I doubled your security anyway, and the rest of the family's.'

'Zara won't like it,' James tuts.

Zara is our youngest sibling, and our only sister. At nineteen years old, she's desperately champing at the bit for freedom, and this increase in security will have her whining worse than Avery.

'At least she'll be alive to form an opinion.' I accept the beer James hands to me. I don't normally drink while I'm working, but after this afternoon, I need it. Besides, my men are everywhere. I don't trust easily, but I trust them more than I trust even myself sometimes.

'Anyway, enough about that. How does it feel to be a married man?'

A huge grin reveals James's perfect teeth. 'It feels fucking phenomenal. You should try it sometime.'

I scoff. 'Yeah, in another life maybe.'

I don't do relationships—the last one I had resulted in multiple deaths. Including hers.

An hour later, Avery's slim arm is linked with mine again as we stroll over the sand towards the only table set on the beach. I'm not used to being touched. I don't do PDAs. But at least if she's hanging on to me, I know where she is. I can protect her. I had hoped to wrap this stalker business up within a matter of hours, if not days, but it's not looking likely—which is concerning on multiple fronts, but mostly because it means being within two feet of the one woman who crawls under my skin like a severe case of pompholyx eczema.

'This is beautiful,' Avery's hand clamps over her mouth,

though even that doesn't stop her talking. 'Did you arrange all of this?'

I cast my eyes over the table that sits on a raised wooden deck over the sand, sheltered by a white linen canopy that drifts lazily in the Caribbean breeze. Crystal glasses catch the dying sunlight, throwing prisms across the crisp tablecloth. Hurricane lamps filled with flickering candles create pools of golden light that will grow stronger as dusk deepens into night. The champagne—Dom Pérignon, 2008 vintage—chills in a silver bucket, beads of condensation rolling down its neck. White orchids and Birds of Paradise spill from a cut crystal vase, their colours intensified by the setting sun that paints the sky in shades of amber and rose. And the ocean provides a perfect date-like soundtrack, waves lapping gently at the shore.

Oh fuck.

This really is romantic.

I asked Thomson to arrange dinner. I should have known better. The man is one of my few employees who is married, and happily married at that. His wife thinks he does private security for celebrities. She's not wrong, but he does a whole host of other questionable duties for my family too. We have a lot of enemies. Dangerous, powerful enemies. My team and I do what we have to do to ensure those enemies don't take us out. Even if that sometimes means taking them out.

I touch my earpiece and hiss, 'Thomson, I'm going to fucking kill you with my bare hands.'

His answering chortle rumbles back.

Avery slides into the high-backed chair as I clear my throat. 'Thomson arranged everything. You can thank him for this flowery bullshit.'

Her smile falters for a second before she fixes it firmly back in position. 'Maybe I will.' There's a defiance in her tone that I'm dying to fuck out of her. 'Where is he?' She scans the surrounding foliage through the twilight.

'He's probably on the phone to his wife, asking how their children are.' I take the seat opposite Avery.

She sighs dramatically, reaching for the white linen napkin in front of her. 'Why are all the good men taken?'

I don't deign to answer. I wouldn't know. I'm not a good man. She's Beauty, and I am unequivocally the beast—not necessarily in the way I look, but in the things I've done.

A waitress arrives with menus before my brain can torture me with my worst memories. Her name tag says Amelia, but I knew that already. I have a photographic memory, which is handy for work, but not so handy now I've seen the face of every man Avery has fucked.

While Amelia pours the champagne and talks Avery through the specials, I scan the perimeter. At least eight of my men are on guard within a two hundred metre radius. Close enough to protect her, not close enough to pry. It killed me that every single one of them had a front-row seat to her sunbathing topless today.

If she were mine, those tits would be for my eyes only. Which is why it's imperative I stop thinking about fucking her, because the woman's entire career revolves around people ogling her almost naked.

Besides, I don't do 'mine'. I do mine for the night. Mine for the weekend. Mine for a week if the sex is supreme.

What would sex with Avery be like?

An image of her handcuffed and spread legged on my bed forms at the forefront of my mind.

For fuck's sake.

'Killian?' Avery clicks her fingers in front of my face and I flinch. 'What do you fancy?'

You. I fancy the fucking pants off you, even if you irritate the shit out of me.

I turn my attention to Amelia. 'I'll have the king prawns to start, then the lobster surf and turf with the fillet rare.'

'I'll have the same.' Avery hands back her menu and reaches for the champagne flute in front of her. 'Cheers,' she raises her glass as Amelia strides away.

I huff out a breath, then reach for my own glass. I don't like champagne, but tonight, I'll drink anything to take the edge off. 'There's a stalker on the loose and you want to raise a fucking toast.'

She leans over the table, clinks her glass against mine, giving me a spectacular view of her cleavage again. My dick thickens in my pants.

There's a stalker on the loose and my dick wants to raise a fucking table.

What the fuck is wrong with me?

'Do you have to be so negative all the time?' She licks her lips and an image of her licking precum from the tip of my cock forms in my fucked-up brain.

'Just keeping things real. One of us has to.' I stare at her pointedly.

'You know, if we're going to be stuck together for a few days, we could at least try to be nice to each other.' Her blue eyes blaze.

'This is me being nice.' I'm not even joking.

'You know what I mean.' There's a hint of a plea in her tone. 'You radiate animosity. I don't know what I ever did to offend you, but if you're hellbent on being by my side for however long it takes to find this psycho, can you please not be so cold?'

If only she knew the truth. I'm cold towards her because she stokes a fire in me that could burn down my world. The woman could ruin me, and despite her fancy fucking doctorate in psychology, she has no fucking clue.

'Fine.' I shrug, feigning nonchalance.

'You said that with as much conviction as a politician.' She runs a finger over the stem of her glass.

'What do you want from me, Avery? I'm here to protect you, not to be your fucking BFF.'

'I know, but do we have to be at each other's throats all the time?'

'I'm not good at small talk.' I take another sip of champagne, watching her over the rim of my glass. What I wouldn't do for a whiskey.

'Really?' She fakes surprise. 'I'd never have guessed.' Laughter bursts from her lips, rich and uninhibited, just like her. The sound does something strange to my chest. 'Tell me, Killian, what *are* you good at?'

'Plenty of things.' The words come out more suggestive than I intended.

'Like what?' She leans forward, and it takes all my willpower not to look at her chest again. 'You know every single thing about me—I had to tell you things today that I've never even admitted to Scarlett! Yet, I know nothing about you except that you're James's brother, and the only emotion you ever display is disapproval, or irritation. Tell me something real.'

I sigh. 'Like what?'

'How many women have you fucked?' Devilment dances in her eyes.

'I'm not telling you that.' I down my champagne, then top up her glass before filling my own.

'Oh, come on. Indulge me.' A strand of hair falls across her face, and my fingers itch to brush it back.

'I didn't keep track.' I lie. I couldn't forget if I wanted to; it's just the way my brain works.

'Liar.' She points a glossy painted fingernail at me.

'Okay, let me ask you a different question. Is your dick as big as Rian claimed?'

'It's bigger.' I deadpan.

'More lies!' she squeals, slapping the table. If only she knew how hard I am beneath it. 'You know, this weird tension between us could all be worked off with a good hard hate fuck and we could move on with our lives.'

What a thought.

But no, Avery is the epitome of everything I avoid in one picture perfect package. Spending time with her like this is even more dangerous than my day job. The way she torments me is worse than any form of torture I've endured. Well— almost.

'Okay, how about this one... Have you ever been in love?'

Her question hits me like a bullet to the chest.

Seconds pass. Avery waits, silent for the first time tonight.

'Once. Her name was Sarah.' I stare into my glass. 'It didn't end well.'

Avery sits back in her chair, all traces of mischief gone from those blue eyes as she studies me with her usual Freudian focus.

'What happened?'

'She died.'

Chapter Seven

AVERY

'I'm so sorry.' I cover my mouth with my hand. 'When? How?'

'A long time ago,' he picks up his drink again. 'I'm over it.'

Jesus Christ. I assumed he had PTSD or something, but not in a million years would I have guessed his grief. Or is it guilt that renders him so arduous? He was a soldier, a hero, yet he clearly couldn't save the woman he loved.

Is his callous demeanour a front to keep people out? Is his indifference actually a self-imposed prison constructed with fear? And why do I feel compelled to fix him or distract him at the very least?

'Stop psychoanalysing me, Avery,' he snaps. 'This conversation is over.'

Probably best not to admit I'm simultaneously psychoanalysing myself—and trying to dissect this weird chemistry between us.

Minutes pass in silence. I swallow down a million questions and glance out towards the sea. The Beckett brothers have seriously suffered over the years. Women tend to get hurt around them. My thoughts drift to Scarlett.

Then to my own situation.

'How long do you think it will take you to catch our lily-loving friend?'

'I thought I'd have him already, to be honest.' Killian rubs his fingers over his razor sharp jawline. 'He's good. Unfortunately. But he'll fuck up. And I'll be there when he does.'

'Are you sure it wasn't just a prank or a hoax?' I hate the hope in my voice. I know as well as he does that the threat is real. Someone went to the trouble of sourcing those specific lilies to send me a message. It's creepy as fuck. A shiver runs down my spine. A couple of times lately, I've sensed someone watching, but I assumed I was either overtired or over-imaginative.

But do they really want to hurt me?

And why?

I believe you reap what you sow. I believe the Universe gives you back the same energy as you emanate, which is why if I can't say something nice about someone, I don't say it at all. I don't have any enemies that I know of. Yeah, I have a few ex-boyfriends, but the relationships ended amicably. When you're in the industry that I'm in, it's safer not to fall out with people who could sell stories to the tabloids about you.

'I'm certain.' Killian's sombre tone leaves no room for doubt.

The waitress returns carrying our starters. The scent of saffron-infused butter and grilled prawns wafts in the air and my saliva pools on my tongue.

I pick up my fork and force myself to put my energy into brighter topics—worrying won't help. I just have to trust Killian is as good as he's supposed to be.

I make small talk as we eat—partly to distract myself from the fact that there's a stranger out there harbouring a weird obsession with me, partly to stop myself from prying further into Killian's past. He won't thank me for it. It's one thing to rile him sexually, but I don't truly want to make him uncomfortable. Especially not when, like it or not, we're stuck together.

At least what he lacks in social skills, he makes up for in eye candy. I watch his mouth work as he chews every morsel, the way his tongue darts out to wet his lips. It's the best distraction from reality a woman could ask for.

By the time we finish the champagne and devour our dinner, the sky has turned inky black. The hurricane lamps cast a soft glow across his face, softening those sharp angles.

'We should head back.' He signals Amelia for the bill. 'It's not safe out here after dark.'

I click my tongue against the roof of my mouth. 'We're on a private beach at a five-star resort with six of your men watching our every move.'

'Eight,' he corrects automatically. 'Sterling is stationed by the beach bar, Walsh at the water sports hut, Thomson and Marco are covering the perimeter. Hughes and O'Connor are monitoring the CCTV feeds, Carter's on the roof, and Davidson's coordinating with hotel security.'

Just as I suspected, the man is a complete control freak. 'Let me guess—you colour coordinate your underwear drawer by shade and designer.'

A vein throbs at his throat. 'They're organised by fabric and occasion.'

I stare at him for a beat, then burst out laughing. Way to lighten the mood. It's only when he doesn't laugh with me, I realise he's not joking. 'Seriously? By occasion? What occasions are we talking about here? Business meetings? Black tie? Hot dates?'

Does he date?

'Organisation saves time,' he says stiffly, 'And lives.'

I stand, smoothing a hand over the front of my dress. His eyes follow the movement, dragging over my body like a hot poker stick. He rises from his seat and sidesteps around the table, leaving less than a foot between us.

'Do you feel the need to exercise control in every aspect of your life?'

His gaze lifts until his eyes catch mine. Dark twin pools burn with a shocking intensity—disdain or desire? Or both? The man is impossible to work out, but fuck, I'm compelled to try.

'What do you think?' His voice is low, almost guttural.

I step closer, leaving less than a foot between us. The air is charged with the sexual chemistry that permanently pulses between us. 'I think you should show me.' I wet my lips and tilt my face upwards to where his huge frame towers over me. Silence hangs heavily between us as my heart hammers in my chest. His face dips closer, so close the scent of his heady cologne wafts between us.

Just when I think his plump lips are about to brush mine, he pulls back. 'Not a good idea, Avery.'

He's probably right. But when he backs away from me, it feels so fucking wrong.

Sterling and Thomson escort us back to the suite. When they've secured the suite, I step inside, glancing around the open plan area.

'I'll take the couch, obviously,' Killian says, as he unbuttons the top buttons of his crisp white shirt. I get a tantalising glimpse of those tattoos and his tanned torso.

It's official; I don't even like the man, but I *need* him to fuck me. Just once. I don't know if it's the threat to my life, the heat, the sun, Killian's sheer presence, his earlier admissions, or the need for oblivion, but I need a release. I'll never be able to sleep with this tension thrumming through me. 'The bed is huge. We could share it and still be in different area codes. Unless...' I pause for effect, watching his throat work as he swallows. 'You don't trust yourself?'

His eyes darken to midnight. 'I don't trust you.'

'Me?' I perch on the arm of the sofa, letting my dress ride up to reveal a dangerous amount of thigh. His gaze tracks the movement, and satisfaction curls through my core.

'Avery.' The sound of my name on his lips sets a fresh burst of lust coursing between my legs.

'What?' I widen my eyes innocently.

He steps closer, and I stand again. The air between us crackles like a live wire. His chest is inches from mine, and the heat radiating off him makes it hard to breathe. He feels it, this potent, inexplicable attraction between us. Our bodies are begging to bang. I'm vibrating with the need for him to touch me. Smoothing my hands over the fabric of my dress, I reach the hem. I hesitate for a split second before pulling it up, yanking it off, and tossing it to the couch.

'What are you doing?' A rush of hot breath whooshes from his mouth and his eyes drop to my lingerie. 'Are you trying to kill me?' His voice has dropped to a dangerous whisper that sends shivers down my spine.

'No. I'm trying to make you feel alive.' I trace my finger over the broad slope of his shoulder, over his tricep, before catching him by the hand.

'Have you no shame?' Coal-coloured eyes bore into mine.

'Honestly?' I inch closer. 'When it comes to my body, and giving it what it wants——no. I have zero shame.' This close, I have to tip my head back to meet his gaze, and the position makes me achingly aware of how much bigger he is, how much strength and power is contained in that muscular frame.

'I knew you were dangerous the second I laid eyes on you at the club.' The words rumble through his chest, and I swear I can feel them in my bones. His eyes are molten as they drop to my lips, lingering long enough to make my pulse race.

'You're the trained killer, yet I'm the one who's dangerous?' My voice comes out breathier than intended. I inch closer, slowly.

'You're lethal,' he whispers a split second before his mouth crashes onto mine, hot and heavy and urgent. His tongue bursts between the seam of my lips, demanding entry. Every stroke of it stokes a fire deep inside my core. Huge, hot hands grip my waist, fingers digging into my skin roughly before sliding up to my breasts. He swallows my feral moan as he rolls his palms over my nipples. His erection strains against my stomach—fucking hell, Rian wasn't exaggerating.

He's the one who's lethal. I might actually combust with lust if he doesn't thrust his enormous cock into me in the next three seconds. I reach for his ass, fingers dragging his pelvis hard against mine.

'Fuck.' He rips his lips away and leaps back like he's been burned. Black eyes blaze with both lust and disgust.

'What's the problem?' My heart pounds through my ears and there's a pulsing in my panties that's practically painful.

'You. The problem is you, Avery. You've spent the day torturing me with your transcendent tits, and now this.' His eyes rake over my transparent lingerie and his hands flex at his sides, like he's fighting the urge to reach for me again. I pray to fuck the urge wins because my own urges are eating me alive.

'We're two consenting adults. We can do whatever we like.' I take a tentative step towards him again, but he turns his back to me.

'I'm supposed to be protecting you. Not railing you with my cock,' he spits.

My hands fall to my hips. 'Can't you do both?'

'No, Avery, I can't. You might be reckless, but I'm not. Go to bed.' He doesn't turn around again.

'Reckless? That's what you think of me?'

'I don't think; I know.' He blows out a heavy breath and

stalks towards the terrace doors, staring out into the darkness.

'Reckless is watching life from the sidelines because you're too afraid to enjoy it. Reckless is assuming there's always going to be a tomorrow. Reckless is dying without having fully lived.' I strut towards the bathroom. I need a cold shower.

Chapter Eight

KILLIAN

I fucked up on the first day. That's why I can't be around Avery. She does things to me. Things I can't control and I despise not being in control. I despise being weak. When she slid her body against mine, I snapped.

It won't happen again.

I sit outside on the terrace while she showers. There's no way I'm going back in there. Not until I'm certain she's asleep. I don't trust her, and I don't trust myself. The woman is bewitching, beguiling, feminine and feral. And has the smartest mouth of anyone I've ever met. It's a fatal combination.

Part of me envies her carefree attitude, another part despises it.

I snatch my phone from my pocket. The background checks on Avery's ex boyfriends all came back clean. Doesn't mean I've ruled out eradicating every single one of them for touching her when I can't—won't.

I rake my fingers over my scalp.

Who the fuck is the stalker?

Houdini?

I need to find him, kill him, and put an ocean between Avery Williams and me before I do something I'll regret.

Even if I wasn't supposed to be protecting her, Avery is Scarlett's best friend. I can't just fuck her and fuck off, like I normally do. We move in the same circles. It would be weird and awkward, as well as utterly inappropriate.

My phone buzzes in my hand.

Thomson.

'Report.' My team are used to my bluntness.

'Perimeter's clear, boss. But the drummer from the wedding band—Raven McCormac—was asking for Miss Williams at the barbecue. He was quite insistent apparently. Told Scarlett he wanted to catch up about old times.'

'Old times at the Luxor, no doubt.' He used to frequent the place often. Did Avery dance for him? Did she let him touch her? My jaw clenches.

At least he wasn't on her fuck list—he won't be joining it anytime soon if I have anything to do with it... For security reasons. Obviously.

'Don't let him out of your sight. If he so much as farts, I want to know about it.'

'Yes, sir.'

'How are things in Dublin?'

I ordered our Command Centre to deploy a Tier One residential security package to Avery's house. Specialized installation teams will integrate our proprietary system—motion sensors, infrared cameras, and military-grade facial recognition software—directly into our European Operations Hub, where over two hundred security specialists monitor our clients' properties around the clock. The same setup we use for foreign dignitaries, with direct alerts routed to both the central monitoring floor and my personal security team.

'Installation will be complete before you return.'

'Good. I want eyes on every entrance, every window,

every possible point of access. As soon as the cameras are live, send me the link.'

'Yes, sir.'

'And don't bother me with anything else until this business is tied up. Ask Dixon to oversee all other operations for the immediate future. I can't risk any distractions.' I have my hands full with the obvious one.

'Yes, Sir.'

'How is our paparazzi friend doing in Wicklow?'

'He's had better days apparently,' Thomson sniggers.

'Make sure they keep him fed and watered. I want to deal with him myself when I get back. And Thomson?'

'Yes, sir?' he clears his throat.

'Bring me over a bottle of Beckett's Gold.' After watching everyone on the beach—including my brother and my men—drooling all over the only woman I've wanted in years, I need it. I wanted to tear their eyes out—all of them. Which is why I need to get this thing wrapped up, before I do something crazier than the stalker.

Two hours and two double whiskeys later, I force myself to head back inside, moving silently across the marble floor. The suite is dark except for moonlight streaming through the floor-to-ceiling windows, painting silver stripes across the furnishings. The scent of Avery's peony perfume lingers in the air like a sweet torment, mocking me for pulling away when every cell in my body begged me to stay.

My eyes gravitate to the bed. Avery's asleep, curled on her side like a content cat. Her blonde hair spills across the white pillow in golden waves, catching the moonlight like spun silk. Her long sweeping lashes flutter against her porcelain cheeks as she dreams.

Is she dreaming of me?

I couldn't bring myself to look at her after that kiss.

Couldn't face seeing the hurt, rejection or disappointment on her face, knowing I was responsible for it. But there's no trace of it now. Her flawless face is worry-free.

Even in sleep, she's stunning—all silky skin and soft curves. The flimsy fabric of her nightdress has ridden up, revealing a dangerous amount of thigh. I stare for a long beat as the steady rhythm of her breathing fills the quiet space. I could watch her all night—which is fucking terrifying. I'm worse than the stalker, but I can't seem to tear my eyes from her—from the gentle rise and fall of her chest, the soft parting of her full rosy lips, the way she burrows deeper into the pillow. It all screams vulnerability. I lean in closer, my fingers tingling with the need to touch her. The urge to protect her wars with the need to run as far as fucking possible.

I eye the suede couch. Another sleepless night stretches ahead of me, but that's nothing new. Sleep and I haven't been on good terms since my last tour. Most nights I manage three, maybe four hours before the nightmares hit. On the really bad nights, I don't sleep at all. At least tonight I have a good excuse for staying awake—keeping her safe.

A soft murmur escapes her lips, and my entire body tenses. But she just shifts slightly, the silk of her nightdress whispering against the sheets. The sound sends my mind places it shouldn't go—again.

I'm in for a long night.

Chapter Nine

AVERY

'You have a cat?' Killian scowls at me from across the glass-topped table. We ordered room service for breakfast, opting to eat it out on the terrace. I wish he'd eat me out on the terrace, because after our hot and heavy kiss the other night, it's *all* I can think about.

'Don't pretend you're interested in my pussy now,' I snap, partly out of frustration and partly to goad him into some sort of reaction. He's been positively stoic the past three days, sitting beside me at the beach, sleeping on the couch, and generally refusing to look my way at all. Though that hasn't dispelled the sexual tension between us. No, if anything, it's only escalated—for me at least. I'm fit to physically burst with it thrumming between us.

He ignores my quip and continues to stare at his laptop. 'Cats are possibly the most disloyal creatures on the planet. If you insist on keeping a pet, you should get a dog.' He lifts his coffee cup to his lips and my gaze follows. The way he kissed me was rough, urgent, like he was drowning and I was his last breath. Then he just stopped.

My eyes drop to the stubble lining his jawline. What I

wouldn't give to feel the friction of it between my thighs... wait... my head whips up and my eyes narrow. 'How do you know I have a cat?' I leap forward to peek at his screen. It's split into eight boxes, all showing high- resolution images of my house in Dublin. 'That's my house!'

Could I sound any stupider?

'Not just a pretty face, are you?' he drawls.

'That's a violation of my privacy!' I didn't agree to that. Mind you, I didn't really agree to any of this. It just sort of happened. Killian isn't a man you say no to.

'It's a necessity.' He finally looks up from the screen. My boobs are in direct line with his eyes. He closes them slowly, and grimaces like he's in pain. Good. Being here with him, wanting him and not being able to have him is pretty fucking painful too.

I drop back into my seat and huff out a breath.

'Do you want to say goodbye to Scarlett and James before they go on honeymoon today?'

My eyes snap to his. Talk about whiplash. One minute he's kissing me, then tearing himself away like he's repulsed, then he's plain ignoring me, then he's nice again. I can't keep up.

'Yes please.' I stab my fork into a piece of pineapple. 'But it'll need to be early; I've arranged a private yacht charter.' It's another cracking day in St. Barths and, seeing as it's my last full day, I plan on making the most of it—stalker or no stalker.

His fingers freeze over the laptop keyboard. 'You did what?'

'You heard me. A luxury day trip with snorkelling at Colombier Beach.'

'When exactly did you book this?' His voice has that dangerous edge I'm starting to recognise.

'The other night, while you were brooding out here.' I had

to cheer myself up somehow. *And distract myself from wondering about the girlfriend who died.*

'For fuck's sake, Avery.' He slams the laptop shut. 'Did you use your credit card online?'

'Yeah, now I think about it, I should have used yours, moneybags,' I joke. I do pretty well for myself, but I haven't quite reached billionaire status yet.

'As usual, this is a fucking joke to you, isn't it?' He shakes his head. A vein pumps furiously at his temple. 'You might as well have sent the stalker a fucking invitation.'

'Don't be so ridiculous. There's been no sign of our flower-loving friend for the past few days, and with your small army surrounding us, no one can get within ten feet of me anyway.'

'You're not going.' He folds his arms over his chest.

'I am. Come, or don't come, but the only way you'll stop me is by handcuffing me to the bedposts.'

'Don't fucking tempt me, Avery,' he growls, and it reverberates through my entire body.

'The choice is yours.' I flash him a sarcastic smile.

Three hours later, we're cruising along St. Barths' rugged coastline on a sixty-foot Sunseeker Manhattan. The gleaming white yacht cuts through crystal-clear waters, its polished decks catching the Caribbean sun. Captain Marcel and his crew of three are discreet professionals. Thomson personally vetted each of them before letting us board.

Sterling and Walsh are positioned starboard, trying to look inconspicuous in their swim shorts. Thomson is at the port. Two more of Killian's men are on a smaller boat, trailing us at a respectful distance. I'm surrounded by hot, hard men and I'm not even going to lie, I'm fucking lapping it up. Although, none of them hold a candle to their boss. In a pair of Tom Ford shorts and a short-sleeved white shirt, the man looks like a fucking model—and I should know. Killian

Beckett is hot enough to melt off my bikini. I picked out a tiny black one for today but as usual he's doing that thing he specialises in again—avoiding looking at me. Sterling doesn't have the same restraint, I notice.

I stretch my legs out on a cushioned lounger on the flybridge. I'm pretending to read a magazine, but I'm actually perving on the eye candy from behind my sunglasses. Killian hasn't stopped scanning the horizon since we left the marina. As usual his jaw is clenched tight enough to crack his molars.

The scenery is spectacular—and not just my hot security team. Emerald cliffs drop into turquoise waters, majestic looking luxury villas peek through tropical foliage, and there's barely a cloud in the bright blue sky.

'Relax,' I call. 'This is supposed to be fun.' Killian's gaze keeps returning to Sterling and his sly glances my way. If looks could kill, we'd be one security guard short.

'For who? Fun isn't getting murdered at sea because you're irresponsible and reckless.'

'I am not.' I snort indignantly. 'Irresponsible and reckless would be sneaking out alone.' I gesture around the boat, 'This is called Living. The. Fucking. Dream. All I'm missing is a martini.'

'I'll go get somebody to make one for you,' Thomson offers from his position. Unlike Sterling, Thomson appears uncomfortable with my lack of clothing—a sure sign he is as happily married as Killian suggested.

What's the big deal?

It's only a body.

We all have one.

Poor Thomson, you'd swear he thinks I'm liable to leap on him. He's safe. Killian, on the other hand, I can't make any promises about.

Killian doesn't want me, but he clearly doesn't like Sterling looking at me. It's time to see exactly how far I can push my brooding bodyguard. I can't help myself. I reach for the SPF oil from my beach bag beside me and tug the string of my bikini top. I bite back my smirk as it falls to the ground beside me.

'Avery,' Killian snarls.

'Yes?' I bat my eyelashes in his direction.

'Put your top back on.' He strides towards me and picks it up from the ground with pinched fingers.

'No.' I glance at Sterling, who is watching intently.

'Don't make me make you, Avery,' Killian warns in a low rasping tone.

'Why does my sunbathing topless bother you so much?' I smooth a hand over the side of my breast and bite back the urge to snigger.

'It doesn't,' he snaps.

'Good, because in case you forgot, I'm a glamour model who happens to have back-to-back photo shoots next week— I can't have tan lines. Here, can you rub this on my back?' I toss him the oil. His reflexes are razor sharp, catching it before it hits the ground.

'Do it yourself. Or better yet, put a t-shirt on.' Killian's glare could slice through ice.

There are more ways than one to skin a cat. 'Sterling, perhaps you wouldn't mind helping me? Or maybe Walsh could?'

Walsh smirks like all he's missing is a bag of popcorn. Sterling steps forward and Killian's eyes narrow to slits. 'Don't even think about it,' he hisses. 'In fact, go to the front of the boat. I've got things under control over here. You too Walsh.'

Sterling glances at me before marching off. Walsh follows on his tail—all trace of humour gone from his expression. Killian tends to have that effect on people.

'Why do you insist on torturing me?' Killian stares at the bottle of oil in his hands. 'Are you so desperate for attention that you need every man in a five-mile radius salivating over you?'

I swallow thickly, push my sunglasses up on top of my head and tilt my face up until our eyes meet. 'Honestly, I like feeling desired. It makes me feel alive.'

'Well, congratulations. You got what you wanted.'

'I didn't,' I admit. 'The truth is, the only man here that I want to want me is you. How fucked up is that?'

His throat bobs as he swallows hard. 'It's fucked up.'

'Stop fighting it, Killian. Never mind a fucking stalker. This chemistry between us is killing me.' I get up from my sun lounger until we're face to face, chest to chest. 'We're a world away from everything out here. Give in to it.'

'What do you want from me?' He asks in a low, strangled voice.

'I want you to fuck me into next week.' My chin juts upwards so our lips are millimetres apart. I breathe in his scent, and the junction between my legs throbs.

He scowls, but his eyes remain fixated on mine. 'I can't lose myself in you *and* protect you.'

'Let Sterling watch out for twenty minutes.' I place a hand on his arm, and for once, he doesn't flinch.

'Sterling is watching everything, believe me,' he mutters darkly.

'Why does that bother you so much?' I sweep my thumb over the curve of his bicep.

'What is it with you and the questions?' He hisses. 'You're relentless.'

'Answer them, and I'll stop.' I tilt my head to the side. 'Why does it bother you when other men look at me?'

Tension lines his neck, his shoulders and even his forearms. He pauses for a long beat, so long that I'm not convinced he'll answer me at all, but then he shocks us both. 'It bothers me because I want to bend you over that fucking deck and fuck you so hard you won't be able to sit down without thinking of me for a full week.'

Finally.

'But I can't.' Torrid flames burn in his irises.

'Can't, or won't?' I place my other hand on his hip.

'Both.' His focus falls to my lips. 'You and your fucking pheromones and silky fucking skin and killer curves wreak fucking havoc on my senses, and I don't like it. Not one fucking bit.'

'Believe me, the feeling is mutual,' the words slip from my lips. 'I don't even know if I like you, but I can't stop thinking about having your fingers, tongue and weeping cock inside of me.' Desire pulses through me. 'It's torture.'

He hisses again. 'Torture is watching all of my men drooling over your tempting tits. Torture is not being able to touch them, claim them, mark my territory and make them mine.'

'Do it then.' I push my chest forward until my breasts are resting on his chest. My nipples are taut, furled peaks, screaming for his attention. 'Please, Killian, give me something. This fucked up attraction between us is killing me.'

He steps back and disappointment soars through my soul until he raises the hand holding the SPF oil. He flicks open the lid and squirts it straight between my breasts. We both watch as it trickles over my skin.

He tosses the bottle on the sun lounger. 'This what you wanted?' His fingers sluice through the oil, smearing it over each of my breasts in maddening circles around my rock hard nipples. My back arches and hips slam forward to meet his, seeking some sort of friction, but he steps backwards, so his hands are the only part of his body that's touching mine.

'Sterling, Walsh, and the rest of the crew are watching. They're all wishing they were me right now. Does that turn you on, Avery?'

'You turn me on.' I blurt, blind with lust.

'I'm not doing this for your benefit. I'm doing it for mine.' He weighs each breast in his hand and squeezes to the point of pain. 'I'm doing it so my men will think twice about looking at you again. So that they'll think you're mine, even though you're not. Because they wouldn't dare so much as fucking peep at you if you were.'

The man is a walking red flag, and I am here for it. My bikini bottoms are ruined. 'Kiss me,' I demand.

'I'm going to,' his pupils triple in size. 'You wanted my attention, Avery. I'm going to give you so much attention that no man here will fucking dare look at you again.' He pinches my nipples, and I push my lips on to his. A wicked laugh slides from his mouth into mine. I think it's the first time I've ever heard him laugh. A ripple of anticipation slides over my spine. 'Not there, sweetheart.'

I inhale sharply.

'I'm going to kiss your perfect little cunt, in front of all these men, and then they'll know for sure that you are off limits,' he whispers. 'Unless you don't want me to, of course?'

Lust courses through every single cell in my body. I glance over to the front of the yacht. Marcel is facing away from us, steering as Colombier beach crests on the horizon. Sterling, however, is resting against the decking and facing this way. So is Walsh.

'As much as I'm enjoying the momentary reprieve from your smart mouth, we don't have all day.' Killian sweeps one hand lower, dragging the slick oil over my stomach, while the other teases my nipple.

I knew he'd be filthy, but this? I had no idea he was capable of this. And I'm shocked at how soaked I am for it.

'There are two conditions, though.' His lips brush over the sensitive skin on my earlobe. 'Firstly, this is a one-time offer. Now or never. Take it or leave it.'

Saliva floods my mouth. I want it so badly, but I've always prided myself on not flashing what's inside my knickers. Some things are meant to be sacred, even after the Eyeful Avery scandal.

It's like Killian can read my mind. 'I'll pull these flimsy little things'—he dips a finger inside the waistband of my bikini bottoms—'to the side. The only thing Sterling and Walsh will see is the back of my head, and your face when you come on my tongue.'

I almost come just thinking about it.

'You'll look at me. You'll watch me, and the image will torment you forever, the way the image of you and those perfect tits torments me.'

Saliva floods my mouth. Two strokes of his tongue and it'll all be over anyway. That won't give anyone a lot of time to look at much. 'What's the second thing?'

'If I give you this, you put your bikini top back on. The only place you take it off is on our private terrace.'

I love his possessiveness. His need to claim me. It's fucking primal.

I part my legs and give him my answer.

'Good girl.' He ushers me backwards until my ass hits the half height wall along the edge of the deck, then lowers himself to his knees.

Chapter Ten

KILLIAN

Avery Williams brings out the caveman in me. My men have seen me do some fucked up shit, but they've never seen me like this before. I'm on my fucking knees for her. I have never got on my knees for *anyone* before.

The scent of her skin seeps into my nose and crawls into my lungs. I brush my nose over her clit and she gasps. If she thinks this is going to be over quickly, she's wrong. Sterling and Walsh, and every other man in the vicinity will be left in absolutely no doubt that she is mine. That I'm the only man who gets to touch her, to taste her, and to ogle her breasts.

'Killian,' her voice is breathy with need.

I tilt my head back until our eyes lock. Hers are pure molten lava. I trail my finger from her knee, up the inside of her thigh slowly, to the black Lycra triangle covering the junction between her legs. When I reach the hem of the fabric, I trace all the way down again.

'I fucking hate you.' She bucks her pelvis and satisfaction slivers into my soul.

'I never said I'd make it quick, sweetheart.' I grab her peachy ass cheeks and hold her squirming pelvis still, rubbing my nose over her clit in a circular motion. She writhes and moans and again, I find myself laughing. This is the most fun I've had in years.

'If you don't pull my bikini bottoms out of the way soon, I'm going to die,' she complains.

'Drama queen.' But I take pity on her and yank the fabric out of the way. It's my turn to hiss. Her arousal glistens like an invitation. Fuck, she's so fucking perfect.

'Everyone is watching,' she whispers.

'Eyes on me.'

Her pupils are enormous as they lock on mine. Electricity short circuits between us. My cock is so fucking hard it's painful. I inch forward, without breaking our stare, and glide my tongue over her seam. Fuck, she tastes as good as I knew she would. Her pelvis jerks and she hisses, but I hold her hips firmly in position while I lick her, savouring every languid stroke like she's my favourite flavour ice cream.

'Killian,' she pants, parting her legs further for me.

I love the way she says my name. I love the way she spreads her thighs for me. I love her like this, surrendered to me and writhing with need. All trace of attitude obliterated by sheer animalistic instinct.

I pause and she moans. 'Don't you dare come yet.' If this is one time only, I'm nowhere near ready for it to be over yet.

'I won't be able to help it.' Her hand reaches for my hair and she threads her fingers through it, which oddly enough feels almost as intimate as sliding my tongue through her sex. I don't want to analyse why. Instead, I capture her clit with my mouth and suck. She moans so loudly they can probably hear her on the moon. I trail my fingers up her inner thigh. Her arousal is dripping from her. I knew she'd be responsive, but fucking hell, she is soaking for me. I dip my tongue lower, lapping up every drop while she watches through hooded, lust-filled eyes.

Her thighs tighten, quads tremble. She's teetering on the edge of oblivion, which is why I slow to a stop.

'Don't you dare leave me hanging.' Her voice is part desire and part demanding.

'I'm just enjoying the view before it's gone for good.' I offer her another slow, thorough lick and she mews like a fucking cat.

'Is that another compliment?' She wets her lips. 'I think I'm growing on you.'

'Don't get carried away now.' I roll the tip of my tongue over her clit, which rapidly puts a stop to her smart remarks.

I push two fingers inside her tight little channel and pump. She's so tight, so wet, so fucking magnificent I'll be fantasising about sliding my cock in her every minute of every day for the rest of my life.

'Please,' she begs, when I slow to almost a stop. I'm still not ready for this to be over, but I think I've made my point —both to Avery and my men. She is off-limits.

'Please, what?' I snap my head away.

'Please let me come now.'

I add a third finger and she parts her legs further again. Easy to tell the woman was a pole dancer; she's lithe and flexible and supple. Sex with her would be sublime. Shame I can't go there. 'Are you going to be a good girl and put your top back on?'

'Yes.' Her voice cracks with desire.

'Good.' I flatten my tongue against her and increase the pace with my fingers. It takes less than three seconds for her to erupt. Her tight channel squeezes my fingers in a vice-like grip as her hands tug my hair.

'Fuck,' she screams, just in case anyone hadn't quite noticed that she's exploding from the inside out. I smile against her sex, lapping up every single drop without breaking eye contact.

Avery Williams is the most beautiful woman I've ever seen. I have every single picture she ever posed for in my office at home—not that I'd ever admit that to her—but this? With her starry eyes and orgasm flushed cheeks, this is the most sublime image of her I've ever seen. It will live rent free in my head for the rest of my days.

When she finally stops shaking, I pull her bikini bottoms back securely in place and give her one more little kiss there —for my benefit, not hers.

I stand, towering above her. The warm breeze wafts her loose lustrous hair behind her, exposing her long slender neck. What I wouldn't do to sink my teeth into her—and my cock—but no.

Enough is enough.

'Can I...?' Her gaze falls to the bulge in my shorts.

'Absolutely not.' Even if my poor dick is disgusted with me. I head back towards the sun lounger and snatch up Avery's bikini top between my fingers. 'A deal is a deal.' I hand it to her, staring at her pointedly.

She blows out a breath. 'Fine. But if I have tan lines next week, I'm blaming you.' She slips the black strings around her shoulder and ties it, securing those perfect tits with two triangles. She leans back on the half-height wall, fingers gripping the chrome bar lining the top of it like she doesn't quite trust her legs not to give way beneath her. A fresh wave of satisfaction curls in my core as her perfect white teeth dig into her lower lip. She hesitates, like she wants to say something but can't.

'Spit it out, Avery. It's not like you to be quiet.'

'I, er...' She glances at the wooden decking, then back up to meet my eyes. 'Thank you,' she whispers, almost shyly. Her gaze darts to the front of the yacht where Sterling and Walsh suddenly appear engrossed in something ahead of them.

'It was my pleasure.' I just hope it's not my undoing,

because even though I was the one that said "just once", now I've had a taste of her, doing that again might be something even *I* can't control.

Thomson arrives back on deck from below with Avery's cocktail in one hand. Great timing. I don't give a fuck what any of my men think of me. They once watched me remove a rapist's fingers one by one, but Thomson's married happy heart would probably have felt violated at the show I just starred in. Though I don't doubt he'll hear every depraved detail from Sterling later.

One look at Thomson's furrowed features informs me we have a problem.

'What is it?' I bark, striding towards him.

'There's something below deck you should see, boss.' His tone is low and hushed.

Every muscle in my back tenses, every single hair on my neck pricks to attention.

'Sterling.' I beckon him over.

'Take this to Miss Williams,' I snatch the drink from Thomson and push it into his hands. 'Do not leave her side until I return.' I turn to Walsh, who's hovering next to me. 'You too.' The graveness of my tone has them standing a little straighter.

I follow Thomson down the narrow winding stairs below deck. My Glock presses against my thigh as I pull it from the pocket of my shorts, nodding for Thomson to do the same. The master cabin door is ajar. On the crisp white bedding lies a single black calla lily, its stem wrapped in cream cardstock. The message hits like a tactical round to my chest.

You let him taste what's mine. It won't happen again.

I check my watch.

Ten minutes.

That's how long I spent with my face between her legs. Which means this sick fuck was watching, waiting.

'How?' I whisper to Thomson. This psychotic bastard is terrifyingly good at evasion.

'I heard footsteps earlier, sir. Assumed it was one of Marcel's crew. I checked the entire yacht before we left. There was no one here but us.' His face is ashen.

'Time frame?'

'Eight minutes ago.'

I motion toward the stern exit. 'Take port side. I'll go starboard. Full sweep.' My voice is low but lethal. 'Then we get her the fuck off this boat.'

We clear every cabin, every storage space, even the engine room.

Nothing. Which means our stalker is either a highly skilled diver, or I've got a serious fucking problem in my ranks.

No. That's impossible.

How could I have been so careless? He was within shooting distance, a fact which I might have noticed had my face not been buried between Avery's legs. Her killer curves and my own obsession with them could have been the literal cause of her death.

I will never touch her again.

Not because *he* said so, but because I can't afford one second of distraction, because in one stupid moment of weakness, I handed this psychopath exactly what he wanted —proof she's vulnerable. Proof I can be distracted.

And I had the cheek to call her reckless. Fuck.

Back on deck, Avery's sprawled on the sun lounger, martini balanced between manicured fingers, completely oblivious to how close danger came. For a moment, watching the sunlight play across her peaceful features, I hate that I have to shatter her tranquillity. But better a broken bubble than a broken neck. Maybe now she'll finally understand the gravity of what we're dealing with.

'We need to get back to the hotel.'

Sterling and Walsh start gathering Avery's things.

'What? But we haven't even reached Colombier Beach—'

'And we're not going to.' I bite. 'There was another lily. With another message.'

I watch as confusion sweeps over her face. 'But how?' She sweeps an arm around the deck at my team. 'Where?'

'Below deck.' I hate myself for putting her in danger because of my own selfish needs.

Her blue eyes dim. 'What did it say?'

I debate how much to tell her, then opt for everything. Maybe it will terrify her enough to stop goading and distracting me. 'He was watching us on deck. Saw everything.'

'Everything?' A blush stains her cheeks. Her hand flies over her mouth in horror. 'What did he say?'

'His exact words were, "You let him taste what's mine. It won't happen again."' Rage rips through every fibre of my body.

The colour drains from her face. 'How did he even get onboard?'

'That's what I intend to find out.'

I motion to Sterling and Walsh. 'Call ahead. Have forensics waiting when we dock.'

This fucker is even more dangerous than I gave him credit for.

Chapter Eleven

THE WATCHER

Rage pulses through my veins as I strip off the diving gear, my movements precise despite the fury threatening to tear me apart. The small boat rocks beneath my feet, anchored safely beyond the yacht's sight line.

I watched them through my scope all morning.

Watched her stretch like a cat in the sun.

Watched her tease him, tempt him—she knows she's irresistible. She wields her body like a weapon, but she hasn't worked out that it was made for me alone.

She let him touch her.

Let him put his filthy mouth between her legs.

Let him taste her.

Let him take what belongs to me.

She'll have to be punished for that.

And so will he.

Avery will learn who she belongs to.

He doesn't love her.

He'll never love her.

No one will ever love her like I do. The black lilies are elegant, rare, impossible to ignore. Like my love for her. Like the destiny we share. But soon... soon I'll show her that everything she thinks she wants—the glamour, the fame, even him—is nothing compared to what I can give her. To what we could be together.

I've watched her for so long. I know every habit, every gesture, every expression. The way she sleeps with one hand tucked under her cheek. The way she brushes her hair exactly one hundred times. How she hums when she thinks no one's listening. The little smile she gets when she says something smart. And now he's there, stealing these moments from me. Taking them for himself. My hands shake with the need to wring his neck. To make him suffer. To make him watch when I put my face between her legs.

I want—no need—to be the only man to give her pleasure.

And I will be...

Because you can't fight fate...

I've never been on a private jet before. Don't get me wrong, I'm used to the good life—I haven't flown coach since I started dancing at The Luxor Lounge all those years ago, but the Beckett brother's plane is something else entirely.

I glance around the cabin, soaking in every detail. Rich wood veneers and gold accents line the walls. The lights are controlled with integrated touch panels. There's a state-of-the-art entertainment system with a retractable ultra-HD screen and surround-sound speakers. A built-in bar with a wine chiller, crystal glassware, and every type of whiskey Beckett's has ever produced. A high-gloss lacquer dining table doubles up as a conference table in the space behind me, where Killian is furiously tapping away on his laptop.

Walsh and Thomson sit at the bar stools talking amongst themselves. Sterling stayed behind with the others to search the resort and apparently check the whereabouts of their top suspects—Thorne Blackwood, and Raven McCormac, who are both apparently staying on the island until tomorrow.

My gut tells me it's not either of them. Yes, Thorne and his micro penis are weird, but loads of artistic types are. And as for Raven... Well, he's a drunken drummer with a crush. Does he have the skills it takes to pull off something like this?

I don't think so...

Which leaves me sitting on a cream, custom leather seat wondering who the fuck is so obsessed with me that he'd scuba dive to the private yacht I rented, just to leave me a fucking flower? It's a comfortable twenty degrees in here, but I've been chilled all the way to my bones since Killian told me there'd been another note. Which is why I didn't protest when he said we're leaving St. Barths early.

There was no forensic evidence—or if there was, it was washed away by the water soaking every surface.

Who the fuck is this guy?

And how the hell did he keep the note and the lily dry? His attention to detail is alarming, yet impressive.

Killian is vibrating with anger—at the stalker and probably at himself for being distracted while he was that close. If he wasn't putting on a show for Sterling and the others, perhaps they wouldn't have been distracted too.

'When we land, we'll go straight to my place. You'll be staying with me for the foreseeable future,' he barks, without lifting his eyes from the screen. We're back to him stoically refusing to look at me again.

Pity.

The best part of my entire trip to St. Barths was having his eyes on me while I came on his face.

Sorry Scarlett, it was great to witness your happily ever after and all, but my own happy ending blew it out of the water—even if it was so short lived.

A part of me is horrified the stalker witnessed that, even though I was ok with having Killian's men as an audience— the badness of it was half the fun. But the defiant part of me is glad he saw it. Glad he knows I don't belong to him. Glad he knows he can't control who I let touch me. That

I'm still living my life, despite the terrifying situation he's put me in.

And then there's another part of me that's so fucking angry that because he—whoever *he* is—gate-crashed my boat trip, Killian will never touch me again. Frankly, that's the prospect that scares me the most because it was the single-best experience of my life, and despite my broody bodyguard insisting it was a one-time thing, I know I could have worn him down.

'I thought we were staying at mine. You didn't put all those cameras in my house for nothing.'

'Change of plan. My place is safer. I'll have your clothes couriered over.' His tone leaves no room for debate, but that never stopped me before.

'I need to go home, Killian.' I drag my fingers through my tangled hair. I didn't even have time to brush it as we hastily gathered our belongings and flung them into our cases.

'Not gonna happen, Avery. This psychotic bastard is even more dangerous than I thought. Who knows how long he's been watching you for? The chances are, he knows your house as well as you do.' He finally looks up from the screen and the second our eyes lock, that intense electricity surges between us again.

'I just need ten minutes to grab a few personal items, and Jasper.'

'You seriously want to bring that creature to my apartment?' His nose wrinkles in disgust.

'Wait until you meet him. You'll love him.' I bat my eyelashes, and he scowls.

'Is it toilet trained?'

'*He* is litter tray trained.'

He pauses for a long beat, like he's thinking about it. 'Fine. But if it shits all over my apartment, it's going to the nearest cat shelter—via the window.'

Two hours later, we land in Dublin airport, where a black SUV waits for us.

'Collins, this is Miss Williams.' Killian introduces me to his driver. I nod politely, as Killian slides into the seat beside me, his cologne wafting around me. I'm dying to lean closer, inhale his neck, throw myself on his lap, and beg him to put his arms around me until this whole fucking ordeal is over.

But of course, I don't.

Walsh hops in beside us and Thomson gets in the front. Killian reels off my address to Collins. The fifteen-minute drive is silent, bar the November rain hammering off the windscreen. It's just after seven in the morning and I feel like I haven't slept in weeks. I need a hot bath, a cup of camomile tea, and to fall into a comfy bed.

'Pull up on the opposite side of the street,' Killian orders Collins, then motions for Walsh and Thomson to check the perimeter. I stare through the dim morning light at the house I bought two years ago—a five bedroomed detached, red-bricked house in Skerries, one of Dublin's most desirable locations overlooking the Irish Sea.

A shiver runs down my spine.

He's been here.

When will I be able to stay here again?

And will I want to when it's suddenly gone from being my safe haven, to a place where I've been watched like prey? A deep sense of violation twists my stomach.

I stare silently out of the window, wondering who the hell is crazy enough to follow me to St. Barths? Just as we're about to exit the vehicle, a car approaches in the distance, its head-lights blinding. I instinctively raise my hand to shield my eyes.

'Get down.' Killian's hand lands on my shoulder, and I jolt as he pushes my head down into his lap. I might enjoy having my face in his crotch if he hadn't just snatched his gun from his suit pocket.

The car engine cuts out right beside us. Fear trickles over me. Killian doesn't take his hand from my head, brushing a thumb over my temple with a tenderness I never would have believed he possessed. I take a tiny bit of comfort from his touch and from the heat of his body. He won't let anything happen to me. He won't.

'Who is it?' Would the stalker be brazen enough to pull up outside my house? No. Unless he had a private jet, he has to be halfway across the world.

'Red BMW, registration plate D52 MILF. Thomson and Walsh are in position.'

A snort erupts from my mouth. 'That's my mother! She's here to feed Jasper!'

'Your mother has a registration plate that spells out MILF?' Killian sighs. 'Why am I not surprised?' He removes his hand from my head, and I reluctantly lift my face from his lap. I kind of liked it down there. 'Next you'll tell me she's a glamour model too.'

'No, she's a wedding planner.'

He huffs out a breath. 'Stand down.' He says into his watch. 'It's Miss Williams's mother.'

I reach for the car door handle, but Killian catches my wrist. 'Don't tell your mother about the situation. The less people who know, the better. I'll have security installed at her house in case our flower-loving friend decides to target you in other ways.

Panic rises in my chest. 'You think he'd hurt the people I care about?'

'I have no idea, but the man clearly has the means to, if he takes the notion.'

'What shall I tell her?'

'Tell her there's a leaky pipe and you're staying with a friend until it's fixed.'

I cock my head. 'And that friend would be you?'

'Obviously,' he snaps, dropping his grip on my wrist. 'I'll tell Walsh and Thomson to make themselves discreet. Come out my side.'

Collins is hovering outside the back door, waiting to open it. He's dressed like Killian and the rest of his men in a black tailored Armani suit. I watch as my mother clocks him as she gets out of her car. Her lips pop open as her eyes eat him up from head to toe.

Killian gives Collins a nod, and he opens the door for us.

I slide over the plush leather and out into the chilly morning. 'Mam,' I call from behind Killian's huge bulky frame. He steps aside and her expression morphs from surprise to delight.

'Avery!' she squeals. 'I wasn't expecting you back until tomorrow. I was just about to check on Jasper before my Hot Pilates class.'

My mother is a fitness freak. She does Pilates daily. In fairness, for a woman of her age, she has an amazing figure. She takes care of herself physically, and isn't shy about the fact she gets botox. When dad left her for his PA, she channelled all her heartbreak into self-improvement. Now she's that fiftysomething woman who gets mistaken for being in her thirties and has more energy than most twenty-year-olds. She has a huge Instagram following, and half her followers are boy toys sliding into her DMs—which she takes full advantage of.

She races towards us; Killian sidesteps a split second before she flings her arms around me. I sag into her embrace, the weight of the past twenty-four hours finally catching up with me.

'How was the wedding, honey? I bet Scarlett looked amazing. Did you have a good time? What was the resort like? The

pictures looked fantastic. How was the food?' This incessant
stream of conversation is totally normal for my mother. 'Did
you have a hot and heavy holiday fling?' Eventually, she
releases me from her arms to squint at my face.

My gaze drifts to Killian.

'Oh my,' My mother waggles her perfectly shaped
eyebrows. 'Who do we have here?'

'This is Killian.' I clear my throat. 'He's a... friend.'

Killian nods in acknowledgement but doesn't extend a
hand. His issues with personal contact are painfully obvious.
Which is what made yesterday so much more special—until
my stalker ruined it.

'Friend, huh?' My mother parrots in a voice that drips
with disbelief. She didn't read the room long enough to deck
Killian's issues and flings her arms around him. 'Any friend of
my daughters's is a friend of mine. It's a pleasure to meet
you.'

He stands rigid for a few seconds; an expression of horror
pinches his features. The urge to laugh rises in my chest like a
tidal wave. Finally, he offers my mother an awkward back pat
before wrenching himself free.

'So, what are you kids doing home early?' Her cobalt blue
eyes dart between us.

'I have a leak in my house; I spotted it on the cat cam.' I
shrug. 'Killian kindly offered me a space on his jet.'

'His jet,' my mother's jaw swings open as she stares at
Killian again. 'You're Killian Beckett.'

'I am,' he confirms.

The Beckett brothers are notorious in this country.

My mother pauses for a long beat. 'Well, shall we go inside
and check it out? I can't say I noticed anything yesterday.'

'Actually, I'm not sure it's safe. We've arranged a plumber
to call, so we're waiting outside for him.' Killian's smooth lies
roll from his tongue as his face remains poker straight.

'Oh, well,' Mam turns her attention back to me. 'Come and stay with me until you get sorted. We could...'

'That won't be necessary,' Killian cuts in before my mother can launch into another monologue the length of *War and Peace*. 'I've arranged for Avery to stay with me.'

'I see.' My mother drags out the word *see* like it's an entire song. Mischief dances in her irises. She leans in to whisper, not so discreetly in my ear, 'Are you sure it's not him with a leaky pipe that needs attention?' Her shrill laughter pierces the air. 'He's kind of intense, isn't he? But I wouldn't kick him out of bed.'

'Mam!' I cover my eyes with my hand.

'I see the apple doesn't fall too far from the tree,' Killian remarks drily. 'You're welcome to wait in the car with us until the plumber comes,' he offers with a sweeping motion towards the SUV.

'No, thank you, this was literally a flying visit.' My mother's blonde high ponytail swings from side to side as she shakes her head. 'I really do have pilates.'

She turns her attention to me again. 'I'm glad you're home safely.'

A ripple of guilt bursts through my stomach. If only she knew. Killian's right though, it's better she doesn't. She'd be worried sick.

'Thanks for taking care of Jasper while I was away.' I kiss her cheek.

'No problem. He's a little dote.' She backs away, towards her car with a wave. 'Let's do lunch soon.'

'Sure. I'll call you. Love you.' I blow her another kiss.

'Love you too.' She slips into her car and zooms away with another wave.

'Let's get the flea-ridden fur ball and get out of here ASAP.' Killian places a huge palm on the small of my back as he scans the street. Interestingly, I seem to be exempt from his personal contact issues after yesterday. I know his hand on me is protective, but it's definitely a little possessive too. And I like that knowledge almost as much as I like the shooting sensations he's sending rippling over my skin.

'He's not flea-ridden, he's fabulous.'

The prospect of living with Killian Beckett sets stupid little butterflies soaring through my stomach. Which is probably far more dangerous than any stalker, because Killian will never be what I need.

But try telling that to my vagina.

Chapter Thirteen

KILLIAN

The cat litter tray is a fucking eyesore in my hallway. And don't get me started on the weird fucking scent. And that's before the little shit's even used it.

Fuck. My. Life.

'Wow, this place is unreal.' Avery peers around the open plan living area of my penthouse apartment. She's doing that psychoanalysing thing again. Like my Feng Shui might reveal my past trauma. Like she might be able to see it and fix me. Which is categorically not going to happen.

'It's kind of bare though, don't you think?' She struts around like she owns the place, swaying her pert ass like she's on the catwalk.

'I don't like clutter.' Or chaos. Or having a fucking ginger cat sitting on my chrome kitchen top. Or having to live with a woman who crawls under my skin and steals my senses, so much so that I think it's acceptable to go down on her on the deck of a yacht while my men are twenty feet away.

Avery gravitates to the floor to ceiling windows overlooking the River Liffey. 'You know what this place needs?'

'Nothing.' If she's getting ideas about filling my apartment with flowers and photos and shit, she can think again. I need to catch this stalker creep before Avery gets comfortable here. It was one thing seeing her beautiful body on my TV, in the newspapers, and on repeat in my fucking head for the past couple of years, but now I have to live with her too. I must have been a raging cunt in my previous life. Although, admittedly, I've done some pretty bad things in this one too.

My mind wanders to the rapist paparazzo sitting in the warehouse in Wicklow. Anton Roche's hours are numbered.

'Make yourself at home. There's a gym. Swimming pool. Sauna and Jacuzzi. A cinema room. There's only one room that's off limits—my office.'

Her pupils flare. 'Why? What are you hiding in there?'

'Nothing.' Liar—one step inside that fifteen foot space and she'll know exactly how obsessed with her I am—and always have been. Every photo shoot she's ever posed for is pinned to the wall like I'm a groupie with a crush. Or a stalker. The irony isn't lost on me. The difference is, I wouldn't actually stalk her—clearly. I was perfectly content admiring her from afar. It was safer for both of us.

I bristle. 'I'll show you your room.' I motion towards the wide staircase. Walsh and Thomson put Avery's belongings up while she was setting up that god awful cat tray.

'Thanks, I'm whacked.' She yawns, and I get a glimpse of the pink inside her mouth a split second before she covers it with her hand. What I wouldn't do to slide my tongue in there again. Or better yet, the permanent semi I have when she's around. I've fantasised about her plump lips wrapped around my cock for years. But it can never happen.

Yesterday is irrefutable proof of that.

Living with her is going to be torture.

'It's been a long day.' I stride towards the stairs, my shoes sinking into the plush grey carpet.

'Yep, and it's barely eight a.m.'

'Get some sleep. I have some errands I need to run.'

'You're leaving me?' Her eyes widen and a flash of fear flickers over her face.

'This place is like Fort Knox. No one can get in, bar me, Walsh, Thomson, Sterling and Collins. There are cameras everywhere. Fingerprint and facial recognition are the only ways to access this entire building.' I stride along the wide corridor towards the nicest guest bedroom, coincidentally right across the hall from mine. I need to be able to keep an eye on her, after all. 'Walsh and Thomson have their own rooms here. They'll take care of you.' *While I take care of the rapist pap.*

I open the bedroom door for her. She gasps as she takes in the décor, all silver, greys and soft furnishings. Sliding patio doors boast the same view as the lounge area. There's a forty-foot walk-in wardrobe and an ensuite bigger than most people's houses.

'This is stunning.' She steps in. I deliberately don't follow her. I lost control once; I don't entirely trust myself not to do it again. Especially now she's essentially locked in my apart-ment. Which is why I need to put some distance between us.

'My housekeeper, Anabelle, will be back this afternoon. She'll fix you something for dinner.' I pull the door closed, but before I can shut it properly, Avery calls me.

'Wait!' She closes the distance between us, lingering in the doorway. 'You're not going to be home for dinner?'

'I'll eat alone in my office.'

'Do you usually eat in your office?' She places a hand on her hip.

'No.'

'So, what, you don't want to eat with me?' She pouts.

I exhale heavily. 'Avery, we are not friends. We're not anything, so let's not pretend. I have a job to do. And I intend to do it, so we can both get back to our normal lives.'

'We might not be friends, but we are stuck together—like it or not.' She smooths a hand over her crumpled dress. Dark shadows linger beneath her eyes. She looks like how I feel—wrecked. 'You're the only person I have for company right now. Please don't make me eat alone.' Her voice wobbles slightly as she says the word alone. Vulnerability flickers over her face, yanking something deep inside my chest.

What is it about this woman that's so fucking hard to say no to?

What is it about her that makes me want to burn down the world for her?

To want to watch her while she sleeps.

To want to listen to the soothing rhythmic rise and fall of her full chest.

To eradicate every single person who ever wronged her–or fucked her.

I swallow hard. 'Fine. We can eat together. I'll ask Annabelle to have dinner ready for seven. But this'—I gesture between us—'is not happening. It's not a date. We are not friends. And you don't get to ruin my dinner by asking me three thousand personal questions.'

Her lips tip upwards in a small smile. 'Deal. I won't ask you three thousand questions.' She places a hand on the curve of her hip. 'I'll ask you three.'

'Not happening Avery.' I tut.

'Oh come on, indulge me. I'm stuck here with you; we have to pass the time some way.' Her gaze trails over my torso and lands on my crotch. 'Unless...'

I groan. 'Fine. Three questions—but that's your daily limit.' The woman should have been a terrorist negotiator. Which is worrying on so many levels, given my past. 'My ex is off limit. And don't even think about psychoanalysing me.'

'See you at seven,' she sings gleefully before slamming the door in my face.

By the time I get back from Wicklow, Annabelle has set the huge dining room table. The scent of garlic and thyme floods my nostrils as I wander through the apartment. The ginger fucking fur ball runs towards me and butts its furry fucking head at my ankles.

Huh. So, it's true what they say; pets really are like their owners. This flea-ridden fucker is just like Avery—determined to get my attention and has zero boundaries.

I didn't drag things out for too long at the warehouse. Our rapist friend confessed very quickly when I took a bolt cutter to his finger.

I don't enjoy torture.

I'm not a sadist.

Some things, however, are an unpleasant, but necessary, means to an end. I would have killed him for what he did to Avery, but knowing that he got off with raping a minor made what I had to do a little easier on my conscience.

I check in with Thomson and Walsh, then head to my en suite for a shower. I wash the blood from my hands, then scrub my entire body from head to toe twice to ensure I removed every trace. The water pounds against my back, the heat and pressure relieving some of the tension in my shoulders. My mind drifts to Avery in the room across the hallway.

Is she still in bed?

Or is she in the shower too?

The idea of her naked and soapy has my cock rising quicker than a flagpole. I sigh and wrap my hand around the thick base, gripping tightly. It was always going to happen after yesterday on the boat.

I summon the image of Avery's perfect, glistening pink cunt to the front of my mind. Having a photographic memory is useful sometimes. I can still taste her arousal on my tongue. Feel it gliding between her soft, slippery folds.

I pump harder, imagining it's *her* hand working me. *Her* hand dragging me to the edge of oblivion. Precum trickles from my tip. I picture her on her knees in front of me, licking me with heat and hunger in her eyes. My balls tighten. My quads shake. My orgasm explodes at the precise second my ensuite door opens and Avery bursts in, wearing nothing but a tiny white towel around her torso. Her blue eyes widen as they fall to my cock. Cum shoots from my tip in rope-like spurts.

'Fuck.' Her eyes dart from my dick to my face and back again with fascination while I'm trapped in the final tremors of one of the best orgasms of my life—with the woman I'm fantasising about as a witness.

Yeah. Fuck is the only word for it.

I don't bother turning away. It's too late. There's no point.

Her hand flies to her mouth and as she lifts her arm, the towel around her torso drops to the marble floor. Avery's famous curves are bare in front of me. She really might be the death of me. I just hope to hell I'm not the death of her, because if she keeps distracting me like this, it's a very distinct possibility.

I sigh as she snatches her towel up from the floor.

'Ever heard of the word "boundaries"?' I spit.

'Ever heard of the word "lock"?' She tucks the towel around her again, but her eyes shamelessly rake over every inch of my body like she's committing it to memory for later.

'What do you want, Avery?' I force an air of boredom into my voice. She needs to leave before I drag her in here, bend her over, and fuck her so hard she won't be able to walk straight for a week.

'I er...' she wets her lips, then tears her eyes away. 'Shower gel. I was looking for shower gel.'

I reach for the bottle on the built-in shelf and toss it to her. Surprisingly, she catches it.

'Thanks.' Her focus returns to my cock again, and she shifts from one foot to the other.

'Goodbye, Avery.' I stare at her pointedly as the water cascades over my contours.

Her throat bobs as she swallows. She makes no attempt to leave. I arch a single eyebrow in question.

'I mean I could...' She waves a hand at my shower.

'That won't be necessary.' Even if it's tempting as fuck. 'As you can see, I've already finished.'

'But...'

'If you don't get out in three seconds, you'll be eating dinner alone for as long as it takes me to catch your psycho stalker.'

'You're no fun, you know that?' She tosses her glossy blonde hair from her shoulder.

'I never claimed to be.'

She spins on her heel and storms out.

I should be happy.

It's what I wanted.

Yet, there's no denying the disappointment in my core.

And in my dick.

Chapter Fourteen

AVERY

I've been at Killian's for five days now. He's tailed me to meetings, to photoshoots, to the gym. He accompanied me to lunch with my mother—much to her delight. He even sat patiently in the salon while I had my highlights done. Unfortunately, he's also started locking his bedroom and bathroom door—more's the pity. I've been getting myself off to his image every night since, but almost a week later, I'm greedier than ever for the real thing.

There's been no sign of the stalker, and no more flowers as yet. It's like he's disappeared into thin air. Killian has absolutely zero leads and is growing more frustrated by the day. True to his word, he's eaten dinner with me every night this week, and allowed me three questions per night while we devour whatever delicacy his talented housekeeper produces.

I've deliberately been easy with the questions, luring him into a false sense of security before I drop the big one—the one that's been eating me up inside since the shower incident. It's literally crawling up my throat tonight, though that might have something to do with the half a bottle of Bandol I consumed with my venison. The wine is a product of the

Beckett family vineyards in Provence; it's so good even Mr Control Freak let down his guard to have one.

'Spit them out then, Avery.' He swirls his wine around his glass. 'Let's get this over with.'

'You love it really.' I hold out my empty glass for a refill.

He takes it, reaching for the bottle with his other hand. 'I don't.'

'Don't you ever get lonely?'

'Is that your question?'

'No.' I accept the full glass he passes over the huge cherry-wood table. Our fingers touch and a jolt of electricity sears my skin. He yanks his hand away and hides it under the table. 'It was *a* question.'

Our eyes lock and the chemistry pulses between us. How he can ignore it is beyond me.

'No,' he says, bluntly.

'That's it? You're not going to elaborate?' Jesus, it's a good job this man is easy on the eyes because his conversational skills are shite.

'It's the psychology doctorate, isn't it?' He doesn't break eye contact. 'Maybe if you got a job using it, then you wouldn't feel the need to practice on me.'

'Does it make you uncomfortable?' I inch forward over the table. His eyes drop to my scoop neck top and a ripple of satisfaction surges through me.

'No.' He lifts his wine to his lips and drinks. I watch his throat work as he swallows. He really is a piece of art. 'That's two questions you've used up now.' A hint of a smile ghosts his lips.

'That wasn't a question, it was—'

'It was a question. And think carefully before you waste the next one, because that's your lot until tomorrow.'

In that case...

'Fine.' I straighten my spine. 'But you better be honest.'

'Shoot.' His expression gives absolutely nothing away, as usual, but I'd almost swear he's enjoying these evenings together more than he lets on.

'What were you thinking about the other evening?'

Confusion mists his eyes.

'In the shower.' I clarify.

His nostrils flare as he thrums his fingers off the table. 'Avery...' there's a warning in his tone.

'You said you'd be honest,' I remind him.

'It won't change anything.' He stares stoically at my face.

'It's only a question.'

'Fine.' He pauses for a long beat. 'You want the truth?'

I nod, frightened if I open my mouth I might scare him off.

'I was thinking about you, but you knew that already, which is why you're asking.' He rests an elbow on the table, his dark dilating pupils boring into mine. Hot flames lick over my skin. 'What you don't know is that I was thinking about your lips around my cock, imagining you lapping my cum from the tip, and loving every fucking second of it.'

The air whooshes out of my chest. Desire pools in my core and lower. Wow. The speed at which he can flick from being verbally stunted to downright filthy and uninhibited is an impressive talent. He should drink wine more often.

It's not often I'm lost for words—but tonight, I have none.

That was his intention though, wasn't it?

I wet my lips. My underwear is ruined. I'm fucking ruined. How is it possible to want someone so badly? If we ever did have sex, I know it would blow every other experience I've had out of the water. But Killian Beckett is off limits, physically and mentally. Even if I could convince him to take my body, he'd never give me his heart or mind.

Fuck, where did that thought pop from?

For all I know, the man might not even have a heart.

He downs the remainder of his wine, then stands. 'I'll be in my office.'

'I'll be in my bedroom with my vibrator.' I'm not even joking.

'Avery,' he hisses as his eyelids fall closed.

'Unless you've got a better suggestion?'

His fingers curl into tight fists. Tension radiates from him as his eyes snap open. 'I suggest we catch the stalker.'

I watch his firm sculpted ass as he storms away.

A few days later, I'm perched at a chrome bar stool at Killian's massive kitchen island. He struts in looking positively fucking edible in one of his trademark black Armani suits which sculpts his shoulders in a way that should be illegal. He strides towards the coffee machine with a grunt that I've come to interpret as 'morning.'

Over the past couple of weeks, I've learnt that Killian is even moodier than usual until he's had a double espresso. And when he gets himself a caffeine fix, he usually gets me one too, just the way I like it. He doesn't even ask anymore—just does it. Two shots of espresso, steamed oat milk, two sweeteners. The man might be emotionally stunted and repressed, but he pays attention to detail.

My phone chimes with a message notification from the counter. I'm under strict instruction not to even open one of my social media apps and the withdrawal symptoms are starting to kick in. The FOMO is real. I suppose I'm lucky I still have a phone.

'Who's that?' Killian asks gruffly.

'Kenzi.' Kenzi is one of my school friends who's making it big as an actress in America after a Netflix series she starred in blew up. I click open the message.

'Kenzi O'Brien?' Killian's dark eyes narrow as he reaches for the oat milk. I'm pretty sure he knows where this is going.

'She's wrapped up filming and she's in Dublin this weekend only. She wants to meet for cocktails at Elixir.'

'Absolutely not.' As usual, his tone implies that it's not up for debate.

Has the man learnt nothing about me in the copious amount of time we've been forced to spend together?

'It's not in your schedule.' He necks his espresso, then stirs the sweeteners into the coffee he's making me, hard enough to rattle the silverware from the mug.

'It's called spontaneity. You should try it sometime.' I motion for him to hand me the mug, preferably before he cracks it with the spoon.

'Spontaneity gets people killed.' He passes me my drink, then places the spoon in the top tray of the dishwasher on its side, exactly one centimetre apart from the first spoon I used this morning. Then he turns that one on its side too, so it's sitting at exactly the same angle as the other one. My billionaire bodyguard has OCD as well as control issues.

'People die of boredom too.' I take a sip, watching him over the rim. 'Come on, Killian. I've been cooped up in here since we got back from St. Barths. Elixir is exclusive, has great security, and your men can come too. Though maybe not Sterling...he's kind of intense.'

Despite the yacht incident, Sterling continues to stare at me with some sort of weird fascination when he thinks I'm not looking.

'Not happening.' Killian slams the dishwasher door closed.

'You misunderstand me.' I hard ball him. 'I'm not asking your permission.'

He straightens himself and I feel the full impact of the glare he's aiming at me, but I refuse to back down. 'Avery...'

'Would you prefer I go completely stir crazy in this fancy penthouse prison of yours?'

He plants his palms on the counter, leaning forward. 'You have a seriously educated, and apparently affluent stalker leaving you death threats.'

'They're not death threats. They're creepy love notes. And I refuse to let him win by hiding away.' I stand, smoothing down my silk robe. Killian's eyes track the movement. 'Besides, I might get lucky tonight. It's been way too long since—'

'Enough.' The word comes out as a long low growl that sends heat pooling low in my belly.

'What's wrong?' I step closer, close enough to catch the scent of his ovary combusting cologne. 'Worried I might find someone who's actually willing to fuck me?'

His knuckles go white against the marble counter. 'You're not going.'

'I am, with or without you.' I turn to leave, letting my robe swish around my thighs. 'Question is, are you going to let me walk into potential danger alone?'

* * *

The bass line thrums through the soles of my Louboutin's as we step into Elixir. Crystal chandeliers drip from coffered ceilings, casting rainbow prisms across chrome and velvet. The air is thick with expensive perfume, fruity cocktails, and bad decisions waiting to happen.

Killian scans the space with military precision, probably cataloguing exits, threats, and vantage points. His hand hasn't left my lower back since we left the car, fingers splayed possessively against the barely there fabric of my gold dress. And I'm not going to lie, I'm loving his attention. I should have insisted on going out days ago.

Walsh and Thomson flank us, Collins waits outside in the car, and Killian orbits me like I'm the sun, shifting his body whenever someone moves too close.

I spot Kenzi holding court in our usual curved booth, the VIP section elevated above the main floor with a perfect view of the dance floor below. She's with Sophia, our other friend, and on the table in front of them are two bottles of Dom Pérignon glinting under the chandeliers because Sophia never does anything by halves. Sophia and I met three years ago at Milan Fashion Week. We were both new to the indus-try, terrified and trying not to show it. She caught me stress-eating mint chocolate gelato behind a curtain before the La Perla show and shared her emergency flask of tequila. We've been firm friends ever since.

'Finally!' Kenzi grins, but her step falters at Killian's thun-derous expression.

His fingers flex against my spine; the heat of his palm burns through the fabric of my silk Rebecca Vallance dress.

'Dios mío!' Sophia's voice carries over the music as she sashays towards us, drawing every male eye in the place. Well, every male eye except Killian's. His gaze hasn't left me since I stepped out of my room in this outfit.

'Oh my god, I didn't know you were coming!' I squeal at my stunning friend.

'I texted her the second you said could make it!' Kenzi throws her arms around me and Killian reluctantly sidesteps without taking his hand from my spine, continuing to scan the vicinity

'Is that Killian Beckett?' Sophia openly stares at my billionaire bodyguard.

'The one and only.' I shrug. 'Scarlett asked me to babysit him while she and James are on honeymoon.' The lie rolls from my tongue. 'He brought a few friends.' I glance around at Killian's men.

'Hot. As. Fuck.' Kenzi pretends to fan herself.

'Ladies.' A smooth, deep voice cuts through the music from behind us. 'Can I buy you a drink?'

I spin on my stiletto to find Austin Falcon smiling down at us. Venture capitalist, and regular on Dublin's most eligible bachelor lists.

Killian's fingers dig into my skin.

'Austin!' Sophia launches herself at him. 'When did you get back from New York?'

'Yesterday.' But Austin's eyes home in on me. 'I saw your GQ magazine shoot, Avery. Stunning.' He shakes his head like he's mind blown and wets his lips.

'Thanks.' Red hot tension radiates through Killian's palm. 'How long are you in Dublin for?'

'Long enough to take you to dinner.' Austin steps closer and places his hand on my bicep. 'How about it?'

Chapter Fifteen

KILLIAN

'Remove your hand before I detach it from your body,' I swat Austin Falcon away hard enough to make him step back. Walsh and Thomson move in, but I halt them with my hand.

Who does this jumped up prick think he is?

Austin's eyes flick to Avery, then to my hand that's now firmly wrapped around her waist, then back to me with a raised eyebrow.

'She's unavailable.' My voice could freeze hell.

'Is that right?' Austin's smile doesn't quite reach his eyes. 'Are you two a thing?'

Avery's two friends stand open-mouthed like they're watching a soap opera from the front row, while she turns slowly to face me, deliberately dragging her breasts across the side of my chest. Every cell in my body vibrates with the need to take Avery right here, right now in front of everyone and show the world she's mine.

Except she isn't.

'I don't know. Are we a thing, Killian?' Her indigo eyes glitter like she's loving every second of this.

Of course she is.

It's probably her wet dream to have men physically fight over her. If she had her way, we'd probably be fighting naked too.

How would she feel if she had any idea I killed for her the other day? That I'd kill for her every damn day if it meant keeping her safe, keeping her happy.

But right now, I could cheerfully kill *her* for putting me in this position.

If I say no, she'll accept his dinner invitation. I won't let her past my front door to attend—but that's irrelevant. It's the principle of the matter.

If I say yes, the woman has me over a barrel.

I brush her bouncing blonde curls back from her face and inch my lips lower until they brush against the sensitive skin of her earlobe. She's not the only one who can fight dirty. 'What do you want me to say, sweetheart?' I whisper-shout. 'You want me to tell him that I licked your pretty cunt last week? That I'd do it again in a heartbeat if I wasn't preoccupied trying to find a man who clearly wants to do the same thing to you?'

A tiny gasp slips from her pink painted lips as they part into a pronounced O.

In my periphery, Austin shifts from one foot to the other beside us. I tighten my grip on Avery's waist, brushing my thumbs over the curve of her hips.

'I want you,' she whispers into my ear. The scent of her peony perfume floods the air between us. 'But if I can't have you, I refuse to hang around like a spare part.'

Brat.

She'd go out with him to fucking spite me. To make me watch. And she'd probably get off on every damn second.

That's what she wants, to get off. She pretty much told me that in my kitchen this morning.

An idea forms in my mind.

'Tell him you're mine.' I graze my lips lower, peppering tiny kisses along the column of her throat as Austin stares on, sporting an expression of half horror, half intrigue.

'Why?' Avery inclines backwards, offering deeper access to her throat and pushing her hips against mine in the process. Her eyes widen as my rock solid erection presses into her.

'Because if you do, I'll take you somewhere private right now and make you come so hard you'll see stars. Again.' I press my dick harder against her to prove my point.

'You promise?' Desire flickers in her dilating pupils as she rolls her hips against me. 'Right now?'

'Right now,' I repeat with a nod.

The things this woman drives me to.

This is the last time we're going out until I catch the stalker. Because I refuse to be forced into this position again.

She twists her head towards Austin. 'Sorry, Austin,' she shoots him an apologetic smile. 'Apparently, we are a thing—at the moment.'

I slide my hands over the pert globes of her ass and pinch hard enough to make her jump. *At the moment.* I've a good mind to put her over my knee.

Austin sighs. 'I'm devastated.' He clutches his chest like he's wounded. He fucking will be if he doesn't get out of my sight in the next three seconds.

'Looks like the baby sitting's going well,' Kenzi teases, as Austin disappears into the crowd. I make a mental note to run a background check on that brazen fucker the second I get home.

'We're going to need details,' Sophia squeals, picking up her champagne glass.

'I'll give you all the details,' Avery promises with a smirk, 'Once I've had a private chat with Killian. Something's come up and we need to deal with it quickly.' Her gaze shifts back to me and that invisible, illicit charge powers between us again.

I said I'd make her come—I didn't say I'd fuck her.

There's no way I'm going to reward her brat-like behaviour with my cock. No matter how much I want to. That would only encourage her to do it again. I drop my hands from her waist the second Austin is out of sight.

'Thomson.' I touch my earpiece. 'There's an office on the third floor. I need you to give it a sweep. Avery and I need to have a private conversation.'

'How do you know there's an office on the third floor?' Avery pins me in a curious stare.

'One, I wouldn't be much good at my job if I didn't have a blueprint for every venue you drag me to, and two, who do you think owns this place?'

Realisation lights in her eyes. 'You?'

'Technically Rian does, but it's under the Beckett umbrella.' I shrug.

Kenzi pours Avery a glass of champagne and hands it to her. 'Just in case you need to wet your lips.' She grins knowingly, then turns to me. 'What about you? Do you need something to wet your lips?' she teases.

I don't dignify her with a reply.

I brush my lips over Avery's earlobe again. Austin might be gone, but I love to watch the way I make her skin ripple with goosebumps. 'Don't drink too much. I don't feel like putting you to bed. Again.'

'I thought that's what people did when they're a thing.' She winks and uses her free hand to make air quotes.

I'm going to enjoy watching her beg me to make her come.

'All clear.' Thomson's voice sounds through my earpiece.

'Stay there. We're on our way.' I nod at Walsh and he's by our side in seconds.

'Back shortly,' Avery tells her friends.

That's what she thinks. I fasten my hand to her lower back and escort her to the nearest exit through a throng of people. I scan the crowd. We attract a few stares, both of us, but this place is notorious for celebrities and there are way more famous people than either of us here tonight.

We take the stairs to the third floor, Walsh first, his hand resting on his holstered gun. Avery follows behind, with me guarding her back. Thomson is waiting outside the office doorway, one hand in his suit pocket. I don't need to see it to know it's wrapped around a pistol at the ready.

'All clear for the... Private conversation.' A ghost of a smirk steals over his lips before he catches himself. I roll my eyes.

'Both of you stand guard. Do not leave this door. Even if the place is on fire, understood?' I glance between the two men.

'Absolutely boss.'

I usher her in through the deep mahogany door and into the dimly lit room. There's a large desk with a tall leather chair tucked behind it, a corner lamp, and a metal filing cabinet. I was here with Rian a few weeks ago when he signed the paperwork to this place. This is his private office, not that he uses it much. We each have our own floor in the Beckett office building near Grafton Street. Still, if I wasn't so adamant about not fucking Avery, I'd take great pleasure in bending her over my baby brother's desk.

The door clicks behind us ominously. I turn the lock, not because I don't want anyone coming in, but because I don't want her getting out until I'm finished with her—which if I'm honest, could be never. As infuriating as she is, there's something about her that ignites a primal hunger in me which steals all rationale.

She stands in the middle of the room in those goddamn

stilettos and that dress which barely covers her fantastic ass, and it's a battle not to pounce on her like the predator I am. She takes a long slow sip from the champagne glass she's clutching like a lifeline. 'Where do you want me?' She runs her fingers languidly over the dark wooden desk.

'I hate that you put me in this position,' I growl, prowling closer. 'I hate that I let you. But most of all, I hate this wanton chemistry between us. You might have won whatever round of this fucked-up game we're playing, Avery, but you will never win the war. There's only one soldier here, and that's me.'

She sucks in a breath, her teeth digging into her lower lip.

'What are we fighting over?'

'*You* are fighting to distract me from my job. I am fighting for my fucking sanity.' I lift my hand up and wrap it around a lock of her golden hair, pull it to my nose and inhale the scent of her exotic shampoo.

'You just need to get better at multitasking.' Lust clouds her eyes as she sucks in a deep breath.

'I already mentioned that's something I excel in.' I step closer so we're toe to toe, hip to hip. She grips my bicep, wrapping her fingers around it and squeezing. It hits me like a hammer. Avery is one of the very few people I can tolerate touching me. Nobody gets close. Ever. I don't let them. Yet in the space of a couple of weeks, she's wheedled her way in.

Okay, it hasn't been weeks—not really.

We've known each other for years.

I've wanted her for years.

Which is why I can't take her—not properly, anyway. Not with my cock. Because I already know if I do, if I stake that claim on her, I'll never be able to let her go. I'm worse than any stalker. Way worse.

I dip my face towards hers and trace the outline of her lips with my tongue, savouring the plump rise and fall of her

Cupid's bow. She stands rigid, eyes wide open, boring into my mind like she can see my soul. Like she can see how much it wants to possess her—not just her body, but her heart, her mind, her everything.

But Avery will never give up her job as a glamour model, and I'd never ask her to, but no woman of mine could ever be plastered naked over every glossy magazine for every other man to see, to stare at, to wank over. Not a fucking hope.

So, I'll just take what I can, give her what I can. And maybe, eventually, my craving for her will wear off... Maybe.

I run my hands up over her stomach to her beautifully formed breasts and squeeze. She hisses.

'You're fucking stunning.' I bite out. 'But you're a brat for putting me in this position.'

Her body tenses a hint of wariness clouding the hunger in her eyes. 'Take your lingerie off and get ready to take your punishment.'

Chapter Sixteen

AVERY

My core clenches with need as I place my half empty glass on the desk, then wiggle my silk thong down over my thighs. It hits the floor with a soft swish. I sidestep out of it and raise my gaze to meet Killian's. A cocktail of desire, anticipation, and nerves pool in my stomach. I saw how big he was that day in the shower. If he decides to punish my behaviour by giving it to me hard, I'm not sure I'll survive it. Then again, if he doesn't—I'm not sure I'll survive that either.

He drops to the floor, snatches up my lingerie, brings it to his face and inhales. 'It's no wonder you have a crazed fucking stalker, woman. You'd drive any man demented with lust.'

I part my thighs slightly in invitation.

'Oh, no, sweetheart.' He chuckles—actually chuckles. 'I said I'd make you come, but I'm not going to make this easy for you. Plus, the longer I keep you in here, the less time anyone out there will have to ogle you.'

'Bastard.' I spit, but there's something really fucking hot about him wanting to drag this out. About him wanting to keep me away from his competition—not that there is any. How could any man compete with this hot, brooding bastard?

His finger darts beneath my dress and he swipes at the arousal between my legs before pulling it away again. He brings his finger to his mouth and sucks. I inhale sharply. I could be in for a long night. His dark haunted eyes exude the heat and carnality of an untamed beast.

I need him to unleash himself on me.

I need to feel him pummel into me so hard it'll feel like he's breaking me.

The truth is, he actually might. The man might be a walking red flag, but I want him more than I've ever wanted anything or anyone.

'Killian, please.' I'm not above begging. 'Bend me over that desk and fuck me until I can't see straight.'

A wolfish smile rips across his face. 'I said I'd make you come. I never promised you my cock. That's for good girls.'

Disappointment powers through me.

His fingers reach between my legs again. I'm dripping. A whimper slips through my lips as his thumb glides over my clit.

He fights dirty.

But so do I.

The next chance I get to go out with any man, I'm going to take it and drag him along to watch.

'So wet,' he purrs into my ear as his fingers continue working me.

I suppose a release is a release. For now. But he *will* fuck me if it's the last thing he ever does. I'm going to spend every minute of every day that we're together teasing him, tormenting him and making sure it's the only thing he can think about, until he eventually snaps.

Because he will do.

He retracts his hand again and I hiss.

'Take your dress off,' he commands.

Thankfully, I've got an alpha kink and not a praise one. I

grab the hem of my dress, tug it up over my shoulders, and toss it to the floor. I'm naked bar my stilettoes. It's his turn to hiss. His fingers glide over my nipples. There's something so fucking carnal about being naked for him. About surrendering to whatever pleasure he deems suitable to deliver— whichever form it comes in.

'If you were mine, nobody but me would see these spectacular tits.' His mouth dips down to catch my nipple, and he sucks hard enough to make me cry out. His laughter vibrates against my breast.

'If I were yours, I'd be riding your gigantic cock on that leather chair right now.' I shrug, feigning nonchalance but fooling neither of us.

He stands straight, challenge blazes in his eye. 'Such a pity we can never be.'

He reaches between my legs again, this time he slides two, no, three fingers deep inside my core and pumps as his thumb circles my clit.

Sensory overload.

It's official—the man can multitask.

'Imagine how good my cock would feel, sweetheart. Imagine all the deep, delicious spots I could hit in here.' His fingers still, and I cry out in frustration.

I'm drooling, actually drooling. 'Please, Killian.'

'Please, what?' A wicked glint gleams in his eyes.

'Give it to me.'

'Absolutely not.'

'Bastard.' My need for him is actually painful.

His low laughter fills my ear. 'I love it when you curse me. It tells me that I've crawled as far under your skin as you've crawled under mine.'

My legs are trembling like a newborn fawn, my orgasm shimmering on the horizon, just out of reach. 'Make me come. I need to come.'

'Only when you promise not to threaten me with dating other men while I'm trying to protect you.'

'Fine.' I'd promise him any damn thing he wanted right now; once he gives me what I need.

'Say it,' he demands.

'I promise I won't threaten to date other men while you're trying to protect me.' I'm so close. I need him to finish the job.

'Good girl.' His fingers resume their decadent movements. Lust blinds me. He watches intensely, for once it's with approval. When a moan bursts from my mouth, he places his lips on mine and swallows my screams. My tongue thrashes against his, greedy and grateful all at the same time. He sucks and licks and explores the inside of my mouth as I shudder and shake through the most devastating orgasm of my life.

The truly devastating thing about it is the knowledge that I need so much more from the man who has nothing to give.

When my legs finally subside their shaking, he breaks our kiss. I slump forward onto his chest, inhaling his cologne, his masculinity. The rapid hammering of his heart echoes through my ear.

'Can I...?' I reach for his buckle.

'No,' he disentangles himself from me. 'That wasn't the deal. We should get back to your friends. The quicker you see them, the quicker we can go home.'

He scoops my dress up from the floor and wiggles it over my head.

I won. I got what I wanted—sort of anyway. So why does it feel like I lost?

Maybe, just maybe, every time he touches me, I lose a bit more of myself to him. And so far, he's given me nothing of himself.

I genuinely wonder if he's capable?

'Where's my underwear?'

'In my pocket.' His lips twitch slightly. 'And that's where it's staying. I need a souvenir, seeing as this will categorically never happen again.'

He strides across the office, unlocks the door and opens it cautiously. The sound of the heavy base pumps from the floors below. He sticks his head out and says something to Thomson and Walsh. I smooth my dress back into position and follow Killian back out into the hallway and down the stairs back to the bar area. Killian says something inaudible to Walsh, and Thomson fires me a knowing wink. I shake my head in a poor attempt at denial. Thomson leans close enough to speak into my ear. 'He likes you.'

'He doesn't, trust me.'

'You get under his skin.'

'I'd like to get under him.' I grin at Thomson and he sniggers.

Killian's head whips round. 'What's so funny?'

'Nothing.' I flash him an innocent smile as he falls into line beside me.

'You're the future Mrs Beckett,' Thomson whispers.

My stomach somersaults. Why, I have no idea. I'm not even sure I believe in marriage. I brush off Thomson's remark with a subtle head shake.

Walsh takes the front as we cross the crowded bar to get back to Kenzi and Sophia. They're chatting animatedly over the music, but both turn expectantly when we approach.

'There you are! I was about to send out a search party!' Sophia calls, her eager eyes jumping between Killian and me.

'Where's your glass?' Kenzi lifts the almost empty bottle of champagne from the bucket.

'I must have put it down somewhere. I'll get another one and get us another bottle.'

'No need. Some guy sent one over to our table.' Kenzi

waves behind her and my gaze lands on a silver bucket. Resting on a bed of ice beside an unopened bottle of Dom Pérignon is a black calla lily and a tiny white card with my name scrawled on it.

Killian spots it the same second I do; his entire body tenses.

Before we have time to think about what to do next, an ear-splitting siren pierces the club.

The shrieking of the fire alarm sets adrenaline surging through my blood.

He's here.

And his aim is to cause chaos, and get Avery out into the open.

Panicked patrons flock to the exits, trampling over each other in a desperate bid to break free.

Avery clings to my arm, while Thomson and Walsh reach for their weapons.

'Come on,' Kenzi beckons Avery to move.

'It's a drill. There's no fire,' I shout over the high-pitched wailing.

'How do you know?' Sophia demands as her eyes dart around, wild with suspicion.

'Call it a hunch.'

When the exit is clear, Walsh, Thomson, and I escort the girls back to the office on the second floor. I grab the note from the bucket on the way. I'm not stupid enough to think it's worth dusting for prints. The stalker has already proved he's too smart for that.

If I hadn't been so preoccupied getting Avery off—again —maybe I'd have spotted him.

How did he know we were here?

I've put a block on Avery's mobile. Her location can't be traced. She hasn't opened a social media site; I know for sure because she's whined incessantly about it every day since we've been stuck together. He must be watching my building. It's the only way. He must have followed us.

When we're all firmly locked in the office, I power up the computer on the desk. Rian's passwords are always the same, and this one is no different. I key in IlikebigbuttsandIcan-notlie, and shake my head. I click into the club's security cameras, but funnily enough, the system apparently has a fault and has been down for the last forty minutes. How convenient.

I reboot the system and power the cameras back up. The building is empty.

I switch off the fire alarm remotely and the wailing comes to an abrupt halt. The silence rings through my ear canals louder than the alarm. The women, who are all huddling together in the corner of the room breath a collective sigh of relief.

'Are you sure the building isn't on fire?' Kenzi eyes the door like she's expecting smoke to start wafting under it any second.

'Certain.' I tear open the note. Rage ripples through every cell in my body.

Them fighting over you is pointless—we all know you belong to me.

See you soon.

My molars clang together hard enough to hurt.

I missed him.

Again.

'Who sent the champagne?' I snap at Kenzi and Sophia. 'Did you get a look at him? Did anyone approach you? Did you see anyone you recognised, or did anyone stand out as suspicious?'

They glance at each other, alarm creeping into their heavily made up features.

'No,' Sophia says. 'A waiter wearing an Elixir embroidered shirt brought the bucket over. Austin was around somewhere, but I didn't recognise anyone else. What's going on here?' She glances at Avery, whose cheeks are unusually pale.

'Avery has an admirer. There's nothing to worry about, but we're monitoring the situation.' I'm such a liar. There's everything to worry about. This guy is ridiculously fucking good. If I didn't hate him with every fibre of my being, I might actually be in awe of him.

After running every one of Avery's thousands of Instagram messages through our most sophisticated detection software—cross-referencing linguistic patterns, analysing IP addresses, and deploying behavioural prediction algorithms—we've found absolutely nothing concrete to identify the stalker, which is almost more concerning than finding something; whoever this is knows precisely how to operate just beneath the digital radar.

And now this.

'Comes with the territory.' Avery attempts a weak smile, playing the situation down to her friends. The last thing we want is to incite panic and fuel the rumour mill.

'I hear you,' Kenzi shakes her head. 'When you're in the public eye like we are, people think they have some kind of connection with us. Got to keep the boundaries firm.'

'Speaking of boundaries,' Sophia's eyes widen, 'did you see the news?'

'What news?' Kenzi inches closer for whatever meaning-less gossip Sophia's about to vomit.

'Remember that body they found on the outskirts of the Wicklow mountains last week?'

My ears sharpen, muscles tighten. I told my men to dispose of it discreetly. Apparently they weren't as discreet as I hoped.

'What about it?' Kenzi demands.

'You'll never guess who it was.' Sophia flicks her hair from her shoulder.

'Who?' Avery asks quietly.

'Anton Roche.' Sophia twists her gold tacky rings around her fingers. 'Clearly he pushed one too many boundaries—again. Wasn't he the guy who papped you at Paris fashion week?'

'That's him.' Avery's eyebrows crease into a frown; her gaze darts to me but I keep my focus on the note in my hand.

'Was he murdered or what?' Kenzi demands the details.

'There was so little of him left, it was inconclusive.' Sophia shrugs.

I wait, frozen in motion for Avery's reaction. If she expresses even a hint of horror or disappointment, I'll know the darkness in me is too much for her. That the beast I've become is incompatible with the beauty in her.

The silence stretches like a blade between us.

Her eyes meet mine, curious, clear, and unflinching.

'Karma's a bitch,' she says finally, her voice steady. Not celebrating his death, but not mourning it either. 'He made a lot of enemies.' Her make-up is smudged beneath her eyes and she looks beat. 'Can we go home?'

I exhale the breath I'd been holding. 'Yes.' I cross the room and take her into my arms, instinctively. The urge to protect her possesses every inch of me. I press a kiss to her temple and she slumps against my chest. If she has any inkling I'm responsible for Anton's death, it certainly hasn't put her off.

'You're okay. I've got you,' I murmur into her ear and she snuggles tighter.

'How did he know we were here?' She tilts her face up to meet my gaze.

'I have no idea. But I will find out.' Even if it's the last thing I do.

Chapter Eighteen

KILLIAN

Two hours later, Avery is safely nestled beneath the Egyptian cotton sheets in her bedroom at my apartment. She asked me to wait in her room while she showered and got changed for bed. Normally, I'd run the other way at being trapped in a bedroom with her—it would test any man's restraint, but given the fact that she was visibly trembling and it's a comfortable twenty-three degrees in here, I couldn't say no if I tried.

I lean against the doorframe, deliberately keeping the distance between us, because as much as I know that distraction nearly cost us earlier, I can't trust myself not to let it happen again. Not when I know she's only wearing a silk slip beneath those covers. And not when she's looking at me like I'm the only man in this world.

Devoid of make-up, she's every bit as beautiful as she is with it. More so, in fact. Her blonde, lustrous locks fan out across the pillow as she readjusts herself beneath the covers.

Her blue eyes are dark with uncertainty. 'Will this ever be over?'

'It will, I promise.' And as much as I want that day to

come soon, I'm glad she's here under my roof. Even if she does awaken a ravenous, irrational need that is frankly terrifying and exhilarating.

Being near her is like standing too close to a flame—knowing I'll get burned but unable to step away from the warmth. For years I've existed in a self-imposed frozen state, emotions locked down, senses dulled. Tactical. Strategic. Safe. But Avery... she makes my pulse race in a way it hasn't since Sarah. Makes my skin hypersensitive when she enters a room. I hate it. I crave it. This sudden, visceral reminder that I'm still human beneath the armour I've constructed.

The professional in me knows this is a catastrophic breach of protocol.

The soldier knows attachment is vulnerability.

The man who buried his heart in the desert knows exactly how this story ends—in blood and regret.

Yet here I stand, watching her breathe, memorising the shape of her lips, and wondering what kind of man I might have been if I'd met her before Sarah, before the hostages, before I became this hollow, dangerous version of myself. Avery makes me feel alive again—and that terrifies me more than any threat I've ever faced. Because being alive means having something to lose.

I shift from one foot to the other. I should let her sleep. I have work to do, starting with a background check on Austin Falcon, then hacking Kenzi and Sophia's phones to see if they spoke to or texted anyone of interest today. Someone who they might have mentioned in passing that they were meeting Avery. Thomson and Walsh are currently scanning the CCTV cameras on the streets surrounding Elixir and surrounding this building, but I'm not hopeful on that front.

'I'm sorry,' she says, blinking hard. Her thick eyelashes sweep over her delicate cheekbones.

'What for?' I step closer, drawn to her like a goddamn magnet.

I'm not used to this version of Avery. I'm used to the bolshy,   in-your-face-don't-tell-me-what-I-can-and-can't-do version. Tonight, she's swathed in a vulnerability that tugs at my heartstrings.

'For dragging you to Elixir. You said it wasn't safe. I thought I knew better.' She sighs.

'I understand your frustration at being cooped up here with me, but for now, it's for the best. No nightclubs. No bars. We stick to your schedule until this is over, okay?'

She makes a salute sign. 'Yes, sir.'

Those two words shoot straight to my dick.

'No variation from routine.' I bristle. 'You've had your fun.'

'I'll admit, goading you started out as a bit of fun.' Her eyes catch mine and she hesitates for a long beat. 'But now... I can't help it.'

I cock my head to the side in question.

'Have you ever wanted something so badly that it's all you can think about? Like thoughts of it literally ravage your body?'

'You want to get out of this apartment that badly?' I scrub a hand over my jawline. I tried my best to make this room nice for her. When I knew she was coming to stay, I had Annabelle go shopping for the softest sheets. I had her stock the fridge with all the foods I saw Avery enjoy in St. Barths. I even ordered in her favourite brand of coffee and that mint chocolate ice cream she loves. I know I'm not exactly fun to spend time with, but fuck, I didn't think things were that bad.

'You misunderstand me.' She wets her lips. 'I don't want to get out of the apartment. What I want is you.'

My heart beats double fast in my chest. She glimpsed the

darkness in me, even if she hasn't fully processed it. On some level, she knows what I am, and she still wants me. Every bit of my body begs me to move closer. To close the distance between us, wrap my arms around her chest and give into this thing between us, but I can't—for so many reasons.

Every time I touch her, I miss a chance to catch the creep who wants her for himself.

And even if I do catch him, Avery will never be mine. She belongs to a different world—a world in the limelight, a world I can't share her with.

And I promised myself after Sarah, I'd never let another woman in again. I'd never be weak again.

But realistically, I've already epically failed on that level because Avery has clawed her way under my skin. There's fuck all I can do about it. Except try to keep my hands off her.

'Avery...' I sigh.

'I know, I know...' she shrugs. 'But can I ask you one favour?'

She could pretty much ask me for anything right now, and I wouldn't be able to say no. She has me by the balls and the only person who doesn't know it is her. Thomson's exact words to me earlier were, 'that's your future wife'. Sentimental, delusional bastard. But yeah, in another life, one where Avery didn't parade around naked for a job and I didn't feel like murdering every man who looked at her... I might not be as quick to rule it out.

'I'm not having sex with you.' *Not because I don't want to, but because it terrifies me how much I do want to.*

She rolls her eyes, but not nearly with as much sass as usual. 'Will you stay with me for a while until I fall asleep?' Her voice cracks with need and it splits open my chest.

My gaze drifts to the chaise lounge to the left of her bed.

'No funny business, I promise,' she says.

I exhale heavily, take off my tie and toss it onto the vanity station littered with every cosmetic known to man.

Just when I'm about to sink into the plush velvet, there's a scratching noise at the door. Every hair on my body pricks. Avery bolts upright in bed, clutching the covers over her chest.

The realistic part of me knows there's no one in my apartment bar my men, who I trust with my life. But the part that's on edge, unsettled after this evening's events, can't be sure. I grab my gun from my pocket and push the door handle down slowly. It bursts open and a ginger furball darts in between my legs, scurries across the room and leaps onto the bed.

I exhale heavily as Avery squeals in delight, lifting her cat into her arms as he butts his head against hers.

'Fucking cat.' I kick the door closed and drop into the chaise lounge.

'We both know you love my pussy.' Avery's eyes latch onto mine, a hint of devilment flashing through that vulnerability.

'Go to sleep.'

'But I didn't get my three questions today.'

I pinch the bridge of my nose. I just have to say one word —no. Two tiny letters. One consonant. One vowel. But as usual, I just can't bring myself to annunciate them. 'Make them quick.'

She snuggles into the pillows, readjusting herself with a thoughtful expression on her face. Oh god, she's liable to come out with anything. And if it's "can you get me off again?" how the fuck am I going to say no?

'How did you end up in security?'

So, she's going for the psychoanalysis route. Here we go again. I take off my cufflinks, place them on the vanity station, and roll up the sleeves of my shirt. Her eyes follow the movement with a hint of hunger. 'I joined the military when I was eighteen, much to my parents' dismay.'

She sits quietly, waiting for me to elaborate.

'They'd rather I went to college like my brothers. I didn't have the patience for that. I wanted to see the world. My grandfather was in the military before the distillery came to fruition. He always told me the best education you can get is on tour. He wasn't wrong.' I crack my knuckles, forcing back the memories.

Sarah.

My final tour.

The hostages.

The blood.

Multicoloured pixel-perfect images, as clear in my head today as the day they happened.

Avery stares, quietly, drinking me in.

'The skills I learnt weren't exactly appropriate for banking, or investments, so when I got home, I channelled them into an area they were appropriate for–security–and started my own business.'

'Makes sense.' Avery rubs a hand over the ginger furball. Lucky bastard.

'Try and sleep.' I tell her.

'But I still have two more questions.'

'Go on then.' Who knew Avery Williams would turn out to be one of the few people I could talk to all night? Still, I have work to do.

'What do your tattoos mean?' Her eyes linger on my neck.

'They mean my parents disapprove of me,' I snort.

'That's a cop out if ever I heard one.' She tuts.

'Final question, then you need to sleep.'

'Fine.' She rolls her eyes at me. 'Why won't you let me touch you?' Her gaze drops to my crotch. A flicker of something like hurt flashes through them.

Does she seriously think I don't want her?

Does she have no idea how I feel about her?

I squeeze the bridge of my nose. If I tell her, she may never give up. If I don't she'll live with that uncertainty forever.

'The truth is sweetheart, if I let you touch me, you'd take more than I'm prepared to give.'

'What does that mean?' Her eyes snap to mine.

'You're all out of questions, princess.' A smug smile splits open my face. 'Goodnight.'

Chapter Nineteen

AVERY

Killian has slept on the chaise lounge in my bedroom every night since the Elixir incident a week ago. He's never here when I wake, but the scent of his masculine cologne lingers in my bedroom. It's both comforting and confronting. The more time I spend with him, the more I want him, which is problematic because he's more closed-off than a Carthusian monk. He hasn't once surrendered to the physical attraction between us for his own pleasure. The man's self-control is iron clad. Until it comes to giving *me* pleasure.

Jasper purrs on the pillow beside me. I rub his soft fur. 'Of all the men in the world, why do I have to want the one I unequivocally can't have?'

I sigh, throw back the covers and go in search of coffee. It's been another week of stylists, photoshoots and interviews and I'm frankly exhausted with the whole thing. Yes, I love some elements, but a lot of it is mundane. Repetitive. Mind numbing. I'm praying that things work out with ELEGANCE. I've got so much more to give than just my body. And besides, my time as a glamour model will come to an end one way or another, and I'm determined to lead the narrative on the when and how.

We haven't deviated from the schedule once and there have been no more lilies or notes. I still don't know what the one in the club said and I'm not sure I want to. What I do know is that when Killian is breathing the same air as me, I feel safe. Safe—but sexually frustrated. He hasn't touched me since the club, and I haven't even been able to touch myself with him sleeping in my room.

Ha, I should do it anyway and make him watch. Now there's an idea.

I pad barefoot into the kitchen. It might be mid-winter outside but in here, it's hotter than hell, mostly due to my hot bodyguard who's perched at the island with his laptop and a coffee. He's wearing navy suit pants and a white shirt with the sleeves rolled up to reveal his muscular forearms again.

Who even knew forearms could be sexy? The urge to lick every raised vein and artery is primal.

He looks up from the screen as I enter. 'Do you have to walk around half naked all the time?' He says gruffly.

I glance down at my short silk slip. 'If you think this is half naked, wait until we get to Tuesday's photoshoot. It's for a new Angel Nova perfume. And guess what I'm wearing?' I waggle my eyebrows at him as he stares back with that deadpan expression. 'The perfume—just the perfume. It's called Nova Natural.'

'I see it's our friend Thorne who's taking the photos.' Killian scowls, but he rises from his seat and heads to the coffee machine, grabbing oat milk from the fridge as he passes it. 'He was out of the country last week when we were at Elixir, so I suppose that rules him out, but I still don't fucking trust him.'

'He's harmless. Weird, but harmless.'

'I've cancelled your appearance at Hustle tonight.' He pauses, like he's waiting for me to stamp my feet or shout.

'Good.' I exhale a sigh of relief as I slip into the seat opposite the one he just vacated.

'I thought you'd fight me about it.'

'Not after last week.' A shudder rips over my spine. 'You didn't tell me what the note said.' Knowledge *is* power, I suppose. Maybe this creep will reveal something about his identity by accident.

The coffee machine whirs to life. Killian adds my sweeteners to a white china cup. It's a shame he's so off-limits. The man would make an amazing boyfriend, arrestingly attractive and thoughtful—not to mention he has the biggest dick I've ever seen. I press my legs together just thinking about it. There's no point trying to deny it—even to myself.

I want him more than I've ever wanted anyone.

I want his body, but I also want to break into his head, and I want to tug his heartstrings, the way he tugs mine. Beneath his hard exterior, there is a man with a huge heart, a man who's loyal beyond belief, a man who sleeps upright on a chaise lounge to make me feel safe, makes my coffee just the way I like it, who claims me when he thinks someone else is edging in... but I need more, so much more. I need him to claim me because he wants to, not because he's making a point.

'Sure you want to know what it said?' He stirs the coffee, then places it in front of me, sliding back into his own seat opposite.

'Not really, but tell me anyway.' I cradle the cup in my hands, but even that doesn't take away the chills washing over my skin.

Killian reaches into his trouser pocket and tosses the white tiny card over the table.

Their fighting over you is pointless—we all know you belong to me.

See you soon.

'He's wrong, you know.' I blow on my coffee and take a sip. It's dark, strong and decadently rich. Just like the man I'm becoming increasingly obsessed with.

'I know he's wrong.' His eyes hold mine with that alarming intensity. 'I wasn't fighting over you. I would though, if it came to it. I'd kill every man on the planet for you.'

An image of Anton Roche flashes through my mind. Did Killian…? I shake it away. Ignorance is bliss. 'You'd kill every man on the planet for me, but you won't have sex with me.'

'It's not won't, sweetheart.' A pained expression flickers over his features. 'It's can't.'

'Why not?'

'We've been over this. You know why.' He swallows and I watch as his Adam's apple bobs.

His remark the other night replays through my mind. *'If I let you touch me, you'd take more than I'm prepared to give.'*

'We both know you're not being honest with me. There's a lot more to it than the "I'm your client". You won't even let me pay you—so that excuse won't stand with me. And I know you think I'm irritating and reckless, yada yada yada,' I roll my eyes. 'But I also know that you're as attracted to me as I am to you.' I cover my eyes with my hands. 'Oh my god, I can't believe I admitted that out loud.'

'No point pretending you're shy now,' he says drily.

'I'm not shy, not when it comes to my body anyway, but when it comes to other things…'

He thrums his thick fingers on the island with a faraway look in his eye.

'Okay, I want my three questions. I'm calling them in early today.' I inch closer over the counter.

'Then you won't be able to ask me anymore for at least another twenty-four hours,' he reminds me. 'Sure you'll be able to last?'

'I'll have to.' I study his face, taking in his strong bone structure, Roman nose, square jawline peppered with a generous amount of stubble that I am dying to feel between my legs again. Dark soulful eyes that a woman could drown in.

'Fine. Shoot,' his tone sounds bored, but a flicker of interest registers in his pupils. I think he's secretly beginning to enjoy this game as much as I am.

'If I wasn't your client, would you have sex with me?'

His gaze dips to my lips for a second, then back to meet my eye. 'No.'

Ouch. His rejection stings like a slap. 'Why not?'

'That's question number two.' He slams his laptop closed. 'You sure it's the one you want to ask?'

'It's the one I *need* to ask.' I swallow the lump forming at the back of my throat.

'We're too different.' He clasps his fingers together in front of him, the tips turn white with how tightly they're interlinked.

'Bullshit.' I bang my coffee cup down on the table. 'That's not an answer. You're fobbing me off.'

Different shouldn't matter if it's just sex. Different is only a problem when it comes to relationships—and even then, they say opposites attract. Sure, there's the obvious Scarlett and James connection. We'd run into each other from time to time afterwards, but I don't think it's that.

What is he hiding from me?

Is it that he can't have casual sex with me without it meaning something?

Is it the loss of his previous girlfriend? Is he terrified to let anyone close again in case he loses them?

Or something else entirely?

'You have one more question, Avery. Then I'm going to shower—alone.' He grimaces.

'Final question.' I stare into his deep dark eyes. 'And I want a full answer. Not three words. I want an explanation.'

He blows out a long, slow breath. 'Fine.'

'What are you so afraid of? Is it letting someone in? Is it losing them? Is it losing control?'

He rests an elbow on the table like he's steadying himself. He's silent for several long seconds and I hold my breath, wondering if I pushed him too far.

'That's four questions.' He arches an eyebrow pointedly. 'But the answer to all of them is that I'm not afraid of losing anyone or anything.'

'Liar!' I yell.

'I haven't finished.' He holds up his palms in a peace sign. 'I'm afraid of finding something that I never wanted, or looked for. Of stumbling across the one thing that I've actively avoided. *Love*. And I can't love something—someone who will never truly be mine.' He stands then and storms out of the room.

He has no idea.

Whether I want to be or not, I'm already his.

He has me hook, line, and sinker.

Chapter Twenty

AVERY

The following Tuesday, I'm padding barefoot across the plush carpet of The Merrion Hotel's presidential suite wearing nothing but a silk Ivy-shaped scrap of material over my vagina.

'Darling, you're positively ethereal!' Thorne calls dramatically. Killian is fit to kill him, even if for the first time in history, Thorne seems to be keeping his micro boner in check. He claps his hands as I emerge. 'A goddess made flesh.'

I try to ignore my bodyguard's burning gaze from his position by the door. His jaw is granite, his eyes steel, but there's something else there too. Something that makes my pulse skip. A muscle ticks in his cheek, and I know he's fighting every instinct to throw his jacket over me and drag me out of here. But this is my job. This is what I do. And I get paid a ridiculous amount of money to do it.

I've deliberately kept my questions vague since Killian's shocking admission in the kitchen. *I'm afraid of finding something that I never wanted, or looked for. Of stumbling across the one thing that I've actively avoided. Love. And I can't love something—*

someone who will never truly be mine.' I've spent hours mulling his words over, trying to make sense of them.

Did he mean he could potentially fall in love with me?

Some days I'm still not sure he even likes me.

Although, brick by brick, his stoic barricade seems to be crumbling, I'm treading carefully, cautious of doing anything that might make him re-erect it.

I move the way Thorne directs—fluid, graceful, like water made woman. Nova Natural is all about returning to nature, celebrating the raw and real. Hence my current state of undress. The sweeping staircase curves down to the private drawing room; its marble steps are cool beneath my feet. The decor comprises gilt-edged mirrors and cream silk wallpaper, crystal chandeliers throwing diamonds of light across Georgian cornices. Perfect for selling overpriced perfume to ladies who lunch.

'Stunning!' Thorne calls. 'Now pause there, half-turn. Let the light catch your silhouette.' His hand lands on my bare arm to reposition me. But he doesn't remove it. Instead, his fingers trail down to my elbow, lingering. Something cold slithers down my spine.

'Remove your hand, or lose it.' Killian's voice cuts through the room like a blade. Within seconds, he's beside us, despite the fact I asked him to stand quietly in the corner, or better yet, outside with Sterling and Walsh. Thomson has taken a few days off to spend with his wife. The guy really is a hopeless romantic. That's probably why he's my favourite of all of Killian's men.

Thorne's hand drops away. 'I'm directing my model—'

'Direct with your voice.' Killian steps forward menacingly. 'Or you'll be directing from a hospital bed.'

After a long, exhausting day, we finally wrap things up. I don't know who's more relieved, Killian or me. I get dressed in the presidential suite while he guards the door from the outside. When I emerge with my clothes on, I swear his shoulders relax a fraction.

My phone vibrates in my Chanel clutch and I sift through six shades of Charlotte Tilbury lipstick, three sticks of sugar-free chewing gum, and a cherry flavoured condom, before eventually locating it.

Dad

I suppose I'm due a call. It's been a few weeks.

Killian quirks an eyebrow but says nothing.

I swipe to answer. Awkward or not, he's still my father.

'Dad, how are things?' I rest the phone on my shoulder, pinning it with my ear as I attempt to fasten my bag closed. Killian might be good at multitasking, but I'm not. The phone slips and I instinctively go to catch it and drop the bag upside down, where all its chaotic contents land on the opulent flooring with a clatter.

'Shit.' I manage to catch the phone, at least.

'Avery?' My father's voice is flooded with concern.

Killian motions for me to continue the conversation while he picks up my belongings. The condom causes his eyebrows to furrow, but I don't have time to worry about it.

'Sorry, Dad, I dropped the phone. I'm just finished shooting for the day.'

He clears his throat. 'Do I want to know what this shoot entails?'

You'd swear the man had a deep sense of morality the way he carries on. Now is not the time to remind him that modelling semi naked is much less of a problem than being caught fully naked with your PA. At least I'm getting paid for it. Mind you, so was Tessa. I bite my tongue for half a second, but I can't help myself. 'Same as usual, Dad. Tits and ass. Sex sells.'

He sighs and I can practically see him squeezing his fingers into a fist, his signet ring glinting on his right hand.

'I'm just calling to see if you have any plans for Christmas.'
One thing about my father—he gets to the point.

'Christmas,' I repeat, mulling over the word. 'I haven't
given it much thought. Things have been...' I want to say
crazy, or surreal, but I settle on busy.

'Well, we'd love to have you with us this year. Your
brother is coming and I know Tessa would like the whole
family to have dinner together.'

Eugh. *Your brother.* They're not *my* family. They're his.

As if Tessa isn't bad enough, he expects me to put up with
her painfully awkward, tech-obsessed son, Sebastian. If his
snooty, supercilious girlfriend, Yvonne, tries to slut shame me
again, I'll slap her with my bank statement before stuffing her
like a turkey.

I pause. 'I don't know, Dad, I'll have to speak to Mam.'

'Oh, she's going to a festive fitness retreat. It's all over her
Instagram.' He tuts, disgust rolling across the phone.

I wouldn't know, given my social media ban. I had to use
Killian's phone the other day to check on my beloved British
Princesses and their latest fashion picks.

'She never mentioned it.' Though it does sound like something my mother would do. Spontaneity is her superpower. I
glance at Killian, who's put back the contents of my handbag
bar the condom, which he tucks into his suit pocket with a
glower.

I link my arm through his as we take the stairs to the
ground floor.

'Look, think about it. I know you've never really warmed
to Tessa, but it's been years, Avery. It's time to leave the past
in the past.'

I blow out a breath. 'I'll see what I can do,' I lie. I'd rather
eat kangaroo balls than sit through Christmas day and
pretend Dad and Tessa's affair didn't almost break my
mother.

'Wonderful.' I can practically hear him rubbing his hands together.

'I said I'll see, not yes.'

'I know, I know.' The optimism in his tone splinters my sternum. I can't take it.

'I have to go, Dad, I'm at work. Talk soon, yeah?'

'Goodbye darling.'

I disconnect the call before he can say anything else.

I lean into Killian's huge frame for emotional support this time, rather than physical.

'I know we're not supposed to veer from the schedule, but is there any chance we can have one drink in the hotel bar? Even the briefest conversation with my father stirs the need for hard liquor. The hotel is secure, right? I'd love a martini.'

Killian stares at me appraisingly for a few seconds before finally caving. 'One drink. The hotel's running on skeleton staff today, all of which we've run a background check on. The only guests are the ones associated with this shoot, so it's no riskier than being here, I suppose. And Thorne has left the building. The man is a walking red flag.'

I snort. 'Says the biggest walking red flag I've ever met.'

He reaches for his earpiece, but I grab his hand before he can touch it. Electricity sparks between us. 'Please don't call the others in. Leave them in their positions.'

'Why?' Confusion drifts in his eyes.

'Sterling gives off a weird vibe, you know.'

'He's a moody fucker, but he's exceptionally good at his job.' Killian drops a palm on my lower back as we make our way through the wide corridors into the dome shaped bar. 'We served in the military together. In fact, I offered him the chance to invest in my business when I started it, not because I needed the investment, but because he was like a brother to me after...' he trails off, 'everything.'

I'm about to ask him what everything means, but he swiftly changes the subject.

'I know for a fact he regrets not taking me up on that offer now. I'd put money on that being the reason he's so sullen. You know why they call him psycho Sterling?'

'No.' I'm not sure I want to know either.

'He once interrogated a suspect for seventy-two hours straight, barely stopping to piss or shit. That exhausts me even thinking about it.'

'Do you do much *interrogating*?' I emphasise the word because we both know it's a euphemism for torture. Again, for some reason, Anton Roche's face forces its way into my mind.

'When the need arises. I don't enjoy it, but some things can't go unpunished.' He ushers me into a green, circular leather booth in the corner of the room out of the way. 'When I catch your flower-loving friend, I'll spend a week interrogating him. Until then, I won't leave your side.'

His underlying threat of violence might cause some women concern, but it offers me comfort–knowing that he's got me, that he won't let anything happen to me. That he's as enraged with the stalker as I am.

I order a martini from the waitress, Killian orders a water. I wish he'd have a whiskey; that way I might have some hope of seducing him.

'So...Christmas.' He arches an eyebrow.

'Don't. I can't bear the thought of it. But if my mother really is out the country, what excuse do I have?'

'That you're spending it with my family.' His shoulder jerks in a shrug. 'Your mother already thinks we're a thing. What does it matter if your dad does too?'

'I suppose, but what will we actually do? Sit in your apartment with our matching Christmas PJs watching *Home Alone*?' I tease, but truthfully the prospect sounds fabulous.

'If that's what you want to do.' His eyes catch mine. 'Or we could actually go to my parents. Scarlett and James will be back from honeymoon. It'll be bedlam with the kids running riot, but we both know you love chaos.'

'That sounds amazing. But what if you catch the stalker before then?'

'I'm not exactly going to uninvite you.' He deadpans. 'As a friend, of course.'

'Of course.' Worst fucking luck. 'In that case, count me in. Oh, and we need to talk about San Francisco next week.' I sit back in my chair. He has my schedule. He knows we're going to the ELEGANCE offices. But we've yet to discuss the finer details.

'What about it?' He shifts in his seat beside me and our thighs touch. Even through the fabric of his suit, I'm hit with zinging sensations from head to toe.

'I've booked you a seat on the flight beside me, but the Ritz-Carlton doesn't have any availability, so you'll have to share my suite, but given you've been sleeping in my room for the past week, it's no big deal, right?'

His eyes narrow. 'Cancel the flight.'

'Killian, I don't mind missing Friday night cocktails with the girls, or cancelling guest appearances at nightclubs, but this is one meeting I can't miss. ELEGANCE is bigger than Vogue these days. And even more exclusive. I told you. I've been manifesting this meeting for two years.'

'I know who it's with. I have your schedule, remember? I've already investigated every single person that works in the office building, including the fucking janitors. I'm not asking you to miss it. I'm saying we'll take my family's jet.' He scrubs a hand over his jaw. 'We'll have to take at least two members of my team. And I'm pretty sure Aer Lingus won't permit firearms on board their aircraft, even in business class.'

'Oh.' It never even occurred to me.

The waitress returns with my cocktail. 'Will you be dining with us tonight?' she asks, her eyes roaming over Killian's broad shoulders unapologetically.

I'd love to have dinner out. Annabelle's cooking is fabulous but a change of scenery is as good as a holiday. No doubt Killian will say no. I'm lucky to even get in here for a drink. I look at him as he stares at me intently.

'Sweetheart?' I love it when he calls me sweetheart, even if most of the time it's heavily tainted with sarcasm. But tonight, the tenderness in his tone shocks me.

'Can we?' Hope hijacks my heart.

He shrugs. 'I suppose. We're already here.'

'Thank you.' Away from his apartment, away from his men, this feels almost like a date.

We order a sharing platter to start, and then the lobster. He even has two sips of champagne with me, and I know he doesn't particularly like it, which means he's trying to be sociable. Conversation doesn't exactly flow, but it's nowhere near as awkward as it was a month ago on the beach in St. Barths. That feels like a lifetime ago already.

When we finish eating, he pays the bill and leaves the waitress a hefty tip.

'Thank you.' I link my arm in his as we exit the bar, and he doesn't flinch. Walsh and Sterling are waiting by Killian's SUV. 'You didn't have to buy me dinner.'

'I wanted to.' His irises burn with his usual intensity.

Three simple words.

One tiny admission.

But it's one massive step in our relationship—friendship, I mean.

My heart soars in my chest.

Chapter Twenty-One

KILLIAN

'You look tired,' Thomson remarks as we sweep the lobby of my apartment building for any trace of devices, spyware, bugs, etc. It's almost ten p.m. and we've been on the go since before six a.m. I'm beat. We started the day with a radio interview with Ireland's most popular female DJ, Abby Connolly, followed by a charity lunch at the Shelbourne—an appearance Avery point blank refused to cancel. They're fundraising for single mothers—unsurprisingly, she's a huge advocate, given she was raised by one. Then we met her agent, Zack Kiel, this evening. He's another creepy cunt if ever I met one, but I've resigned myself to the fact the glamour industry is crawling with them. Zack's background check came back clear, and he was in Italy the week Scarlett and James got married.

'Something keeping you up at night?' Thomson continues to tease. 'Or someone, perhaps?'

'Don't,' I snap. When I'm satisfied with our safety checks, I motion for Collins to help Avery out of the SUV.

'I've said it before, and I'll say it again.' Thomson watches Avery exit the vehicle. 'She's your future wife.'

Irritation flares in my chest. Not at Thomson, but because his remark sluices open something inside of me that I've spent years trying to bury. I vowed I'd never enter into a serious relationship again but if the circumstances were different, if Avery didn't crave being ogled naked, maybe, just maybe, there might be a modicum of hope for the future.

But there isn't.

'I pay you for protection, not for you to play Cupid.' I dust off some imaginary lint from my suit, then fall into step beside the woman that even Thomson's noticed I'm falling head over heels in love with.

Fuck.

There's no point denying it. I love listening to the sound of her soft even breaths as she sleeps. I love the way her eyes flash with desire or devilment before she says something suggestive to shock me. I love knowing she's under my roof, only a few feet away from me. I love the way she demands her daily questions like they're her god-given right. I even love how she struts around half naked most of the time, even if it is giving me a case of serious blue balls. Hell, I think deep down I've been half in love with the woman for years.

No one has ever even attempted to infiltrate my defences before. No one until her. Avery is like a circling sniper, determined to capture my heart one way or another. And every day it's getting harder to hold out.

There have been no calla lilies in almost two weeks, which is why I've formulated a plan to lure the stalker out. When I suggested to Rian he should host celebrity nights at the Luxor Lounge, he ate it up like a dog. Given the fact that Avery started her career there, she seemed like the natural choice. By the time I finished with him, he thought celebrity night was entirely his idea. I love my brother—all of my brothers, but the fewer people in on my plan, the more chance it has of success. Given the stalker hasn't had a chance to access Avery in weeks, I'm almost certain he won't be able to resist this opportunity.

Meanwhile, Avery will cancel with a last-minute sickness from the safety of the States—I've already organised for an up-and-coming British burlesque dancer to stand in.

This is the perfect opportunity to grab him without endangering Avery. Because if we don't get him soon, he will get her. This cunt is unfortunately the real deal. I assumed he'd slip up, make a mistake by now, but the only person who's slipped up is me—each time I've succumbed to temptation. Which is why it can't happen again.

But that's easier said than done.

We step into the lift. My men avert their eyes from Avery out of respect. No one, not even Sterling, has dared to so much as glance her way since the yacht incident. She doesn't offer me the same courtesy, though. Instead, she stares at me with that devilment I've come to simultaneously loathe and love. Loathe because I know she's cooking up a new way to test my boundaries, and love because despite the struggle, her relentless pursuit of what she wants—me—is yet another thing I respect about her.

If I was a betting man, I'd say she's about to offer me a nightcap. Attempting to ply me with whiskey or wine is one of her favourite tactics. Of all days, tonight I could do with one.

When we reach the top floor, I tilt my face toward the biometric panel, holding still as the scanner maps the unique pattern of my iris. The penthouse is silent when we enter. Sterling is in his quarters. Walsh bids us goodnight and heads to his, and Thomson heads home to his wife.

The furry ginger fucker is sprawled on my hand-tailored Meridiani couch, with all four legs in the air like he's a goddamn pornstar. I shake my head with disgust while Avery coos over him, tickling his belly and nuzzling her cheek against his.

I slide my suit jacket off and hang it over the back of one of the stools tucked under the island. The spoilt little flea ball takes it as an invitation to pounce over to me and butt his head against my ankles.

'Beat it,' I bark.

'Don't be so mean!' Avery stalks towards us and scoops him up into her arms like he's the prodigal child. 'He thinks you're his daddy,' she coos.

'He doesn't think anything. He'd need a brain for that.' I scowl and the little fucker miaows in protest.

I suppose from certain angles he is kind of cute—if you forget the fact he cleans his own asshole with his tongue.

Avery raises him up into the air and presses a kiss to his nose before setting him down again. He scurries back towards the living area. If he scratches his claws on the curtains, I'm going to have new ones made out of his fur.

'And then there were two.' Avery eyes me like I'm a mint chocolate sundae; her tongue dips out over her lips.

'Aren't you tired?'

'I am, but I'm also restless, you know?'

'No, I don't know,' I lie. 'Go shower. It's late and we've another fun-filled day tomorrow.' My voice rings with sarcasm.

She places her hands on her voluptuous hips. 'Care to join me?'

'The only thing I care for is your safety,' I growl.

'So stoic, as usual.' She rolls her eyes. 'But don't think I haven't noticed the way you've been looking at me all day.'

'And what way would that be exactly?' I roll up the sleeves of my shirt out of habit, and her focus shifts to my forearms.

'Like you're in pain from fighting the urge to pin me down

and fuck me,' she says before sashaying her voluptuous hips out of the room, leaving me to pick my jaw up from the floor.

I give her a fifteen minute head start. It goes without saying that I'll sleep in her room now. I'll sit with her until she's asleep, then shower, throw on a pair of sweatpants and a t-shirt, then creep back to the chaise lounge. I can't wait to sleep horizontally again—naked—but that means no longer sharing a room with Avery, and I'm nowhere near ready to contemplate that right now.

I set the high-tech security system, then pad down the long wide corridor following the scent of peony perfume. I'll miss it when I eventually do catch her stalker. Though the elusive fucker certainly isn't making it easy.

I knock, and wait for her to say enter, then step in, closing the door swiftly behind me before fur-face can come flying in. The door clicks shut and I spin around. Avery is wearing the tiniest white triangle between her legs and nothing on top.

'What are you doing?' I keep my gaze firmly on her face. If I look now, my resolve will break.

'Getting ready for bed,' she says innocently, running her fingers through her hair.

'I knew you were going to be trouble tonight.' I palm my face. How am I meant to sit here with her looking like this?

'I don't know what you mean.' She spins on her bare feet and bends over to flip back the covers, giving me a first row seat to the thong nestling between the smooth globes of the ass I've been fantasising about fucking since I first glimpsed it all those years ago.

She hops onto the bed, tucks her long legs beneath the duvet and pulls it up to her waist. It would be far kinder to my dick if she'd pull it over her tits, but she isn't aiming for kind tonight. Blood floods to my cock as I stalk towards the chaise lounge.

'You could sleep in the bed, you know. It's big enough to fit an entire family,' she says coyly. 'I won't touch you.'

I sigh and avert my eyes, refusing to bite. My back is in fucking bits from sleeping sitting up, but at this point, it's not even her I don't trust. It's myself.

She pats the bed beside her. 'Come on, Killian, your back must be in agony. I swear, I won't touch you. Unless you want me to, that is.' Her finger drops to her clavicle, lingering for a second before drawing a cross over the swell of her generously sized chest. 'Cross my heart and hope to die.'

'No one is dying. Not on my watch anyway.' I'm so tired. Horny as fuck, but tired. Maybe just this once I could sleep next to her—above the covers, of course.

She scents my resolve wavering like a predator sniffing out its prey. 'Please.' She pouts, her teeth digging into her plump lower lip.

For fuck's sake.

I stalk towards the bed. 'Fine. But if you so much as lay a finger on me, I'm gone.'

She smirks, mirth flashing in her eyes. She's up to something, but I have no idea what.

I kick my shoes off and fall onto the bed. It's a battle to bite back the sigh of satisfaction as my shoulders sink into the plump pillows. I touch the lamp beside me and dim it to the lowest setting.

'I didn't get my three questions today,' Avery says, turning on her side to face me. She places her hands beneath her cheek and gazes at me.

With only a foot between us, it almost feels more intimate than when I ate her out on the yacht.

'Get them over with then.' I attempt nonchalance, but I'm pretty sure I'm not fooling either of us. Despite my best efforts, my focus falls to her bare breasts, full and round and so ripe for devouring. My dick is so hard it's fucking painful.

'Is it hot in here, or is it me?'

'That's your question?' I was expecting either another attempt to psychoanalyse me, or given her lack of nightdress, an attempt to seduce me with dirty talk.

'Yep.' She throws back the duvet in one fluid movement and, try as I might, I can't stop myself from looking at the white sheer fabric sheathing her pussy. I'd bet my life she's dripping for me.

I'm so fucked.

'It's hot,' I admit. And it has nothing to do with the underfloor heating.

'Take your clothes off. I promise I won't touch you.' She peeps up from beneath hooded eyes.

There's a catch here. I just don't know what.

'No,' I snap. There, that wasn't so hard after all, was it? Not nearly as hard as my rock solid dick anyway. 'Next question.'

'Do you think about those times you gave in to me? Do they play on repeat in your head like an advert that you don't want to remember, but is just too fucking catchy to forget?'

I slam my eyelids shut, but it does nothing to stop every fucking pixel-perfect image of Avery's sex from flying to the forefront of my mind.

'That was two questions masked as one,' I growl.

'So answer them.' Her eyes glow with defiance.

'Yes. And fucking yes.'

'Good.' Her huge pupils lock on mine as her hand slides inside the white slip of material

'Avery,' I warn. My entire body vibrates with the need to pin her arms above her head and fuck her into next week.

'I said I wouldn't touch you. I didn't say I wouldn't touch me.' She rolls on her back and parts her legs. When her finger finds her clit, she moans. Her eyelids flutter shut, elongated lashes sweeping over the prominent curve of her cheekbones.

Fucking witch.

I can't tear my eyes from her, and she fucking knows it.

My pulse thunders through me, not loudly enough to drown out the sound of Avery's fingers sluicing through her slickness. The noise alone is almost enough to make me come in my pants. That combined with watching her writhe with wanton pleasure.

'You fight dirty.'

'I can be very dirty. Stop fighting me, and I'll show you.' The hand that's not between her legs skims over her breast. I inhale sharply. Watching her get herself off is almost hotter than being the one to get her off. But not quite.

'You want to tease me? You want me to watch you make yourself come?' I reach over and rip the material from between her legs. 'I'm watching.'

The lace is saturated in my hands. My entire body screams at me to mount her like a wild animal, but I can't. I won't. Our eyes connect again, hers clouding with her escalating pleasure. Mine fill with wonder at this woman who wields her sexuality like a weapon. I *knew* she was dangerous. Knew it from the first night I laid eyes on her.

I prop myself on all fours with my face just inches from her pussy. It would be too easy to lick it, suck it or fuck it, but I won't give into her. Not like this. She increases the pace with her fingers, gliding from her clit to her slit and back again.

'Don't even think about coming.' I warn. 'You have my attention. So give me a fucking show.'

Her oval eyes gleam and her fingers slow to a stop. 'Yes, Daddy,' she purrs, waving her arousal covered fingers in front of my face. I grab them and shove them in my mouth before I can stop myself. She tastes like the most decadent mouth-watering dessert known to man. I suck each finger slowly until there isn't a drop left.

'I warned you what happened to the last woman who called me daddy. Get on all fours.'

'I was hoping you'd say that.' Her lips curl like the cat who got the cream.

Dirty, dirty girl. She doesn't hesitate, baring her backside to me like a fucking trophy. Face down, ass up, she is fucking stunning. The urge to swipe my tongue between her open legs is overwhelming, but I refuse to reward her goading behaviour.

What she needs is a spanking.

Chapter Twenty-Two

AVERY

'You're intent on testing the limits of my restraint. What I should do is restrain you. You need to be punished.'

'So do it.' I shimmy my ass and his palm connects with it hard enough to make me squeal. Hot, promising tingles shoot across my skin.

'You want this, don't you? You want me to spank you?' His disbelief melds with something like awe.

'I want you to spank me, suck me, fuck me—I want it all.' There's no point denying it now. My breasts are so heavy with need, my nipples ache for his touch, and my arousal pools between my legs.

No one has ever spanked me before and I love it. There's something so depraved about the whole experience.

Killian hisses out a breath as his hand hits my backside again. The sound echoes through the room like a mating call. My skin stings, tingles race across my thighs and between my legs. It should be demeaning, but instead, it's unbelievably erotic.

'You're determined to break me, woman.' His palm connects with my ass for a third time, this time slightly lower, teasingly close to my sex. I *need* him to touch me there.

'I'm determined to have you—it's different.' I pant, squirming in anticipation of his next move.

'It's one and the same. If I take you, you're mine, and that's something I'm not convinced you want, sweetheart.' A fourth deliciously decadent slap stings my skin and fuck, I'm one step closer to the edge.

'I want it.' I twist my head around to meet his ravenous stare. 'I want you.'

'I'm not a good man, Avery. I'm most women's nightmare.'

'You're my number one fantasy. Being with you, day in, day out, watching you, wanting you, not being able to touch you—it's killing me.'

He runs his palm tenderly over the spot he spanked, like he's stroking the pain away. 'Because of that, and only because of that. I'm going to make you come so hard you see stars, the sun and the entire fucking galaxy.' He lowers his face and presses his lips to my ass, scattering tender kisses over my skin.

'Thank god for that.' The need to come is consuming me.

'Don't thank God, baby, he has fuck all to do with this.' His tongue swipes my slit and I actually whimper in relief. 'You taste so fucking good. How can you be so bad?'

'You make me want to be bad,' I admit, bucking back against his face. 'You make me want to do things I've never done with anyone before.'

He groans as he eats me out from behind. I'm so fucking close. My legs tremble and my thighs tighten, but I fight it. I'm not ready for this to be over. 'If you won't let me touch you, touch yourself.'

His tongue slows to a stop and the sweet sound of metal unzipping floats through the air. I peep around my shoulder to see his fist wrapped around his engorged length. He pumps twice before his tongue finds my clit again. I've never been so turned on in my life.

'Fuck. Me. Killian.' I'm not beyond begging.

'Don't be greedy,' he growls, pumping himself harder.

My fingers twist in the sheets, holding on for dear life, but I can't fight it. My core convulses. My eyes flood with a thousand white-hot stars. And my orgasm crests in wave after wave of transcendent ecstasy.

His low guttural groan is a split second behind mine, then hot ropes of come spurt across my back, marking me with the proof of his pleasure. The sound of our ragged pants permeate the air as we both struggle to catch our breath.

'That is the last time, Avery.'

'Actually, it was the first.' I turn to him and smirk. 'The first time for you, but it won't be the last. I always get what I want, Killian Beckett. And what I want is you.'

He shakes his head, but not nearly as convincingly as he could. I flop onto my front as he backs off the bed and disappears into the bathroom. Two minutes later, he returns with a hot washcloth and proceeds to clean my back with gentle dabs before swiping between my legs.

He might claim he's bad, but whatever he's done, there's a goodness there that he can't hide.

What I wouldn't give to know what goes on behind those dubious dark eyes.

He throws the washcloth on the bedside table and curls his body around mine, wrapping a calloused hand around my waist. Long thick fingers splay across my stomach, and his thumb settles just below my bellybutton, stroking my skin with affectionate sweeps.

His breathing settles into a rhythm I've never heard before. It takes me a second to realise that my beautiful, broken bodyguard is asleep.

For the first time since he agreed to take care of me, it occurs to me I need to take care of him too.

My alarm shrills at six a.m. and it feels like the middle of the night. A million memories from the night before race through my brain. I roll across the bed to find it's empty. Empty and cold.

I pat the bedside table until I find my phone and hit snooze.

'Time to get up sleepy head,' Killian's deep, familiar baritone booms from the far side of the room. So we're back to the chaise lounge.

'Why aren't you in bed with me?'

'You've barely been awake ten seconds and you're already starting with the questions. You sure you want to waste them this way?'

'It's not a waste if you give me a real answer.'

'Fine. I'm not in bed with you because this isn't a romance movie. I fucked up—again. It won't happen again.'

'Ugh. When are you going to get over yourself?' I grab a pillow and slap it over my face to muffle my frustration.

'Never.' Amusement taints his tone. 'And that's your second question gone.'

'Fuck you, Killian.'

His low chuckle rumbles through the air. 'I'll go get you a coffee.'

'I'd prefer another orgasm.'

'That's not on the menu.'

'Well, it fucking should be.' I toss the pillow at his back as he strides towards the door.

A cold shower does absolutely nothing to alleviate my

frustration. I had the best orgasm of my life mere hours ago, and yet somehow I've never felt less satisfied. I need more.

I pull on a black lace thong, deliberately not bothering with a bra, and go in search of my coffee. I make my way along the corridor barefoot, stopping when I reach the kitchen.

Killian's opening a pouch of cat food for Jasper, who is miaowing on the counter beside him.

'I suppose for a flea-ridden ginger furball, you're kind of cute. But don't ever quote me on that.' He rubs a hand over Jasper's head, and my flea-ridden ginger fur-ball leans into him.

Unbelievable.

I clear my throat loudly. Killian flinches, then snatches Jasper up and sets him on the floor. He's not nearly quick enough though. I saw the affection lighting his eyes. I heard the affection in his tone. And it only fuels my hope that that affection will spread to me.

Because it hits me like a smack in the face, that's what I want—his attention, his affection and a shot at a real relationship with him.

Chapter Twenty-Three

KILLIAN

Not fucking Avery is growing harder by the day—as is my poor cock. She continues to waltz around my apartment in her lingerie with furled nipples, occasionally asking if I've made any progress on catching the calla creep. While I'm sorry to say the answer is not yet, but I have a plan in place, I'm increasingly less sorry that she's still under my roof. Even if my balls are ready to explode. I've managed to avoid any more fuck ups the past couple of days, primarily because I've been fucking my hand in the shower at every given opportunity. But it's only a matter of time before I break again. I know it. And she knows it.

The question is, if I break, how devastating will the destruction be—to her and to me?

Austin's background check came back clear. There was nothing on the CCTV on the streets surrounding Elixir. I haven't been able to locate the source of these calla lilies. I'm currently in the process of cross checking every man in the country with a diving qualification or diving experience against anyone Avery worked with over the past three years, so far, I've come up with sweet fuck all.

The stalker is worryingly elusive.

'Are you packed?' Avery asks, wheeling a ridiculously large Louis Vuitton case to the top of the stairs.

'Here.' I run up the short flight of steps from the lounge area to grab it from her. 'Let me.'

'My hero,' she pretends to fan herself.

Little witch.

At least she has clothes on today. Though if she were mine, I'd enforce a naked in the penthouse rule, purely for easy access.

I place the case on the floor by the door. 'I thought this was a four-day trip, not a fortnight.'

'It is, but a girl can never be too prepared.' She beams at me. In an elegant cream cashmere dress and chocolate coloured leather boots, Avery looks simply stunning.

'I hope you packed pyjamas in there.' The Ritz Carlton is fully booked, like she said, but I would have stayed in her suite regardless. There was a cancellation on a different floor to Avery, but apart from the fact I sleep better to the sound-track of her breathing, I can't protect her if I don't have eyes on her at all times. Thomson and Sterling took the other room instead.

'Of course.' She winks, and it does things to my dick. Not helpful.

'You didn't tell anyone about this trip?' I triple check.

'No one. And I used the burner phone you gave me to confirm the details.'

'Good.' Finally, she's taking this seriously.

'Are you sure Annabelle will remember to feed Jasper?' She nips her bottom lip. 'I could ask my mother to stop by.'

'I pay Annabelle a ridiculously generous salary in order to remember precisely these details.' I eye the litter box to the side of the kitchen. 'And she's under strict instruction to change that thing four times a day.'

'That's a bit excessive.' Avery rolls her eyes.

'It's not. Trust me.'

The following evening, we reach the Ritz Carlton near Union Square. The time difference is a killer—for me at least. Avery is bright eyed and bushy-tailed and looking for a cocktail as usual.

'I need to soothe my nerves before the meeting.' She begs, taking my hand and dragging me to the hotel bar. Thomson and Sterling did a sweep while we checked in at reception. I put out a false schedule for Avery, including her appearance at the Luxor Lounge. I deliberately didn't encrypt it as deeply as I could have. Our stalker is highly sophisticated and I don't trust him not to hack even some of my tightest systems. I made sure he didn't have to.

Rian's PA circulated an email to the elite members of the Luxor Lounge detailing that Avery's the celebrity guest dancer this weekend. There will be some extremely disappointed patrons at his gentlemen's club, but should our stalker stumble across the 'schedule' I planted, he won't question it.

It's only a matter of time before my men will have the sick, twisted bastard in my warehouse in Wicklow, which is why I'm feeling slightly more relaxed than I have in weeks.

I glance pointedly at the chunky silver watch on my wrist. 'Your meeting isn't for approximately forty hours.'

'Not the point,' Avery shrugs. 'I'm acclimatising to the time difference. Besides, I need something to help me loosen up.'

I could loosen up every muscle in her lithe body ten times over, and ten more again if the circumstances were different, but they're not. And I'd do well to remember it.

Avery and I are from different worlds.

She lives in the limelight.

I live in the shadows.

I'll never be able to have a relationship with a woman who I have to share with the entire world.

Fuck. Up until recently, I would never even have entertained the idea of having a relationship again at all after Sarah.

But I'd be lying if I denied I like having a woman in my apartment. Well, not any woman. Attention-seeking Avery, of all women. She certainly has my attention, every damn minute of every damn day, whether I want to give it to her or not.

She has my attention—but she also has my heavy heart.

Hell, I even put up with her ginger fucking cat shitting in my penthouse.

My gaze sweeps the room with military style precision. A couple in a heated, whispered debate at four o'clock. A group of women gathered for a birthday celebration at six o'clock. A few suits lurking at seven o'clock. Nothing to cause concern, but I steer Avery towards a quiet corner with our backs to the wall. I'd prefer if she ordered room service. She's not as famous over here as she is in Europe, but still, there's no such thing as too careful.

'I've got a better idea.' I lean deliberately close to her hear so my breath skims her ear. All I can smell is peonies. For the rare few hours I do sleep at night, I even dream about the damn things.

'Please tell me you've finally reconsidered our situation and you're prepared to bang me into next week?' Avery's blue eyes glitter as she turns to face me, pressing her chest against mine.

'No, sweetheart.' I tut. Though I think about it a million times, every fucking minute of every damn hour and her pressing those fantastic tits against my torso isn't helping.

'What then?' She juts her chin upwards until her lips are just inches from mine.

'Let's order room service and have a couple of drinks in the suite.'

'Why would I agree to that?' Her eyes narrow. 'I'm already cooped up in Ireland. Here, no one knows me. I have my freedom back—for a few days, at least.'

'If we head up to the suite, I can relax with you, without having to survey every single person in the room.'

She twists her lips as she contemplates the idea. 'You'll have a drink with me?'

'Maybe even two or three.' God knows, I could use it. And I'll need something to send me to sleep.

'Whiskey?'

I know exactly where this is going.

'Whiskey,' I confirm.

'Fine. You have a deal, on one condition.' She brushes her body against mine and I stand rigid, willing myself not to get hard. Again.

'What's the condition?'

'You dance with me.'

'You want me to dance with you?' I repeat.

'Yes.'

'Fine.' How hard can it be? We already danced at Scarlett and James's wedding.

'And we order champagne.'

'You should probably stick to the martinis.' I steer her back out of the bar and to the glass elevator. 'We both know champagne goes straight to your head.'

'It might stop me thinking about giving *you* head.' She shoots me a sidewards feline glance and my dick twitches in my pants.

Twenty minutes later, room service arrive with a silver trolley transporting a bottle of Dom Perignon in a bucket of ice, and a bottle of Macallan. Sterling and Thomson are stationed outside the suite door. They swept the entire floor for cameras, bugs, and anything suspicious. I'm satisfied that Avery is in no immediate danger, which is why I pour myself a double whiskey after pouring her a glass of champagne.

I scan the suite one last time before bringing the whiskey to my lips. There's a queen-size four-poster bed which Avery has already dumped her handbag on. I eye the cream leather couch—my bed for the night. May as well test it out. I slip out of my suit jacket, toss it on the table and drop on to the sofa. I take a large mouthful of the Macallan before placing it on the huge mirrored top coffee table in front of me.

It's no Beckett's Gold, but it's not bad.

'I'm just going to freshen up quickly, then I'll set up the tunes.' Avery strides across the room towards the en-suite. I reach for my drink again. When I hear running water, I down it and pour myself another double. Anything to distract myself from the fact that every fibre in my body is screaming at me to run to the bathroom and fuck her in the shower.

I shouldn't. I can't. I won't.

When she finally emerges, she's wearing an ivory silk slip that might look virginal, if her dark, taut nipples weren't glaring obvious beneath the thin fabric.

'Put a robe on.' I motion to the wardrobe where two fluffy Ritz Carlton embossed dressing gowns hang. My self-control is already maxed out. I'm teetering on the edge, and she knows it.

'Why?' Avery flicks her hair from her shoulder and pushes her chest out.

'You know why.' I swirl the whiskey in my glass. I'm going to need another one. Really fucking soon.

'You don't like what you see?' She strides towards me, snatching up her champagne glass in the process.

'Is that one of your three questions?' Deflection. I'm the king of deflection.

'No, but this is.' She takes a mouthful of champagne. 'Do you want me?'

I sigh. 'Want doesn't cover it. You're utterly fucking arresting. That's not the issue here.'

She picks up a remote from the coffee table and points it at the TV, flicking until she finds a music station. A low sensual beat floods the room and she turns it up.

'On your feet.' She beckons me over to her.

At times like this, I regret being a man of my word.

She places her drink down, prises mine from my hand and puts it on the coffee table. I step forward, trying to leave a small gap between us, dropping my hands on her waist like I did at the wedding. She presses those big, beautiful breasts against my chest. Her nipples are solid round buttons, and I'd bet my life her cunt is dripping for my touch. My cock is painfully rigid between us, and the satisfied glint in her eye tells me she feels it.

As we begin to move to the music, she slides her hands around my back, then palms my backside. 'Avery.' My warning isn't as sharp as it should be.

'What?' she feigns innocence.

'One dance.' Am I telling her? Or myself?

She circles her hips in time to the beat and with every damn movement, my dick gets harder and harder. When the song finally comes to an end I jerk backwards, grab my drink and slump back into the couch. Avery helps herself to a refill from the champagne bottle, shaking her shapely hips the entire time.

She crosses the room to stand in front of me.

'I miss the old days at the Luxor Lounge.' Her eyes land on my tented crotch. 'It would have been nice to have made that guest appearance.'

'Why doesn't that surprise me?' Of course, she misses dancing nearly naked for hundreds of Dublin's most eligible men each night. 'You are the biggest attention seeker I know.'

That's the problem.

'The only attention I truly wanted was from the one man who refused to give it to me.' She lifts a bare foot onto the coffee table. 'I used to fantasise you'd book a private room and pay me to dance for you.'

I used to fantasise about fucking her on the stage so every man in the place would know she's mine, but she's not mine and she never will be.

I bite my lip, not trusting myself to speak. The final cords of my self-control are frayed, hanging by a fraction of a thread.

'I used to fantasise about getting you all alone, about drowning in your undivided attention as your ravenous eyes caressed my body.' She puts her other foot onto the coffee table and hoists herself up. Her bright blue eyes bore into mine.

'I told you, sweetheart, it's not that I don't want you. Believe me, I do. But us,' I motion between us, 'We'd be dynamite in bed, but we'd be a nuclear bomb in the real world —we'd destroy everything around us.'

Well, I'd destroy anyone who so much as looked at her for too long.

Which is why we can never be.

She stares at me hard for a few seconds. Just when I think she's going to challenge me, she switches tactic. She'd have made a worryingly good soldier.

'Can I dance for you?' The way she asks, it's almost coy.

I observe her from over the rim of my glass. The rational part of my brain knows this is a terrible idea. But I'm not thinking with my brain. I'm thinking with my rock solid dick. The word no suddenly isn't an option again. Not when, from where she stands on the table, I have the perfect view up her nightdress at her perfect, glistening seam. If that isn't enough, it's reflected in the mirror top of the table she's standing on. I don't stand a fucking chance. I was delusional to think I ever did.

'Dance,' I demand, pulling my wallet out of my pocket. I pluck a wad of hundred euro notes from it and toss them at her. I want to make every single one of her fantasies a reality. I can't, not really. But I can give her this.

She smirks at the knowledge she has me hooked on her racy role play. This is a disaster waiting to happen but I can't say no to this woman. She has her claws so far into my skin I can't move without checking where she is first. I'd burn the world down for her if she asked me to.

She bends forward to scoop up the notes, providing me with a perfect view of her beautiful breasts.

I'm fucked.

So fucked.

Her hips circle and sway to the music, as she lowers herself slowly into a crouching position on the coffee table. I watch transfixed as she shimmies her shoulders seductively. One strap of her nightdress falls down. She pauses for a minute before shrugging off the other one. Her full tits spill over the top. An appreciative hiss slips from my lips. She smirks again.

Just when I think I can't take anymore, she spreads her legs and gives me a full frontal of the pink perfection nestled between them. Her arousal gleams like a beacon. I *have* to lick up every drop. It's not even a want, it's a need.

'Is this how your fantasy played out?' I place my whiskey tumbler on the table and shift forwards to the edge of the sofa.

'Not exactly.' Her hand glides upwards over her inner thigh, hovering beside the junction between her legs.

'Have you been touching yourself, thinking about me again?' I straighten in my seat, inching closer to stare at the eighth wonder of the world—Avery Williams' perfect pink cunt.

'Every fucking day.' Twin pools drag me under until I'm drowning in her desire.

'Tell me how your fantasy ends,' I demand.

'I'd rather show you.' She stares at me through hungry, hooded eyes.

My fingers are gliding through her slickness before my brain has a chance to remind me this is a fucking terrible idea.

Terrible—yet apparently inevitable...

The second he touches me, sweet sensual relief floods my entire body. I need him like a fire needs oxygen. I watch as his huge hand disappears beneath my night dress. I need to see. I need to watch his fingers fuck me. Like he can read my mind, he tears the silk from my body with an animalistic rip and tosses it to the floor.

'Fuck,' he spits, as his pupils dilate into his irises. 'Look what you drive me to, woman. I don't do this. I don't lose control, but you make it fucking impossible for me.'

'Give into this, please,' I beg, inching my face closer to his until we're sharing the same ragged breath.

'Tell me how your fantasy plays out,' he demands.

My eyes fall to his crotch.

'You offer me more money for... extras...' I gasp as he sinks two fingers deep into my core.

He stares at me long and hard. A muscle flexes in his jaw. I hold my breath, silently pleading with him to go along with this. My body aches for him to fill it—with his dick.

'Avery.' He inches closer to brush his lips over mine. 'Do you ever offer... extras?' He rolls the word over his tongue.

My throat tightens with desire. Flames blaze in his black eyes, licking over every inch of my naked skin. 'I don't... normally... ever...but...'

'Good girl,' he purrs. 'I appreciate that you don't do this for anyone. But you *will* do this for me. I'll give you everything I own, if you let me lick your pretty wet cunt.'

I'm dripping onto his hand. Actually dripping. And it's hot as fuck. '*Everything* you own?' I need to be sure he's going to give me what I really want and—spoiler alert—it's not money. I need him to give into me. I need him to give himself to me. Because I know, when he does, there's no going back for either of us.

'Everything,' he confirms, sliding his fingers out of me and bringing them to his mouth. His eyelids fall closed as he savours them slowly. 'What do you want, Avery?' His rich voice slides over my skin, sending goosebumps spiralling in every direction.

I wet my lips as my focus returns to his crotch.

'Say it, sweetheart. Tell me what you want.' He swipes a finger over my slit again.

'I want your cock. In my hands. In my mouth. And in my pussy.' A hot flush creeps up my neck. I've never spoken to any man the way I speak to him. Mind you, I've never wanted any man the way I want him either.

He reaches for his belt. 'This is a one-time thing, Avery, okay? Tonight is all you're getting. Tomorrow, we go back to business as usual.'

I expected him to say that. Doesn't mean I like it. 'Fine.' It's not fine, but I'll worry about that tomorrow. All I can focus on is his gigantic cock springing free from his suit pants. Precum leaks from his tip. The urge to taste him eats me alive. I'm on my knees in front of him in a heartbeat.

He laughs, actually laughs, low and long, then pats the couch beside him. I shake my head. He pats it again, more vigorously this time. 'The only way you're getting to suck me off is if I have either my tongue or fingers in your cunt while you do so.' His huge hands circle my wrists and he draws me up into his lap like I'm weightless. I'm tempted to accidentally drop onto his cock, but that might tip him and his control freak tendencies over the edge completely. Instead, I straddle him, perching on his knees, awaiting his permission.

A hot hand wraps around the back of my neck as he yanks my face to his, capturing my lips with his. He radiates the same raw, desperate carnality that resides within me as his hands drop to my breasts and squeeze. I inch along his thighs until his tip presses against my entrance.

Oh my fucking god.

His tongue slams against mine, claiming and commanding. If I move another inch, he'll be inside me. My whole body shivers with need.

He tears his mouth from mine. 'This isn't how it was supposed to play out.'

'I'm on the pill,' I blurt. 'I'm clean.'

'So impatient for my cock, aren't you?' He nudges against my slick entrance but doesn't give me so much as a millimetre.

'You have no idea.' My fingers sink into his shoulders, hard enough to leave marks, even with his shirt still on. 'I wanted it for years. Better late than never, I suppose.'

'Better late than never,' he repeats, rolling the words over his tongue like he's contemplating them individually. 'I shouldn't do this,' he rasps, shaking his head.

'Please.' If he doesn't give into this right now, I might die.

He tsks, eyes burning. 'I'll give you an inch—but that's all you're getting.'

I nod, parting my legs wider.

'Be still, and take what I give you like a good girl, okay?'

'Yes, sir.'

He doesn't kiss me. Instead, he watches. Watches and hisses as he enters me. My mouth drops open and a pure primal moan spills out. 'Fuck.'

'Don't move,' he warns me, fingers reaching for my nipples. They're tight and furled and unbearably sensitive as he rolls them between his fingers.

'How does that feel?' He looks pointedly down. The sight of his enormous erection just inside of me is almost enough to get me off alone. The fact he's still wearing those fucking suit pants, and that crisp white shirt only adds to our game. He looks every bit the billionaire bossman he is, and I look and feel like what I am—a glorified stripper, and it has never been so sexy.

'It feels amazing.' I pant, fighting the urge to slide along his length until I'm stuffed with him. 'I need more.'

'Greedy little thing, aren't you?' He hunches forward to trail his tongue around my nipple. It's too much. It's not enough. 'One more inch. That's all you're getting.' He slides in a bit further and my core clenches around him in response.

'Killian,' I gasp.

'Yes.' He quirks an eyebrow. How the fuck can he look so controlled when this is the single sexiest thing in the universe?

'Please,' I beg, my hands roaming over his sculpted torso.

'God damn it, woman, you know I can't say no to you.' He thrusts in another inch and my whole body shakes with pleasure and anticipation. 'You drive me fucking crazy. I should punish you for parading around in front of me with your tits out, demanding my attention. Punish you for making me want you more than anything on this fucking planet.'

'So do it.'

'It won't be gentle, Avery,' he warns. 'I've wanted you for far too fucking long for it to be gentle.'

'I don't want gentle. I want raw. I want real. I want all of you, Killian.' Our eyes lock and something unspoken passes between us.

Snap.

His resolve breaks. Fingers grip my ass cheeks as he pulls us both up from the couch and impales me on his majestic cock. The movement is swift and controlled, but suddenly he's deep inside me, stretching me all the way to my cervix. I wrap my legs around his waist, and my arms around his neck as he carries me like a rag doll across the suite to the four-poster bed.

The muscles of his shoulders ripple and roll beneath my hands as he lowers me onto the soft silk-blend sheets, nipping and sucking my neck, marking every inch of my skin as his. He rests his weight on his elbows as his hips pin me against the bed. He pumps and the headboard slams against the wall with every life affirming thrust. His lips devour mine as we stare into each other's eyes. His have a look that I didn't expect. Yes, there's heat and hunger and everything else I'm feeling, but there's also something else. Something more. Something that looks like awe, or the affection I craved so badly at the very least.

He ups the pace, rocking into me in a way that hits that elusive super-sensitive spot inside over and over and over again. I scrape my fingers over his scalp, then cup his neck and hold on for my life. My thighs shiver and shake as my release looms like a thunderstorm—sudden and violent.

He rips his lips from mine and inches up higher on his elbows to watch me. 'Look.' He glances down to where his huge length rocks in and out of me in that devastating rhythm. It's the single sexiest thing I've ever seen. 'You're so tight. So wet. So fucking perfect. And you're mine.'

He's so fucking hot when he's all dominant and possessive like that.

Are we still in roleplay?

Or does he genuinely mean I'm his?

I hope to fuck it's the latter. One time is never going to be enough. Hell, one fucking lifetime of this wouldn't be enough. He increases the pace, thrusting harder until I'm so full of him, I'm utterly consumed by his cock.

'I used to fantasise about fucking you on the stage in the Luxor Lounge so every single one of those men knew who you belonged to.' He slides a hand between us and circles my clit. It's too much.

'Say it, Avery. Who do you belong to?' His voice is fucking feral.

'You.' I buck against him, grinding shamelessly, seeking more friction. 'I belong to you.' Isn't that the truth?

'Good girl.' He traces my lips with his tongue without breaking eye contact.

'Killian, I'm going to...' Pleasure blinds me. Delicious, decadent heat builds in my core and white-hot sparks crackle over my skin. My orgasm detonates. Delirious oblivion devastates every single cell in my body.

He plunges his tongue into my mouth and swallows my screams as I shudder through the most intense release of my life. He's right behind me, crying out my name as he spills himself inside of me, palming his hands over my body like he can't believe I'm real.

Finally, he slumps onto my chest, his heart hammering against mine as we struggle to catch our breaths.

'Avery Williams, you will be the fucking death of me,' he growls.

'Thought that came with the job description?' I press a kiss against his tattooed neck. 'I know we said one-time, but can we change that to one night?'

Chapter Twenty-Five

KILLIAN

I'm dreaming that Avery's luscious lips are wrapped around my dick and that her skilful tongue is swirling eagerly around my crown. One slim hand cradles the base of my length while the other cups my balls.

Fuck.

I moan loud enough to drag myself from my sex induced slumber.

And I'm not dreaming.

Avery's luscious lips *are* wrapped around my dick.

And her skilful tongue *is* swirling eagerly around my crown.

What a wake-up call.

I whip the duvet from us so I can get the full view of her stunning, naked body. 'I think there's a law against sex acts on a person who's unconscious. Consent and all that.'

She pops her lips off my tip. 'So call the cops then.' She quirks a brow and her tongue darts out to clean up the precum dripping from my dick. 'Mmm. You taste fucking amazing.'

'We agreed to one night.'

'You want me to stop?' she asks before deep throating me in a way that has my lower back arching from the bed.

'Fucking witch,' I hiss. Her laughter reverberates around my dick. 'Come, sit on my face. This is the last time I'm going to make you come, so you better make the most of it.' I wrap a hand around her silky soft hair, drawing it up in a ponytail, and gently pull her up the bed, letting go only when she straddles my waist reverse cowgirl style. She inches backwards and I watch as the smooth spheres of her ass back up over my chest. I should have fucked it last night when I had the chance.

She takes my cock in her mouth again and I grab her hips, positioning them until she's dripping onto my face. I offer her one languid lick and she moans. The vibrations of it around my cock combined with the taste of her sweet arousal are almost enough to send me over the edge. I sink my tongue into her centre, fucking her with it over and over again as she takes me deep into her throat. There are so many things I'd love to do to her, but I can't.

We had sex four times last night and each time we did, she took a bit more of me—parts that I swore I'd never give to any woman again.

Fire licks my skin. I'm so close to blowing. Avery sucks my dick like she was put on this earth entirely for that purpose. The idea of filling her mouth with my come has my balls throbbing with the need to blow. I'm holding on for my fucking life here.

Her thighs begin to tremble, so much so that I have to hold them steady. I move my mouth to capture her clit and she cries out a split second before her orgasm rattles through her like a train.

Thank fuck.

Mine is two seconds behind her. Pure carnal pleasure steals every fucking sense I have as my come floods her mouth. She swallows and swallows like she's as fucking turned on by it as I am. If the fresh bout of wetness on my tongue is anything to go by—she is.

She keeps me in her mouth until she's milked every last drop, then spins around to face me. Her cheeks are flushed, breasts heavy, and there's a glint of determination in her blue eyes. She places a knee on either side of my hips. 'One more time.'

'Avery,' I sigh.

This woman. She's fucking everything, but she'll never be mine. Not really. Which is why I've got to stop taking her like she is.

'Please, Killian.' Her voice cracks and I'm done for.

'When we get out of this bed, that's it—for real.' Am I trying to convince her, or myself?

Her lips split into a smile that squeezes my heart.

Fuck.

This has to be the last time.

If I give her much more of myself, there'll be nothing left. She'll have every fucking piece of me. I pat the pillow beside me. 'Lie next to me.'

She does as I ask—for once—falling into the space beside me. I pull the heavy duvet over us and turn on my side to face her. Our eyes meet, hers wide and wondrous, mine, desperate to soak in every detail of this moment so I can summon it in technicolour glory for the rest of my life. I brush her hair back from her face, stroke a thumb over her full lips, then run my fingers along the column of her throat and then lower.

'Finally, I have your attention,' she jokes.

'You've always had my attention, sweetheart—whether I wanted to give it to you or not.' The words rush out of their own accord. I trace the curves of her breasts, worshipping her smooth, flawless skin with fleeting strokes. Goosebumps scatter in every direction, and satisfaction surges through my veins.

'I wish you'd lavish me with it all the time.' She reaches for my face, tracing the hard line of my jaw before fingering the tattoos on my neck like she's mapping out every inch of me for her memory too. 'I wish we could do this at home.'

I bring her fingers to my lips and kiss the tips one by one. 'I can't protect you if I'm distracted.'

It's not just that though. If Avery did any other job in the world, I'd break my own rules for her. I'd make her mine. But I can't stand every man on the planet ogling her. The thought makes me positively feral, which is why we can't go there. I'd be sent down for murder.

'Last night...' Her sentence hangs in the air unfinished. She wets her lips. 'You said I was yours. You demanded I say it too.'

'Roleplay.' I'm not fooling either of us.

Especially not with the way I can't keep my hands off her.

'What if...?'

'Don't, sweetheart.' She'd never understand. I'd never ask her to give up her job; I'd never put her in a position where she had to choose between me and her work. It wouldn't be fair. Even if she chose me, she'd only resent me for it afterwards. And it's all very well saying yes, let's give this thing a go between us, but it doesn't take a psych graduate to figure out I have more baggage than a long-haul Aer Lingus flight midsummer.

I kiss her then, partly because there's nothing either of us can say to change the situation, and partly because the need to claim her mouth claws at my insides like a predatory beast.

My hand roams over her hips, then dips between her legs. She pulls her foot up to rest on her knee and opens her thighs to me. I love how unashamedly she seeks my touch. I circle her swollen clit with my fingers and she reaches for my rock solid cock. 'I could play with you for fucking hours.'

'Prove it.' Her breathy tone is weighted with challenge.

A low chuckle rumbles in my throat. 'What about the ELEGANCE meeting you've been manifesting for years? Shouldn't you be preparing for that?' Now I think about it, ELEGANCE isn't Avery's scene, but I don't have time to think about it because she says, 'I've been manifesting my vagina meeting your dick too and look how that turned out.'

'Dirty girl.' I click my tongue against the roof of my mouth. I knew she'd be confident in bed, but fuck, the woman is dynamite.

'Only for you.' She sighs as I nudge her onto her back. She spreads her legs in invitation.

I pause, committing the sight to memory. With tousled hair and flushed cheeks, she's more beautiful than any airbrushed, staged magazine photo and—believe me—I have copies of every single one of them.

I run my fingers over her breasts and her rosebud nipples preen beneath my touch. She's so fucking responsive. I slide my hand over her stomach, splaying my fingers over her flawless skin, revelling in how small, how feminine she looks beneath my huge hand.

'Killian,' her voice aches with need.

'Don't rush me.' I trail my fingers lower between her legs. She's saturated.

'Are you always this wet?'

'Only for you.'

'Just me?' I demand.

'Yes.'

'Good girl.' The thought of anyone else turning her on renders me positively murderous.

'You drive me fucking crazy,' I admit, climbing between her legs, kissing her clavicle and inhaling the scent of her skin, her hair and that damn intoxicating perfume. If I was obsessed with the woman before, I'm head over fucking heels for her now. Which is lethal. It could literally ruin me.

'The feeling is mutual,' she says. 'And imagine, I used to think I hated you.' She reaches for my ass cheeks, dragging me closer until my dick is nestled against her wet, inviting entrance.

'You hated that I didn't react to you.' I nip her neck as I slide myself gently inside her, savouring every sensational second. 'But now you know exactly what kind of reaction you incite in me.' I look down. If I live for a hundred years, I'll never tire of the sight of my cock in her.

Her gaze follows mine, and a low moan rushes out of her throat.

'You feel so fucking good, sweetheart.' I pull out, slowly, before gliding back in, revelling in this rare sense of intimacy. I've never had sex like it. Never had sex with a woman who could make me laugh and lust after her in the same second.

My lips find hers and this time when we kiss its slow and sensual, like we're both savouring every second. Her tight channel flutters as she grinds her pelvis against me. I work her good and slow, drawing it out. I wish we could do this forever.

She stares up at me with glassy, awe-filled eyes, her palms roaming over my pecs. I wish I could freeze this moment. Her quads tense beneath mine and her whole body goes taut. She's about three seconds away from coming on my cock. The knowledge is enough to catapult me into my own cataclysmic oblivion. Pure fucking ecstasy rips through my entire body. We cling to each other, rutting and clawing as we both shudder through life's most basic but beautiful gift—raw animalistic pleasure.

When we finally stop shaking, I roll onto my side and pull her into my arms, cradling her on my chest. She snuggles into me, wrapping an arm around my waist. Something wet lands on my pec. It takes me a minute to realise it's a tear. Avery's tear.

I rock up, cradling her face in my hands. 'Did I hurt you?' Horror takes hold of me.

She shakes her head, and another tear streaks her cheek. It slices my gut like a knife.

'What is it then?'

She shakes her head again and jerks her head back.

'Tell me,' I growl.

'It's nothing.' She wipes her face with the back of her hand.

'Tell me.' I lift her into my lap so she's facing me. Her blue eyes are dull.

'I'm just sad, you know?' She tears her eyes from mine.

'I don't know, woman. In case you haven't noticed, I'm not fluent in emotion.' I brush a thumb over her damp cheeks. 'Why are you sad?'

She hesitates, and I drop my hands to her hips, holding her on my lap. 'That it's over.' She swallows thickly.

I suck in a breath.

She's crying over me?

Fuck.

This is so much worse than I imagined.

All these sensations I'm struggling to process—all the parts of me I've spent years trying to protect, they're the parts that she wants.

'I've been attracted to you for years. It was easier when I thought you were an attractive asshole. But now I know better. I'm sad it's over before we had the chance to begin. I'll be fine when you catch the stalker, but being in this proximity with you, and not being able to touch you...'

'I told you repeatedly, I'm not a good man, Avery.' Case in

point, the recently deceased paparazzi found in the Wicklow mountains.

'I bet you're not as bad as you think.'

'I'm worse.' I tuck a tousled strand of hair behind her ear.

'Because you've killed people?' she blurts. I stiffen, fingers freezing in her hair. 'I have a fucking doctorate in psychology. I can read you, even when you're stoically reserved. You were a soldier. Killing people is part of the job.'

'You don't know the half of it.'

'I have a fair idea, but the past is the past, whatever you've done. I'm more interested in what you choose to do with your future. I know you, Killian. You have a huge heart in there somewhere. Why are you so protective of it?'

'Be glad I am. You've had a narrow escape.'

'What if I don't want to escape?'

'Don't say things like that or you'll find yourself hand-cuffed to this bed for the duration of this trip. You know I find it difficult to say no to you.'

I don't *want* this to be over. But I don't see how we can have a future. Not when I'm the way I am. And I'm not naïve enough to think I can change. Other men ogling my woman, jerking off to her picture in magazines; it's never going to be okay with me.

'Handcuffs sounds good to me.' A strained smile touches her lips.

I can't give her what she wants. I want to... but I can't.

But... we're here for three more days. I can give her that.

I sigh. 'I'm not boyfriend material, sweetheart. But while we're in San Francisco, I suppose we can...' I motion between us, once again at a loss for the right words for what we've been doing. Fucking doesn't cut it. It's so much more, which is problematic on so many levels.

Her entire face lights.

'Seriously though, baby, when we go home, we have to get

back to normal. I'm not good for you. And let's not forget we have a stalker on the loose.' Though, with a bit of luck, he'll be tied to a chair and ripe for torturing by the time we get home.

'You're exceptionally good for my vagina. And I think the safest place I can be is in bed with you. Which is why I think we should order room service and stay here for the day.'

I might not be boyfriend material, but Avery Williams is wife material.

It's official.

Chapter Twenty-Six

AVERY

After another two rounds of soul-shattering sex, I drag Killian out of bed for some fresh air. It's either that or accept the fact I won't be able to walk tomorrow—not ideal given I have the biggest interview of my life; something I might have spent years manifesting, but I've barely even thought about since we got here.

Thomson and Sterling flank our backs as we stroll through the streets of San Francisco. Sterling looks pissed for some reason, like he's swallowed a wasp. Thomson, on the other hand, is positively beaming as his eyes dart knowingly between Killian and me. Thomson has made no secret that he'd like his boss to settle down and find some happiness. So would I, but for now, I refuse to analyse this thing between us, and instead focus on enjoying every second of Killian's attention.

The man is an animal in the bedroom. I knew he would be. His need to take control of my body, my pleasure, is nothing short of primal. Moody, broody, broken Killian, was my favourite Beckett brother long before I discovered what he could do with his mouth, fingers, and every other part of him. I suspect I'm in more danger than I've ever been, and not from some crazed stalker—from myself. It would be so easy to fall head over heels in love with a man like him. A man who's so obviously broken and in need of fixing. I'm innately drawn to the complicated ones, and Killian is not only deeply mysterious, dark, and gifted —he also looks like he was sculpted in the form of a Roman God.

'You okay?' He leans in, and his mouth brushes over my ear.

An involuntary shiver slides over my spine. 'Great, thanks. You?'

He offers a single nod, but his eyes remain focused in front, scanning everything and everyone for danger.

The winter sun hangs low over the bay, casting long shadows across Pier 39's wooden planks. To our left, Alcatraz rises from the water like something from a gothic novel, all harsh edges and dark promises against the honey-gold sky. The air is crisp but not cold, thick with the scent of fresh sourdough mixing with salt spray and coffee from the waterfront cafes. I pull my jacket tighter around me. The outfit I picked out—a white blouse, denim skirt and tan knee-high Louboutin's—is cute, but not practical. If Killian's darting glances are anything to go by, it's worth it.

Sea lions bark in the distance, their raucous chorus competing with the cry of circling gulls and the gentle clinking of yacht rigging. A street performer's guitar carries on the breeze, and for a moment, it feels almost normal. Like we're just another couple enjoying the sunset.

I take my phone out and snap a few photos.

'Don't even think about putting them on social media,' he says darkly.

I roll my eyes. 'Don't insult my intelligence.' I flip the camera so it's pointing at us and hold it high in the air.

He immediately steps back. 'I don't do photos. And I definitely don't do selfies.'

'Please, for me?' I step towards him again. He sighs but doesn't move away.

'Smile.' I give him a perfunctory nudge in the ribs and while he doesn't exactly smile, he loses the grimace. I snap three quick pictures. Thomson sniggers from behind.

I push my phone back into my jacket pocket and we resume our strolling. 'It's easy to forget everything when we're half a world away, isn't it?' Tourists mill around us, also snapping photos of the bridge peeking through the late afternoon haze. I soak it all up, especially the sensation of Killian's hand which has returned to my lower back, guiding me through the crowd.

'I never forget anything,' Killian admits. 'Photographic memory.' He taps the side of his head.

I'm not surprised. His intelligence has always been obvious. He listens hard, speaks rarely, although he seems to have a lot more to say around me lately. 'That must be really helpful.'

'It can be.' He shrugs. 'Sometimes it can be torture. Like when I had to go through your relationship history, including photos of every man who ever touched you.' He growls and goosebumps pepper my skin.

I love his possessiveness.

Love how he hates the idea of any other man touching me, because I detest the idea of him with another woman. My mind wanders to Sarah, the dead girlfriend. He hasn't so much as referenced her since that night in St. Barths and, even though curiosity is eating me alive, I wouldn't dream of bringing her up.

'There's only one man I want to touch me.' I give him an appreciative look from my peripheral. 'And he happens to be my moody, broody bodyguard.'

'I'm not moody or broody.' He scoffs. 'I'm serious. One of us has to be.'

'Given half the chance, I could get serious.' I'm dancing around the edges of a subject I swore I wouldn't bring up—at least until we get back to Dublin.

'You don't know what you're asking for, Avery.' His words are weighted with warning.

'I know what serious means, Killian.' I scowl. 'And the funny thing is, I have a doctorate in psychology, yet some people will never take me seriously, because of my career choices, but I won't always be a glamour model.'

He halts abruptly, his head whipping round to face me. 'You won't?' The full force of his focus blisters my skin.

I glance down pointedly at my boobs, which are hidden beneath a tan leather jacket. 'The likelihood of magazines wanting to pay me for shots of these bad boys in ten years' time is slim to none.'

His expression falters slightly, but he rapidly rearranges his features. We resume our stroll towards the back of the pier, leaving the main bustle of tourists behind us. The Golden Gate Bridge stretches across the horizon like a ribbon of burnished copper in the late afternoon sun, its towers piercing the whispers of fog that roll in from the Pacific.

'But I'm okay with that...' I continue. 'Glamour modelling was only ever meant to be a stepping stone, anyway.' I shrug.

Killian slows to a stop again, this time beside some wooden railings. 'Was it? I thought you loved it.' He turns his entire body into mine so we're face to face, toe to toe, hip to hip—an unusual break in his constant surveillance of our surroundings.

'I love the opportunities it affords; travel, new locations, parties, and, of course, it pays well.' I shrug. 'But it's exhausting. And to be honest, at some point, I'd like to be taken more seriously, which is why we're here.'

'ELEGANCE?' There's a question in his tone.

'Yes. ELEGANCE isn't just another magazine shoot. It's the difference between being seen as a glamour model and being taken seriously in fashion. It's exclusive, prestigious. The kind of models who shoot for ELEGANCE become the face of Chanel and Dior. One editorial could change everything for me. Open doors that have been closed because of my past. It's my chance to be known for more than just looking good in lingerie.'

Killian's dark eyes narrow. 'You want to transition out of glamour?'

'Yes.' Why is he looking at me like I've got two heads? 'Is that so hard to believe?'

'If you could do any type of modelling, what would you pick?' His voice is strained, raspy, like he's asking me something so much more significant, but I have no idea what.

'I thought I was the one who asked the questions around here? Speaking of which, you owe me two from yesterday.' I lean closer so our chests are touching.

'Answer the question, and I'll give you four back today.' An intensity blazes in his pupils.

'Deal.' I don't even have to pause to think about it. I know what I want. 'If I'm going to continue modelling, and that's a big if, I'd choose Bridal couture.'

Kilian coughs, maybe to mask his surprise.

I lean against the railing, watching a seagull dive towards the water. 'When my dad left, my mother threw herself into wedding planning. Turned her heartbreak into a thriving business. The house was filled with bridal magazines. I'd spend hours flicking through them, watching these ethereal women floating down aisles in clouds of silk and lace. They looked... regal. Untouchable. Pure. The opposite of everything people assume about me now.' I pull a face. 'Vera Wang doesn't hire glamour models. Neither does Elie Saab or Oscar de la Renta. But if I could get into ELEGANCE? If I could make that transition? Those doors might finally open. Plus, I'd like to merge my modelling career with something more momentous. Maybe a column or a "Dear Avery" advice page or something. I want to do something meaningful.'

His eyebrows rocket upwards—the most surprise he's shown since I've known him.

Apparently I've genuinely caught him off guard. For once, that laser-focused gaze actually wavers, like he's recalculating everything he thought he knew about me.

'Do you want to get married?' He blurts, rubbing his thumb over his jawline.

'Is that a proposal?' Laughter bursts from my lips. 'Because if it is, you'd want to make a bit more of an effort.'

'No, it was categorically *not* a proposal.' He deadpans. 'I was curious about the obsession with the wedding dresses—other than the *ethereal* part.'

'Relax.' I grip the lapels of his suit jacket and pull him closer to me. 'I was fucking with you. Thankfully, it isn't the eighteen hundreds. One night together doesn't mean you're obliged to make an honest woman out of me. I'm not sure I even believe in the concept of marriage.'

'Why?' He continues to stare at me like I'm a riddle he can't quite work out.

'That's two questions you've asked me. If you want me to answer, I'm going to need five back.'

'You drive a hard bargain,' he huffs, but his hand reaches up to my hair, tenderly smoothing it back from my face.

'Take it or leave it.' I feign nonchalance, but inside my heart is beating double quick. I'm stupidly flattered he's so interested in more than just my body.

'I'll take it.' He nods solemnly. 'Why don't you believe in marriage?'

'You've seen my files. My father ran off with his PA when I was a kid. Broke my mother's heart. I mean, look at her now, she's in flying form and she looks amazing, but yet she's never been able to commit to a man properly again after that. It's one thing dating younger men and cruising around with the MILF number plate, but she never had another serious relationship. She never put herself in line to get hurt again. And that speaks volumes to me.'

'What's your relationship with your father like?' Killian probes.

I arch an eyebrow at him.

'I'll give you another question back.'

'A fair exchange is no robbery, I suppose.' It's a battle to keep my lips from lifting into a grin. I'm dancing inside. Actually dancing. It's one type of intimacy to have sex, but this conversation is next level. And for once, it's him initiating the deep and meaningful discussions.

'You overheard our phone call. Our relationship is stilted. He tries. He paid for my private schooling. When I was a child, he made a point of sending me cards and presents at Christmas and on my birthday. He calls every few weeks to check in. It's kind of awkward.'

'I can't imagine you feeling awkward around anyone. You're the most confident woman I've ever met,' Killian muses.

'He struggles with my... occupation.' I confess. 'You know I have a stepbrother, Sebastian. I'm sure you came across him in my files. My father seems to have a better relationship with him than me. Maybe it's the fact that he raised him, maybe because he's a guy he can relate to him more. I don't know. I've never particularly bonded with him. Tessa tried to make an effort with me over the years, but I just can't have any type of relationship with her. It feels disloyal to my mother. Tessa knew Dad was married. She'd met my mother at loads of corporate functions and still had no problem sleeping with her husband.' I struggle to articulate my feelings towards my stepfamily.

'You have trust issues.' Killian announces with a hint of surprise in his tone.

'I do not!' My quick denial speaks volumes.

'That's why you picked psychology.' Mirth lights his eyes. 'So you'd have a head start reading people. Analysing them. It's why you project this brazen confidence, which is a self-defence mechanism, by the way.'

My mouth drops open. 'Hey!' I poke a finger into his rock solid pec. He's not entirely wrong. 'Leave the psychoanalysing to the person who's qualified. Speaking of which, it's my turn to ask the questions.'

'Fine. But can we go for a coffee or something?' He glances around. 'We're quite exposed here.'

'No, we can't go for coffee, but we can go for a cocktail.' I fall into step beside him, hoping he'll put his hand on my lower back again.

He doesn't.

But he does put a protective arm around my shoulder. I lean into his warmth and inhale his scent. 'Fine, but let's find somewhere quiet where we can relax.'

Thomson fires me a knowing wink from his position five feet away and mouths the words *future Mrs Beckett*.

I shake my head and grin. I'm still not sold on the marriage idea, but I am totally sold on Killian Beckett.

I manage to convince Avery the best place for a cocktail is back at the hotel. Unlike St. Barths—which was a media shit-show thanks to James's high profile and all his high-profile guests—nobody knows we're here. Avery is scheduled to make an appearance at Rian's club tomorrow night. Her phone is protected from hackers using my company's innovative software. She hasn't so much as opened a social media app in weeks, but still, I'd prefer to get her back to the suite. Partly to do with safety, but mostly because I'm dying to get her alone again. Especially after her earlier admissions.

They change everything.

If ELEGANCE don't offer her an editorial tomorrow, I'll make some calls. I'm not below using my family connections to help her. Now I know it's what Avery wants, I'll do everything in my power to make sure she gets it. Especially because it aligns with what I want—her—all to myself.

'I get six questions,' Avery announces gleefully, falling onto the sofa. I've already swept the suite for bugs, camera trackers, anything suspicious. Thomson and Sterling are in the bar downstairs. Room service have made the bed, turned the sheets down and spread rose petals all over the place. They also left a bottle of Dom Perignon in a chrome cooler with two crystal champagne flutes and chocolate dipped strawberries. I'd bet my life Thomson had something to do with this romantic bullshit. I'm not sure whether to punch him or give him a raise.

'You do.' I reach for the champagne, then twist the top until it pops. I'm going to need a drink, never mind Avery. And this shit might not be strong enough for what she is liable to ask.

She rubs her palms together expectantly. 'Why did you ask where I want to end up?'

Trust her to go for the jugular. As ever, she's as subtle as a brick.

'Because I wanted to know.' I pour the champagne into the flutes and hand her one.

'That's not an answer.' She wrinkles her nose in disgust. 'Why did you want to know?'

I smirk. 'That's question number two.'

'Cheater!' She points an accusatory finger my way, and it's impossible to hold back the laugh in my chest.

'It's not cheating. It's called being "tactical".' I take a mouthful of bubbles. Tastes like shit. I'm going to need a whiskey if I'm going to survive this interrogation. Though, truthfully, part of me has come to enjoy this game we play.

I grab the bottle of Macallan from the coffee table— what's left of it anyway. I made a good dent in the contents last night.

'Tactical is playing with my pussy before you penetrate it.' She quirks a brow. What a fucking visual. 'What you just did there is cheating.'

'I'm a lot of things, sweetheart—none of which are particularly redeeming—but I'm not, and never will be a cheater. That's one thing you'll never have to worry about.'

'Why would I worry?' She raises her glass to her lips. I don't miss the slight waver in her tone. 'It's not like we're exclusive.'

'That's not what you said last night when I had my cock buried in you.' I pour myself a double for good measure.

A tiny gasp hisses from her rosebud lips as her focus falls to my crotch. My tactical techniques have nothing on my distraction techniques—or so I thought.

She catches herself and tuts. 'Nice try, big guy. You almost got me. Answer the questions and then we can get back to burying cocks.'

I sigh, and give in to the inevitable—something I tend to do a lot around this woman. I drop onto the couch beside her. 'I asked what you would choose to do because if it involves anything other than glamour modelling, then that changes everything between us.'

Her gaze sharpens as her pupils roam across my features, no doubt trying to analyse me again.

'If you want it to, that is.'

Avery isn't the only one going for the jugular. I've never been particularly articulate, and tonight is no different.

'You want to be exclusive?' She purses her lips together like she's biting back her shock or maybe even a squeal, knowing her. Her reaction this morning, the tears and the *what ifs* were enough to imply she'd like to give this thing a go between us. She might not be so keen if she knew how many bodies I've buried.

I take her small, manicured hand in my large rough one, and angle my face to hers so our eyes meet. 'I'm not exactly boyfriend material, sweetheart, but I'm nowhere near ready to give you up.'

'Thank god for that.' She winks. 'I hate giving you a big head but you're the best shag I've ever had!'

My nostrils flare. 'For the sake of preserving lives, we're going to pretend I'm the only shag you've ever had.'

Her tinkling laughter pierces the air.

I'm not joking.

Her expression morphs into something more serious. 'What is it about the glamour modelling that you don't like? Are you worried what your parents would think?' She worries at her lower lips. 'Your brothers?'

I huff out a breath. 'No. They'll be fucking delighted when they hear about this.' I motion between us. 'Your career wouldn't even come into it.' I throw back the rest of the whiskey, slam my glass on to the coffee table, then lift Avery onto my lap until she's straddling me. This is where she belongs. With me. On me. Wrapped around me.

'What then?' She reaches for the top button on her white blouse with a devious look in her eyes. It pops open and I get a flash of flawless creamy cleavage, which renders my dick solid in seconds.

'I don't share, sweetheart.' I rip open her blouse with one sharp tug. 'And these'—I grab her tits in both hands—'are mine now. No one gets to ogle them but me. You're going to smash the meeting tomorrow. They're going to offer you multiple exposures. You're going to get a phone call from every bridal range you've ever dreamed of working with, and the only person taking photos of these... will be me.'

She smirks and grinds against me in response. 'You know you're a walking red flag, right?'

'I told you already, you don't know the half of it, baby.'

'That turns me on way more than it should.' She reaches for my buckle, yanks it open, along with my suit trousers. My erection springs free. She eyes it with wonder, wraps two hands around it, then pumps. 'I need you to come on my tits. Mark them as yours.'

Fuck.

I hiss.

Avery was my dream woman before I discovered her filthy mouth and ability to read my fucking mind. I tug her bra down until her full, round breasts spill over the top of the luxurious lace fabric. It's almost too pretty to tear. Almost. I rip it from her chest and she pumps me harder. 'I'll buy you more,' I promise. I'll buy her anything her heart desires, because she's the only thing that *my* heart desires. And my dick. And every other damn part of me.

I brush my thumbs over her furled pink nipples. They're mine now. Mine, and mine alone.

She inches her face down, lips hovering millimetres away from mine. 'I'm yours,' she whispers, pumping me harder. Yep —the woman is a mind reader.

'Damn fucking right you are.' I claim her lips, sucking her tongue into my mouth as my hands roam over her chest. She flicks a thumb over my tip, coating my cock in my own arousal. I'm embarrassingly close, but this is too good. She's too good. She's everything I never knew I needed, and now she's giving herself to me. I tear my lips from hers as the first hot burst of cum hits her right breast. White-hot pleasure hijacks my entire body as I experience the most intense orgasm of my life.

'So fucking hot.' She grinds her pussy against my thigh as my cum drips over her skin. Her fingers swipe through the sticky mess and she smears it over both breasts before bringing her finger to her mouth and sucking.

Fuck. She loves it. Loves being marked, claimed, covered in my cum. I was half in love with her before, but fuck me, after that—I'm all in.

'On the coffee table, now.' I hoist her up from my lap.

'Yes sir,' she purrs.

'Lose the skirt. In fact, lose everything.' This is one sight I need to commit to memory. I watch as she rushes to wiggle out of her clothes and clambers onto the cool mirrored surface, head down, ass up.

'Spread your legs.'

She parts them. 'Wider,' I demand, and she obeys.

Her pink cunt is glistening—just the way I like it. I drop to my knees by the edge of the glass. Our eyes lock in the mirrored table top just below her stomach. She'll be able to watch as I eat her out from behind. The thought is enough to send blood racing to my dick again.

I smooth my palms over the curve of her ass, then dip my face between her legs. The first touch with my tongue is long and slow. She moans, but nowhere near loud enough for my taste. By the time I've finished with her, she's going to be screaming my name so loud her stalker will hear her wherever he is in the world.

The thought makes me feral.

I thrust my tongue into her hot tight channel and she bucks against my face. Sliding my hand around the front, I tease her clit and she screams.

Better.

But still not loud enough.

I increase the pressure, and my pace, until her legs tremble like a newborn fawn.

'Killian,' she screams, arching her back and bucking against my face as she comes harder than a train.

I smile against her sex as I lick up every single drop.

Chapter Twenty-Eight

AVERY

The ELEGANCE building soars into the San Francisco skyline, sixty floors of steel and glass catch the morning sun. From here, I can see the Bay Bridge stretching across the water. The Financial District hums with morning energy—designer heels clicking on pavements, sleek cars purring past, the scent of artisan coffee drifting from nearby cafes.

I smooth my hands down my cream Bottega Veneta pantsuit for the hundredth time. The silk camisole underneath catches the light, and my Yves Saint Laurent heels add enough height to make my legs look endless. My hair's swept into a sleek low bun, and my makeup is natural but flawless—exactly what you'd expect from a potential ELEGANCE model.

'Do I look okay?' There's no missing the hint of nerves in my voice. No wonder. This meeting has the potential to change everything—and not just in my professional life, but in my personal one too. I assumed Killian disapproved of my career choice because he found it distasteful, not because he's possessive and determined to be the only man I pose naked for. It makes sense though. He's not a man who'd share.

'No.' Killian's voice is rough as his black eyes absorb every inch of me. 'You don't look okay. You look like an absolute knockout, and every man in that building is going to lose his fucking mind when you walk in.'

Heat blooms in my chest. 'You're just biased now.'

He reaches for my arm and gives it a reassuring squeeze. 'I'm just stating facts.'

Thomson approaches before I can respond. 'All clear, boss. Sterling's stationed in the lobby. I'll take the executive floor.'

Killian nods, but his eyes haven't left me. I'm acutely aware how much my career change will influence our relationship, because after last night, it's abundantly clear we're in one. After the coffee table incident, he ran us a lavender bubble bath, which we soaked in for almost two hours, and he answered every single question I asked him. Although, I couldn't bring myself to ask him the one that still niggles me —what happened to his ex. It shouldn't matter, but it obviously affected him, and I want to know everything that makes him who he is, the good, the bad and the ugly.

'Ready?' Killian checks, scrutinising me.

'Yes. Let's do this.'

I suck in a deep breath as he ushers me inside the revolving glass doors. The marble lobby of ELEGANCE puts most five-star hotels to shame. A cascading crystal installation drops three stories through the central atrium, and the walls are lined with iconic covers from the magazine's forty-year history. Sterling nods from his position near a living wall of tropical plants as we pass.

The elevator is comprised of chrome and mirrors, with a glass wall offering vertigo-inducing views of the bay. My stomach flips as we shoot up to the fifty-eighth floor, though that might have more to do with Killian's proximity than the height.

Even if I don't get offered a slot here, I'm officially retiring from glamour. I thought I wanted to do something more momentous, and what could be more momentous than being with him? There's something profoundly intimate about loving a man who allows so few people past his defences. Every day, I peel back another layer and discover something even more beautiful beneath. It's like excavating a masterpiece—carefully, reverently—with the knowledge that what you're uncovering is both rare and precious.

'This way, Miss Williams.' A willowy assistant leads us through an open-plan office that looks like an art gallery. Everything is white, glass, and chrome, dotted with abstract sculptures and elegant fashion photographs.

The conference room door swings open to reveal four of the most influential people in fashion. Mandy Morrison, Editor-in-Chief, raises one perfectly groomed eyebrow as Killian follows me in. She's exactly as terrifying as I imagined —sharp cheekbones and an even sharper tongue if the rumours are true.

'Avery, darling.' David Chen, the Creative Director, air-kisses my cheeks. His silver-streaked man bun and avant-garde Yamamoto suit are on point from the man who revolutionised fashion photography.

'It's a pleasure to meet you.' I glance from David to Killian. I should probably explain the presence of the six foot five Adonis beside me. 'This is my b—'

'Boyfriend,' Killian cuts in smoothly, his hand finding the small of my back. 'Killian Beckett.'

I almost choke on the heavily perfumed air. Boyfriend? I was going to say bodyguard, but if he wants to declare our relationship status publicly that's one giant step for an emotionally challenged Beckett.

'Beckett?' Kim Rivera, the Fashion Director, perks up. 'Of Beckett Enterprises?'

'The same.' His blunt delivery doesn't invite further questions.

James Barrett, the Photography Director, studies us both with an artist's eye. 'You two should do a spread together. Quite the striking couple. The camera would love you.'

'No.' Killian's sharp response is immediate and final.

I catch Mandy hiding a smile behind her coffee cup. 'Shall we begin?'

For the next hour, they fire questions at me like bullets. My education, my background, my aspirations. When I mention my psychology doctorate, Mandy's perfectly sculpted eyebrows rise.

'A model with both beauty and brains.' David leans forward. 'What made you pursue psychology?'

Killian's lip twitches. Yesterday's conversation hangs unspoken in the air. Trust issues my ass. I studied psychology because it interested me, not because I've got daddy issues. But I'm happy to call him daddy if it means he'll put me over his knee again. That was hot as fuck.

'I've always been fascinated by human behaviour. Understanding what drives people, what motivates them.'

Killian scoffs and masks it with a cough. If he fucks this up for me, it'll be me spanking his ass—with a shovel which I'll use to bury him with after.

'And now you're a glamour model.' Mandy's tone is neutral, but her eyes are brimming with curiosity. 'What motivates you?'

'The need to demonstrate that women don't have to choose.' I meet her gaze. 'You can be intellectual and sexy. Professional and playful. Have boobs, a bum and a brain.'

Kim nods slowly. 'Our readers would relate to that. A woman refusing to be put in a box.'

'What do you want, Avery?' James asks suddenly. 'Where do you see yourself going?'

I glance at Killian, finding unexpected strength in his steady gaze. 'I'm ready for something more elevated,' I admit. 'Something that showcases all of who I am, not just my body.' I keep the bridal couture dreams under my belt for now. I don't want them to assume ELEGANCE is just a stepping stone for me.

Mandy studies me for a long moment. 'Would you mind stepping out while we discuss? Katie will get you both coffee.'

The next twenty minutes are torture. I pace the pristine hallway while Killian leans against the wall, watching me with something like pride.

'You nailed it, baby.' He brushes a kiss over my temple.

'I hope so, but either way, I'm going to nail *you* the second we get out of here.'

'We're going to have some celebrating to do.' His quiet tone exudes confidence.

When we're finally called back in, Mandy doesn't waste time. 'We want you for February's cover.' She slides a mock-up across the table. 'And we want you to write a four-page feature. "Beauty and the Brains: The Model Breaking All the Rules".' Her eyes slide to Killian. 'And if you happen to change your mind, we'll happily include you in the article.'

'No chance.'

'Never say never,' Mandy says wistfully. 'I have a feeling Miss Williams could be persuasive.'

'You have no idea,' he mutters grimly.

I practically float out of the ELEGANCE building, my heels barely touching the marble floor. Even Killian's granite features have softened into something dangerously close to a grin.

'I did it!' I resist the urge to jump up and down—the Bottega Veneta pantsuit probably wouldn't appreciate it.

'You did.' His hand settles on my spine again, his thumb

stroking with a tenderness I could get used to. 'Which is why I've booked us a table at Saison tomorrow night. I suppose it'll be our first official date.'

'Saison?' I stop dead. 'That's impossible to get into.'

'Nothing's impossible for a Beckett.' His eyes glitter with something that looks suspiciously like pride. 'Maybe you'll find out one day... oh wait, no, you don't believe in marriage.'

'I think my exact words were "I'm not sure if I believe in marriage" —you might have a photographic memory but your ears need syringing.'

Sterling trails behind us, his face set in its usual scowl. Something about his expression niggles at my instincts, but before I can analyse it, Killian's opening the car door.

'So what are we doing tonight?'

'Tonight,' his voice drops an octave, 'we're doing each other.'

'I can work with that.' I slide across the cream leather interior. 'But first, I have a date with a different Beckett brother.'

'Rian.' Killian tuts, hopping into the car beside me, dropping a possessive hand on my thigh. 'It's not a date, it's a grovelling apologetic phone call. And I plan on eating you out the entire time you're talking. At least if he hears you moan, he'll believe you're sick.'

'You're the sick one! You're one dirty bastard.'

'That's why you love me,' he quips. The second the words are out of his mouth, his face falls. 'It was a joke.'

'Jeez, relax, I know it was a joke.' I place my hand on top of his as Sterling gets into the front seat. 'I hope you weren't joking about eating me out though.'

Sterling huffs, Thomson laughs, and Killian simply smoulders.

Chapter Twenty-Nine

AVERY

It's our last day in San Francisco and just like in St. Barths, I plan on making the most of it, which is why I'm currently strolling around Neiman Marcus laden down with designer bags and three impeccably dressed bodyguards. The historic building is a shopper's paradise—gleaming floors and sparkling counters, crowned by that famous stained-glass dome that throws rainbow patterns across everything below. The scent of expensive perfume mingles with leather hand-bags and success.

Killian stalks beside me like a panther in a designer suit, radiating his usual mix of lethal grace and overprotectiveness. Sterling and Thomson flank us, maintaining what they think is a discreet distance, but actually screams, 'security detail' to anyone paying attention. Not that the well-heeled shoppers browsing Chanel and Gucci seem to care—this is San Francis-co's premier luxury department store, after all. Everyone here has something to protect.

'You don't have to buy the entire store,' Killian mutters as I pause to admire a display of Jimmy Choos. 'We do have to fly home eventually.'

'I'm supporting the American economy.' I add a pair of stilettos to my growing collection. 'Besides, a girl needs options for her ELEGANCE cover shoot, doesn't she?'

His lips twitch, and I count it as a win. Since yesterday's meeting, he's been... different. More cautiously optimistic. For him to even joke about marriage was a huge leap. Even if he did snap shut like a clam after the tongue in cheek, *that's why you love me,* remark.

'Thank fuck for the jet,' he mutters

The collision comes out of nowhere. A shoulder slams into mine, sending my shopping bags scattering across the marble floor.

'Watch where you're going,' a bald-headed man in his forties snaps, adjusting his Rolex with manicured fingers. Money clearly doesn't buy manners. He sneers, looking me up and down like I'm something he scraped off his Italian leather shoes.

'Excuse me?' I stare at him in disbelief.

Before he can respond, Killian's hand shoots out, catching the man's wrist in what looks like a gentle grip, but is clearly anything but, judging by the sudden shocking pallor of the guy's face.

'Apologise.' Killian's voice is soft. Deadly soft.

'I don't think—'

Killian adjusts his grip. The man's knees actually buckle.

'Let me be clearer.' Killian leans in, flashing a frankly terrifying smile. 'Apologise to the lady, or I'll introduce your face to that lovely shiny floor.'

'I... I'm sorry,' he stammers, visibly wincing.

'You can do better than that,' Killian snarls. Thomson and Sterling hover grim-faced beside us as other shoppers begin to stare.

'Killian, please.' I touch his arm. 'It's ok, leave it.'

'It's not okay, sweetheart. No one disrespects you.' His

face is a mask of rage. The man is clearly petrified. I don't blame him. Even I'm alarmed by this side of my boyfriend. I know what he's capable of, but knowing and seeing it are two very different things.

'Killian, people are staring,' I whisper.

'We've given them worse to stare at.' His steely gaze flashes to me.

'So sorry. It was entirely my fault. I wasn't looking where I was going.' The man whimpers, his face now contorted with pain.

Killian releases him with a little shove, and he practically runs toward the exit, cradling his wrist.

'Was that really necessary?' I ask. He's so tender with me I forget the man is a trained killer. The hot, hard, walking red flag thing does things to me, but seeing him in action is confronting.

'Yes.' Killian's already picking up my scattered bags. 'No one disrespects what's mine.' His possessiveness borders on devotion. Thank goodness I've witnessed the tenderness he reserves only for those he truly trusts—or I'd be terrified.

'It's just...' I purse my lips.

'Spit it out sweetheart, it's not like you to be quiet.'

'Seeing you in action is kind of unnerving.' I glance around. Everyone's gone back to their usual business.

'I'm so sorry.' He cups my chin, angling my face to meet his stare. 'Never be scared of me, baby. I'd kill for you. I'd die for you. But I'd never ever hurt you.'

'I believe you.'

But Christ, I wouldn't want to be on the receiving end of his wrath.

Killian gave Thomson and Sterling the night off. In fairness, they earned it trailing around after me while I shopped all day, and thanks to my pre-booked performance at the

Luxor Lounge, the entire world thinks I'm in Dublin. Here, away from everything, it's easy to forget there's a crazy stalker sourcing black lilies and sending threatening notes.

We arrive at Saison just before eight. It's even more exclusive than I imagined. Tucked away in an unassuming brick building, the interior unfolds like a secret told in hushed tones—warm wood, sleek lines, and understated luxury. The open kitchen glows like a stage, chefs moving in choreographed precision beneath copper pots that hang like art installations.

Killian's hand rests at the small of my back as the host leads us to our table, a private alcove with a perfect view of both the kitchen and the dining room. All eyes follow us—more on him than me for once—as we weave between tables of designer-clad diners. The air smells of smoke and sweet wood, subtle spices and a shit tonne of old money. Soulful ballads drift through the restaurant—the kind of emotional, piano-driven music that acts as the perfect backdrop for intimate conversations. The vocalist's raw, slightly raspy voice croons melancholy lyrics about love and longing.

'Wine?' Killian asks as we settle into our seats. The leather chair feels butter-soft against my bare shoulders. I'm wearing a midnight blue Valentino that dips low in the back —partly because it's stunning, partly because I like watching Killian's eyes darken every time I turn around.

'Would you judge me if I order champagne? This feels like a celebration.'

His mouth curves into that rare smile that transforms his entire face. 'As long as you promise not to pass out on me. I've got big plans for you after this.'

'Big indeed.' I lick my lips as the memories of the past couple of days float through my mind. I'm sore from our previous *plans*, but in the best way.

The sommelier appears and Killian orders without

glancing at the menu, something French with a vintage that makes the man's eyebrows lift. When he's gone, Killian leans forward, his gaze intense in the candlelight.

'I suppose it's not too shabby for our first official date,' I tease.

He strokes a thumb over his sharp jawline. 'Thank fuck for that, because this is the last first date you'll be going on.'

'Is that right?' I love how rapidly he's transformed from distant and stoic to being utterly invested in us. No mind games. No bullshit. No wondering if he'll call. I suppose being forced to live with someone is a quick fire way to find out if you *could* live with them.

'Yes.' Confidence oozes from his every pore.

'If I'd have known you'd ask me out if I quit the topless photoshoots, I would have done it years ago.'

'I was going to ask you out once,' he admits quietly.

Shock soars through my system. 'What? When?'

'Scarlett's graduation. At James's house.' He inclines his head and my gaze is drawn to the tattoos peeking out from under his collar. 'We ran into each other by the pool. I asked if you'd started looking for a job relevant to your degree. You told me you didn't have to, that you'd been signed by Zack. I wanted to hunt him down and throttle him.'

I blow out a breath. I remember it like it was yesterday. 'I can't believe it. In fact, I could have sworn you hated me, even then.'

'I hated you telling me instead of using the doctorate you worked so hard for, that you were going to continue torturing me, and the rest of the male population with your fabulous tits.'

'I had no idea you were interested.'

'Interested doesn't cover it. Remind me to show you my office when we get home.' He shakes his head gently. 'Then Isabella died, and I was grateful I didn't have a woman of my own. Caelon's loss reminded me of...' he trails off, averting his eyes.

I try not to look overly interested, but my ears prick like a dog's at dinnertime. 'Do you want to talk about it?'

'No.' His voice is sharp.

The sommelier returns with our drinks and Killian's shoulders visibly relax.

'To your cover,' he says, raising his glass.

I raise mine and clink it against his. 'To us.'

'To us.' He takes my hand across the table, stroking a thumb over the pulse point on my wrist. 'I wasn't joking about this being your last first date. I know things are moving quickly, sweetheart, but I'm an all-or-nothing type of guy.'

'I noticed.' His intensity is one of the things I love about him. As is his darkness. Witnessing him dissemble his carefully constructed guard is a privilege. I'm finally beginning to see the fullness of who he is—the warrior, and the wounded, the protector and the passionate. 'Luckily for you, I'm an all-or-nothing type of girl.'

'I noticed.' He quirks a brow and smirks, then takes a sip of champagne. His wince makes me laugh out loud. 'I don't know how you can drink this stuff.'

'I love it.' My shoulder dips in a shrug. 'Do you want to order something else? A whiskey maybe?'

'No. I'm supposed to be working, remember?' He glances around the restaurant. I know him well enough to ascertain he's already mentally assessed every person in here, noted the exits and entrances, and I don't doubt he has at least one firearm tucked into his trademark Armani suit.

'I'm still work to you, am I?' I tease. 'If your plan falls into place, in a matter of hours, your work will be complete.'

'*When* my plan falls into place, you mean?' His ebony eyes bore into mine, smouldering. 'And you're not work—you're everything to me.'

It's hard to believe that this is the same man who could barely look at me a few weeks ago. My heart is so full.

I swallow the words bursting to get out. It's too soon. I don't want to terrify him.

Then again, he's the one declaring this is my last first date.

Silence settles between us as he continues to stare at me, that familiar intensity radiating from him in undulating waves. It's like he wants to say something but doesn't know how. I reach across the table and take his hand in mine, brushing a thumb over the back of it.

'You know I've never been into PDAs but if you keep looking at me like that, things could change very quickly,' he says darkly.

'You are totally into PDAs. Remember the yacht?'

'You make me do things I'd never have dreamed of.'

'Like what?'

'Like contemplate putting a ring on your finger and a baby in your belly.'

'Jesus Christ.' I almost spit my drink out.

And to think I was worried about scaring *him* off.

Chapter Thirty

THE WATCHER

From the shadows of the VIP section, my view of the main stage is perfect. The Luxor Lounge is every depraved pervert's dream—low, moody lighting, deep panelled mahogany, crystal chandeliers, and naked, sinful flesh everywhere.

This is where she first bared herself to strangers. Where she started down this sordid path.

Fitting that tonight it ends where it began.

Matthew Donnelly owed me a favour. Instead of asking for it, I took it—his credentials to stroll through the door. The chloroform-soaked rag sits in a sealed bag inside my jacket pocket. The service exit I've mapped leads to the alley where my car waits—engine running, fake plates installed, windows tinted. Three minutes from exit to interstate. I've memorised the security patrol patterns, identified the blind spots in the CCTV coverage. I know which stupid, suited guard takes an unauthorised cigarette break at 11:45.

Her dressing room is the third door on the left down the private corridor. Once previously used by dancers, now reserved for "special performers." The lock was simple. Child's play. I left her one last lily, for old times' sake.

I sip my water, watching the patrons arrive in their expensive suits, pretending this glorified strip club is something sophisticated. They're all here to see her—my beautiful girl who lost her way. She's been letting that bodyguard put his hands on what belongs to me, but all that stops tonight.

In less than two hours, she'll finally be where she belongs—with me.

I check my watch.

It's almost time.

Tonight, I'll rescue her from this life she was never meant for. From the men who look at her like she's something to be consumed. From that Beckett bastard who is stupid enough to think he can take her from me.

It's poetic, really. Taking her from the place where she first started her disgusting career. A perfect ending to this chapter of her life.

And the beginning of our story together.

Rian Beckett might have revamped the place, but nothing can erase the sordid acts that occurred here. I should burn this building to the ground.

The lights dim. The announcer's voice fills the space. "Gentlemen, please welcome to the stage... Ruby Fox."

What?

No.

That's not right.

Ruby Fox is a British burlesque dancer. Right on cue, she slinks onto the stage, with cheap curves, plastic breasts, barely concealed with a ridiculous red feather boa.

Where is Avery?

I scan the crowd, the exits. This is supposed to be her slot. The advertisements in the members-only emails confirmed it. I even cracked Beckett's security software to access her schedule.

But she's not here.

He changed her plans.

He kept her from me.

He played me.

The glass shatters in my grip, crystal fragmenting into my flesh. Blood wells between my fingers, dripping onto the pristine white tablecloth—one drop, two drops, a constellation of crimson stars against snow.

I watch it spread. So red. So pure.

Like the way he'll bleed when I get hold of him.

I raise my hand to my lips and taste the copper warmth.

It's a setback.

Disappointing. But he's only delaying the inevitable.

Plans change. But destiny doesn't.

Chapter Thirty-One

KILLIAN

It's fortunate Avery is already living with me. After our time in San Francisco, I'd have insisted on it anyway—a move that might have seemed unhinged under other circumstances. Though I suspect she has the measure of me by now.

We land in Dublin before dawn, surprisingly rested thanks to the comfort of the family jet—though not as rested as we might have been had we not spent half the night fucking like rabbits. No matter how many times I have her, it'll never be enough. Avery Williams was made for me, of that, I'm certain.

There's been no update on how things went last night at the Luxor Lounge, but no news is good news, so I presume our stalker is sitting tight in Wicklow.

Walsh stands sentry at my building's entrance, flanked by Mason, Lynch, and Donovan—three of my most trusted operatives. Their formation is tight, expressions grim.

'Do you have him?'

'Negative,' Walsh is ashen.

'What the fuck?' My anger reverberates through the air.

Avery tenses beside me; the contentment we found in

the States and in each other evaporates in an instant. I smooth a hand over her waist. The last thing I want to do is startle her, even though I'm fucking livid with these imbeciles.

Truthfully, it's me who is the fucking imbecile. Given the setup at the Luxor Lounge, and how ruthless and skilled my team are, I allowed myself to be distracted. I should have been focused on eliminating the threat personally. An amateur's mistake.

Walsh swallows hard. 'He took the bait. Left a black lily in the dressing room with a note: Plans change, but destiny doesn't. But he vanished before we could contain him.'

'How is that fucking possible?' My voice could cut glass.

'He deployed a sophisticated EMP device. Knocked out our electronics for exactly ninety seconds—just long enough to slip away. By the time the backup systems engaged, he was gone.'

'Tell me we have something.' I keep my voice steady despite the fury building in my chest. 'An identity, at least.'

'We've identified every person who entered the club last night. Cross-referenced with facial recognition and ID verification.' Walsh hands me a tablet with detailed logs. 'One anomaly. Finance Minister Matthew Donnelly checked in at 10:22 PM.'

'And?'

'Donnelly was giving a speech at Trinity College at the exact same time. We confirmed with multiple sources.'

I scan through the guest list protocols. Rian's club requires retinal scans and government ID for membership. 'How did he bypass security?'

'That's where it gets interesting.' Walsh swipes to a security image. 'He used a top-tier synthetic ID and a contact lens that mimicked Donnelly's retinal pattern. The kind of technology only available to government agencies.'

'Or someone with access to them,' I mutter. 'What about footage?'

'That's the other problem. The cameras weren't just disabled—the data was corrupted with a military-grade algorithm. IT says it's the same signature used by certain intelligence agencies to wipe sensitive information. Our techs are still trying to recover fragments.'

'Connection to Donnelly?'

'We're digging. So far we know Donnelly oversees funding for several classified defence contracts. Including one with specialised tech development that our stalker seems to have access to.'

The bastard has resources that go well beyond what a typical stalker should have access to. And he knows exactly how to use them.

'For fuck's sake.' My men form a circle around us, with Walsh at the front. His expression darkens. 'And sir... your car.'

My shoulders tighten. 'Which one?' I have four. A military grade jeep, two black SUVs and an Aston Martin for fun.

'The Aston Martin. It was keyed. Not randomly—with surgical precision. He carved a lily into the driver's door, then disabled the alarm and the GPS tracker. Our guys only discovered it during the morning sweep.'

I feel Avery's breath catch. My grip instinctively tightens around her waist.

'Sir,' Walsh says quietly. 'There's something else. He left this on your seat.'

Walsh hands me a manila folder marked CLASSIFIED in red. I only need to glimpse the first page to feel ice flood my veins. It's a detailed report on the Mali operation.

'What is it?' Avery asks, reaching for the folder.

I close it before she can see. 'Nothing.' I snap, way

harsher than I meant to. I'm on edge, and I don't fucking like it. Not one bit.

'Sorry.' I press a kiss to her temple.

Walsh clears his throat. 'There was a note attached.' He hesitates, glancing at Avery, then passes it over to me.

Who is she truly safer with, Beckett?

Fuck. Somehow, this bastard has accessed information that should be impossible to obtain. He knows about Sarah. The hostages. Everything.

And he's deranged enough to suggest he's the better man.

'Get Avery inside,' I order, voice deadly calm despite my churning stomach. 'Full lockdown protocol.'

'Yes, sir.'

I've hunted men across continents, through war zones and urban jungles. This psychopath has managed to evade me for weeks, but his luck has run out. Back on my territory, with my full resources and my complete focus, I'll find him—if it's the last thing I do.

And when I do, I'll make sure he never thinks about Avery again.

I spend the day in the conference room of my penthouse, methodically dissecting CCTV footage from the streets surrounding the Luxor. Walsh and Donovan stand at attention as we analyse every frame, every shadow, hunting for the Donnelly connection. It's our only lead. Avery occupies herself moving her belongings from the guest room to mine—at my instruction. Giving her this task serves dual purposes: distraction from the situation and a clear statement that she's no longer under my protection as my client. She's under my protection as my entire world.

My phone vibrates against the mahogany table, interrupting the surveillance playback. The screen flashes with

James's name. Back from his honeymoon and straight to business—classic Beckett.

'James.'

'Little brother.' His voice is relaxed, sun-soaked from weeks of cruising around the world with his new wife. 'How are things?'

'Busy.'

'How did that stalker situation with Avery end up? I assume you took care of the bastard mad enough to gatecrash my wedding.'

I pause the footage, considering how much to share. James has been completely disconnected on his honeymoon —exactly as I instructed him to be.

'I'm working on it.' I lean back in my chair, eyes still fixed on the shadow figure on my screen. 'He's sophisticated. Used military-grade EMP to disable our systems.'

A beat of silence as the information registers. 'Shit. That's well beyond your standard obsessed fan. Have you any idea who this person is?'

'No.' It fucking pains me to say it. 'This individual has access to technology and resources that suggest government connections or military background.' *And he has enough dirt on me to sully our entire family and everything we stand for.*

'And Avery? Are you still staying at her place with you as her shadow?'

Obviously James has no idea our arrangement has changed. Has no inclination that Avery is currently reorganising my closet to make room for her things. I've never even had a serious girlfriend since I left the military, let alone move one into my bedroom.

'Security assessment determined her residence was too vulnerable. She's staying here now.'

A loaded pause. 'In your penthouse?'

'My building has superior security protocols and controlled access points.'

'Of course.' His tone suggests he's not convinced. 'And how's that working out? You've never been one for sharing your space.'

If only he knew Avery has been sharing my space for a long fucking time—even if it was mostly in my head. 'It's fine.'

'Fine, huh?' He scoffs. 'I suppose sharing your apartment with an attractive glamour model isn't the worst thing in the world.'

'Avery isn't a glamour model anymore.'

'Since when? Is this because of the stalker?'

'Since she asked me to call her agent yesterday and resign on her behalf.' It was rather satisfying to be honest. Zack Kiel was not impressed at that turn of events, but when he realised who he was talking to, he wisely shut his mouth.

Silence for a long beat, then finally the penny drops. 'Are you and she...?'

'Yes.' No point denying it. He'll find out soon enough. His wife is Avery's best friend.

'Wow.' He doesn't even attempt to hide his shock. 'Is it serious?'

'Yes.' I don't have to explain. My brothers have come to expect my short responses.

'Wow. Scarlett is going to be ecstatic with this development.'

'Oh God, tell her not to order us all matching fucking pyjamas for Christmas Day.'

'I'll try, but I can't promise.' He pauses for a few seconds and I wait for him to process it all. 'Need anything from the family? Resources, contacts?'

'No.' I want my family as far away from this as possible. Bad enough the stalker is already after one person I love.

James pauses. 'Killian... be careful.'

The implication hangs in the air. Amongst all this newfound joy, there's a lunatic out there who wants what's mine, and would likely kill me to take her.

'I will. I have to go.'

'We'll be double dating before the week is out, mark my words.'

I end the call, turning back to the screen. We can double date when I catch this psychotic bastard. Somewhere in these shadows is a man who thinks he deserves Avery. Who believes he's entitled to her; believes he can take better care of her than I can.

He couldn't be more wrong.

When I find him, I'll make sure he understands exactly who she's safest with.

Chapter Thirty-Two

AVERY

Full lockdown in Killian's penthouse is nowhere near as bad as it would have been before we were a couple. In fact, other than there being a lunatic lurking in the shadows hoping to kill me or capture me, I'm thoroughly enjoying being holed up here. I moved into his huge bedroom—a sweeping mass of greys and silver, with huge sliding doors which open up onto a rooftop terrace. Opulence aside, the place was in desperate need of a woman's touch—which is why I asked Thomson to print out the photos from Pier 39 and have them framed and mounted. Fresh seasonal flowers bloom in every room. And I also ordered a sixteen-foot gilded mirror for the bedroom with the credit card Killian insist I use while I can't use my own—not just to reflect the light coming in from the triple glazed patio doors, but because we both like to watch as he takes me in front of it.

Every night, Killian makes love to me six ways to Sunday, and every day we work in the conference room together, side by side. While I work on my article for ELEGANCE, he works on finding the man who's hellbent on taking me from him.

Since we got back from our trip, he hasn't let me out of his sight. We cancelled all my prebooked photoshoots. We eat together, shower together, and sleep together. Well, I sleep—he mostly watches over me, stroking his thick fingers through my hair until I drift off. Despite the drama and the fear of knowing there's someone out there who feels I belong to them, I've never felt so safe. So cherished. So cared for. So loved.

He's yet to say those three little words out loud—but this is Killian Beckett we're talking about. I feel them from every one of his fleeting touches to the way he makes love to me. And I saw proof of his affection for me in the images he keeps of me in his office—yes, I eventually got a peep inside. No, I wasn't horrified—it was beyond flattering to imagine the most stoic man I've ever met acting like a teenager with a crush.

I crawl into my side of the bed and slide under the covers. He removes his suit and tosses it on a plush leather armchair in the corner of the room.

'Can I get a Christmas tree delivered for the lounge?' I ask, as he prowls towards the bed with a predatory look in his pupils. He rarely says no to me, but he never says no when he has that particular glint.

'If it makes you happy.'

'I usually love Christmas, but this year, I've never felt less festive.' No wonder, given the circumstances. 'It's our first Christmas together. I want it to be memorable.'

'Christmas is for kids,' Killian tuts.

'It's also for couples.' Which is why I ordered him a vintage Rolex Submariner from the early 1960s, the same model used by special forces operatives—Thomson assured me he'll love it. Especially because I had it engraved with 'better late than never'—our own personal in joke.

'My parents are expecting us on Christmas day.' He

studies me while he waits for my response. 'James has told everyone about us. You're the talk of the family.'

'Oh God. That can't be good.' I place my palm over my face.

'Relax, they're going to love you...' He trails off with that intense look in his eyes and for a second I think he's about to say 'like I do', but he doesn't.

'I need to tell my father "the entire family" won't be at his place after all.' I'd rather pull my own hair out strand by strand than play happy families with him, Tessa, Sebastian, and supercilious Yvonne. 'He won't be happy I'm backing out now.'

'It's not a matter of backing out. It's a matter of your safety. If your father had any idea of the shit that's been going down, he'd respect that. I can protect you better at my parents' place.' He stares at me for a long beat, towering over me from the edge of the bed. 'Their house is bolted onto a beach. There's only one driveway in. It'll be manned by twenty of my men. The security system is as sophisticated as the one here. There's a panic room with a pool table and a fully stocked bar. And you will never be more than two feet from my side. Blame me for the last minute change of plans.'

I glance at the time, 'Might be too late to call him now. I'll do it in the morning.'

'Leave it until Christmas morning. I know it seems cruel, but trust me, it's far safer this way. Your mother used her credit card to pay for her trip. The stalker knows you're not going to be with her for Christmas. He might even be expecting you to go to your father's place. Either way, we're not taking the chance.'

'My father will be disappointed.'

'Disappointed is better than dead. Say whatever you have to, but it's actually safer to keep him away from this '

'Thank God my mother is out of the country.'

'And she has three bodyguards that she doesn't know about trailing her.'

'Thank you,' I exhale heavily. If anything happened to her because of me, I'd never forgive myself. 'But by the way, if the bodyguards you sent look anything like you, trust me, she'll be well aware of them at this stage—for all the wrong reasons!'

Killian shakes his head. 'Parents hey? Be warned, my own mother can be,' he wets his lips, 'intense.'

Laughter bursts from my chest. 'Says the most intense person I've ever met.'

'She's a different type of intense.' He takes his watch off and places it on the bedside table.

'I'm looking forward to getting to know your family.' It's true, while I've met all the Beckett brothers over the years, and met Killian's parents at the wedding, I'm excited to see them in a different capacity.

'James and Scarlett will be there, obviously.'

'As if I needed any more persuasion. It'll be nice to get a change of scenery.' I rock into a sitting position beneath the covers and hug my legs to my chest. 'Any progress on the other thing?' I hate putting pressure on him when he's every bit as frustrated as I am about the stalker situation, but I have to know if we're any closer to normality. We can't stay cooped up in here forever, even if it suits me down to the ground right now.

'I have a meeting tomorrow with the Finance Minister, which I hope will be...' He pauses, choosing his next word carefully, 'informative.' He climbs into bed wearing only a pair of fitted black boxer briefs. If I get my way, they'll be on the floor in less than two minutes.

As he slides under the covers beside me, his expression morphs into a solemn one. Sorrow touches his huge coal coloured eyes.

'What's up?' I reach for him, sliding my hands over his taut, rippled torso.

His fingers catch mine and thread between them. 'I hate letting you down.'

'What are you talking about?' I slide closer, pressing my body flush against his. 'You've never let me down.'

'I was sure as hell I'd have found him by now. I hate knowing there's someone out there who is determined to take you from me. I hate that he's still breathing.' He nuzzles the top of my head and inhales my hair.

'No one is going to take me from you.'

'Damn right they're not.' His fingers tighten. 'I'm going to find this deranged fucker and I'm going to kill him.'

'You'd kill for me?' I suck in a breath.

'I warned you multiple times that I'm not a good man.' He shrugs.

'Three questions.' I demand.

'I thought we were past this.'

'Indulge me.'

'Open your legs and I'll indulge you anyway you like.'

'Please,' I beg.

'Go on then. The quicker we get this over with, the quicker I can make you come on my cock.'

'You've killed men before.' I blurt.

'That's not technically a question.'

'Okay, let me rephrase. Outside of your military tours, have you...' I hesitate, unsure if I really want to know the answers, but also needing to unlock the darkness inside of him. Share the burden of it with him. 'Have you killed anyone?'

His pupils blaze into mine with maximum intensity. I hold my breath as I wait for his answer.

'Would it bother you if I had?'

I roll my lips together. 'Not as much as it probably should.'

'I'll be honest with you.' His fingers stroke me with a tenderness that completely contrasts this entire conversation. 'As long as you promise not to run screaming from the room.'

'I promise.'

'I've never killed anyone who didn't deserve it.' His tone is so matter of fact. It's hard to believe we're talking about him ending a person's life.

I swallow thickly, processing his words. I should be horrified. Terrified. Appalled. But I'm none of those things. Does that make me as deranged as the stalker? Or simply a woman who is sick of being hunted like a baby deer?

Killian gives me a minute to digest. 'My family have a lot of enemies. Enemies who want to hurt us, who want what we have and will do anything to get it.' His lip curls in disgust. 'Caelon's wife, Isabella, being the most recent and tragic example.'

He reaches up to gently sweep his thumb over my cheekbone, his eyes never leave mine. 'It's not what any woman wants to hear about their partner, but I suppose it's better we have this conversation sooner rather than later.'

I nod quietly, still digesting. I'm not surprised. On some level, I knew he had that capability in him. Deep down, I knew, and I think a really dark, primal part of me is attracted to it. Like animals in the wild are drawn to the strongest alphas to mate with. Deep down, I'm innately drawn to him, secure in the knowledge he's a powerful mate. That he's capable of protecting me and providing for our family.

Fuck, the man just admitted to killing people and I'm thinking about having his children?

'I'd never hurt you, sweetheart. I told you before, I'd kill for you, I'd die for you, but I will never, ever hurt you.'

I press my forehead to his. 'I know that.' The truth of that statement rings with every word.

'I'm going to catch this deranged maniac who thinks he can take you from me. And I'm going to kill him—slowly.'

'Personally, I'd like to thank him.' I palm his chest, skimming over the hard ridges of his abdomen.

'Thank him?' Killian's tone is incredulous.

'Yes.' I tilt my face up to meet his stare. 'If it wasn't for that lily in St. Barths, we wouldn't have been forced together, and I wouldn't have been able to woo you with my spectacular p—'

'Pussy,' he growls, and slides a hand lower, skimming my stomach and reaching between my thighs. I'm already soaked for him.

'I was going to say personality.' I smile, parting my legs wider for him, as my hands roam lower over his torso, reaching for his length which is growing harder with every passing second. 'But the time for talking is over. Lose the boxers.'

He slides the black cotton down his thick quads. I watch, entranced, as his engorged length springs free. My mouth waters. My boyfriend might have just confessed to being a killer, but he's also the most beautiful man I've laid eyes on. Every line of his body is a defined, sculpted example of masculine perfection, but his true beauty is what lies underneath that perfect packaging. It's in the way his eyes light when they lock with mine. It's the way he trusts me enough to let me in, to lay his truths bare to me, to let me touch him without flinching. I stare at him in open fascination, and he gazes back like he still can't quite believe I'm his.

When his lips find mine, they're warm, firm, and sensual. His tongue steals into my mouth, swiping in languid sweeps as his eyes hold mine. I could kiss this man for decades and never tire of it.

He nudges me until I'm flat on my back without taking his mouth from mine, working me with his fingers while his lips drop lower, trailing tiny kisses over my jawline, down my neck, over the curve of each breast. My back arches as I writhe beneath him.

'I want you,' I murmur.

'Even now you know how bad I am?'

'Especially now I know how bad you are.' There's something undeniably arousing knowing what my man is capable of, knowing that, and having him treat me like his prize possession, the thing he'd give his life for. I pray it never comes to that.

'You know my truths and you still want me.' He kisses his way back up my body and climbs between my thighs. 'Maybe you're the bad one.'

'You wouldn't have me any other way.'

'I would.' His eyes darken. 'I'd have you exhausted, flushed and spiralling from an orgasm that wrecks you.' He positions his cock at my entrance and enters me inch by-life-affirming inch. My eyes roll back in my head.

'I love the things you do to me,' I pant as he drives in and out of me. Slow, deep thrusts hit that sensitive spot with military precision. His devastating assault on my body is methodical. He knows every inch of it inside out, and he knows precisely what every inch needs.

'I love doing the things I do to you.' Black eyes burn into mine with lust, but there's that earnestness again. I swear I can see his soul and I love it. I love him so fucking much. I've been holding back those three little words because I want to hear them from him first, but it's only a matter of time before they come tumbling out.

Maybe he's waiting for me to say them first.

Maybe he needs me to be the one to voice my feelings for him before he allows himself to get any deeper.

Or maybe he doesn't need to hear them at all because some things transcend words.

Our eyes remain locked in fascination as our bodies move together, grinding and arching towards the same epic finale.

A tiny bead of sweat forms just above his Cupid's bow. I

run my tongue over it and his eyelids flutter closed like he's in ecstasy. When they open again, they're filled with awe.

'Killian.' My voice cracks with need as my core clenches around his cock.

'Yes.' A small smirk curls his lips.

'I need you to do this to me forever.' My entire body vibrates with the shimmering promise of pure primal pleasure.

His low chuckle travels from his mouth into mine. 'That goes without saying, baby. You're mine.'

He kisses me again and I can't hold it back anymore.

I don't want to hold it back anymore.

A brutal, vicious orgasm captures my core and has me exploding around his cock. My nails pierce his ass cheeks, driving him harder into me as I buck against him, revelling in every decadent second. In turn, he spills himself into me with a low moan. Rough hands grip my hips, pinning me in position beneath him until we're both utterly spent.

He falls onto my chest, resting his cheek against my breast, splaying a huge hand over my stomach. My fingers gravitate to his head, scraping over his scalp.

'I can hear your heart,' he says, his thumbs thrumming out the beat of it just below my belly button.

'What does it say?' I pause, playing with his hair.

'It says you see me.' He angles his face to look up. 'You see me, and you love me, despite everything I just confessed.' Our eyes lock. 'And I love you,' he blurts, almost awkwardly, and I swear my heart misses a beat.

Tears threaten the corners of my eyes, not for the first time in front of him, but with a starkly different emotion. I blink them back. 'I love you so fucking much, baby. You *are* a good man, despite what you've had to do.'

'Anton Roche...' He says the name with slight hesitation.

I did wonder.

I probably should have made the connection immediately.

A man is dead because of me. Killian waits for me to speak, but I have no idea what to say.

Finally, I swallow my shock. 'You?'

'I looked into him because of what he did to you.' His fingers flex against my stomach. 'But I told you, I never killed anyone who didn't deserve it. That man was an abomination. He walked away from several rape cases, one related to a minor. I have a little sister, a mother, a girlfriend, women I love and care about. Taking out a man like him was practically a national service.'

I agree, but still. 'But how can you be sure he did it?'

'There's no smoke without fire, sweetheart. He confessed, and it was over quickly.'

'Shit.' It's a lot to take in. Does it change the way I feel about Killian?

No.

Like I said, on some deeper level, I knew this about him. And I still love him.

'I'm not some sort of vigilante. I don't go out of my way looking for scumbags to wipe from the face of this earth, but in my line of work sometimes they trip across my path. And I'd never forgive myself if a man like Roche hurt another woman, and I could have stopped him.'

I understand, but it's a lot to process. But he opened up to me, so I refuse to leave him hanging. 'I love you.' The second time around, it comes out smoother.

He pulls me tighter again. 'I love you too. So much. Sometimes, when I watch you sleep, I still can't believe you're mine.'

'I'm yours. And I wanted to be for a long time.'

'I didn't put you off?' He reaches up to brush a thumb over my cheekbone.

'No.' I shake my head.

'I thought you were reckless, but opening up to you—falling in love with you has to be the most reckless thing in the world.'

'Why?'

'Because I feel like I'm surrendering control or something. Like I'm detonating the one weapon capable of killing me and hoping it won't blow up in both of our faces.'

I swallow thickly, my fingers resume raking over his scalp in slow, soothing movements. 'Nothing is blowing up in anyone's faces. The only thing detonating is multiple orgasms. You said you'd never hurt me, know this—I'll never hurt you either.' I promise.

His expression turns dark. He opens his mouth like he's about to say something, before clamping it shut again. Rome wasn't built in a day, and he's already shared so much tonight. The good, the bad and the ugly.

And isn't that what true love is all about? Sharing everything, loving every part of a person, even the darkest parts.

But now the urge to lighten the mood eats at me. I love yous are supposed to be romantic, not brooding. I need to turn this around. 'And now I know what an epic shag you are; you're stuck with me.'

His thick eyebrows lift. 'Now I know what an epic shag *you* are; *you're* stuck with me.' He presses a kiss against my stomach and it flips in anticipation. 'But don't ever call me baby in front of my men, or my brothers.'

'Would you prefer it if I call you daddy again?' I'm only half joking. The memory of him spanking me is up there with my top five in the wank bank.

'That depends on whether you want me to put you over my knee again.'

'I want you to do everything to me again.' I nestle into him and sigh with contentment. We've still got a long way to go, but one thing I'm sure of, we're taking the journey together.

Chapter Thirty-Four

THE WATCHER

I'd prefer to keep the family out of it, but I have no choice given she's permanently bundled up in that barbarian's penthouse. I haven't been able to hack the cameras, but it doesn't take a genius to work out what he's doing to her in there.

What she's letting him do to her in there.

I'll take pleasure in cleaning every trace of his touch—with my tongue.

Avery will know true pleasure when she surrenders to me, but first, she'll have to be punished.

With three days to go, the house smells of pine, cinnamon, and expectation. For years, Avery has rebuffed every overture—declining invitations with practiced politeness, sending gifts that speak of obligation rather than sentiment, constructing elaborate professional alibis. But this year, she accepted.

Father believes it's forgiveness.

I recognise it for what it truly is: inevitability.

She's coming because our trajectories were always meant to converge. The universe has a fundamental tendency toward order, toward completion. She feels it pulling at the edges of her conscious-

ness—this inexorable gravity between us—even if she hasn't yet developed the vocabulary to articulate it.

The black calla lilies were never merely flowers. They were semaphores, elegant in their simplicity. A sophisticated mind understands the power of symbols, how they bypass the rational and speak directly to the subconscious. Each lily was a brushstroke in a portrait she's beginning to recognise.

I adjust my Brioni tie with meticulous attention, examining my reflection. Appearances matter. Beneath the cashmere sweater, my shirt and tie remain impeccable—like the contingency plans layered beneath my apparent acquiescence.

Beckett will accompany her, naturally. With his private militia and their unimaginative protocols. His security measures are impressive but predictable—the fatal flaw of men who mistake violence for intelligence.

The compound is already prepared, precisely measured and waiting in the Baccarat crystal decanter that was my grandfather's prized possession. One drink. Just enough to disrupt Beckett's influence, to extract her from his evil manipulations.

I observe my expression in the mirror—composed, refined, nothing like the hesitant smiles she once dismissed with casual obtuseness. This is the countenance of a man who understands that patience is not merely a virtue, but a weapon when properly deployed.

Soon, Avery will understand as well. That everything—the lilies, the messages, the calculated pursuit—has been an elaborate prelude to the inevitable. Our convergence.

This Christmas, she's finally coming home to where she belongs.

It's time.

Chapter Thirty-Five

KILLIAN

With only a couple of days until Christmas, and no sign of the stalker, I'm learning the meaning of patience the hard way. I've thought about trying to draw him out, but I refuse to put Avery at risk. His silence is worrying, especially given what he uncovered about my past.

The finance minister was fuck-all help. The dirty bastard worked his way through a string of prostitutes in the last few months. His apartment had more comings and goings than Dublin airport.

Avery is putting the final touches on the sixteen-foot pine tree in the living area. I've lived in here for seven years and I can safely say, it never once occurred to me to put up a tree. Mind you, it never once occurred to me that Avery Williams would be my live-in girlfriend.

Girlfriend.

It's such a childish description for a woman like her.

Which is why as soon as this shit is behind us, I'm going to make her my wife. Especially now she's seen my truths and can still find it inside to love me. She might not be convinced about the values of marriage, but I am. My parents are a stellar example of what marriage can and should be, and James and Scarlett are now too. Avery will be wearing my ring before next Christmas. I'll make sure of it. Now I finally have her, there's no way I'm letting her slip through my fingers.

Soft classical Christmas songs play from the surround system. The scent of peonies mixed with cinnamon and citrus candles wafts in the air. In a matter of weeks, Avery's transformed this house into a home, something that I never thought was possible. I think deep down, part of me felt that with everything that happened in Mali, I didn't deserve to be home, to even *have* a home, when so many others lost their lives out there.

But still, I'm here. I have to live, so I've resigned myself to doing it right, regardless of whether I deserve it or not.

'What do you think?' She makes a *voila* gesture at the silver and blush pink baubles imported from the Christmas shop we stumbled across on the far side of the Golden Gate bridge.

'Stunning.' I'm not referring to the tree. In a pair of baby pink sweatpants and a tight white tank top, Avery is the epitome of casual sophistication. Her blonde hair is piled on top of her head in a messy bun and she's not wearing a scrap of make up. She doesn't need it. Never did.

'I think this calls for champagne.' She claps her hands together and waggles her eyebrows.

'Fine, but don't expect me to drink that shit.' I pull out a bottle from the fridge, pop the top, pour her a glass, and get myself a double whiskey—Beckett's Gold.

Sterling and Walsh are in my games room. Ten other men patrol the building and grounds. Thirty-eight cameras monitor the property. There's not a lot else we can do but sit and drink. Well, I could happily spend the evening with my face buried between Avery's long lithe legs, but Scarlett and James are on their way over—a surprise I arranged. And it *would be* one hell of a surprise if they were to walk in on that. The thought makes me laugh out loud.

'Something funny?' Avery swivels on her bare feet and plants a hand on her hip.

'No.' The lingering smirk on my lips suggests otherwise.

I cross the room with our drinks. The need to have her within my reach all the goddamn time is like a disease. I pass her glass to her and she clinks it against mine.

'To our first Christmas together.' She beams and her smile is warm enough to infiltrate even the deepest, darkest cracks in my soul. She's a balm I never knew I needed.

'To your last first Christmas with a new boyfriend.'

Her eyes flare. 'It's a good job I find your possessiveness hot.'

'Good, because this time next year you'll be wearing my ring—it's not up for debate.' I pull her against me and kiss the sensitive spot on her long, slender neck.

Her mouth parts in a tiny O. 'Christ, Beckett, one minute you're more buttoned up than a nun's knickers, then you're blurting stuff that makes my stalker seem sane.'

I snort. 'He's deranged. I'm deadly serious.'

'I love your confidence, baby.'

'And I love you, which is why one day, you will be my wife.' We've said those three little words every day over the past week, but they still send a shocking sharp thrill through me every damn time. What started as an awkward, bluntly delivered admission—on my part—has now morphed into a daily ritual of being the last thing that leaves my lips each night.

'You know how I feel about marriage.' She sighs. 'I'm just not sure it's for me. It's nothing personal.' She takes a mouthful of champagne, eyeing me over the rim of the glass.

'Let's have this conversation again after Christmas, okay?' I have full faith in my family's ability to sell the virtues of marriage to the only woman I've ever wanted to march down the aisle. 'Besides, I think we already have a stellar wedding planner, and we both know you're eager to wear a white dress.'

Her mouth opens, but before we can get any further into it, the intercom buzzes. She startles.

'It's okay, it's just a little surprise for you.'

'A surprise? For me?' Her features relax instantaneously. 'I love surprises.'

'Which doesn't surprise *me* at all.' I press a kiss to her temple, then guide her towards the hallway with my hand splayed across the base of her spine. 'For future reference, I hate surprises.'

'I know.' She clicks her tongue against the roof of her mouth. 'If anything even slightly veers from schedule, you start twitching.'

'I do not.' I scoff, even though she's uncannily accurate. Seems I'm not the only observant one in this relationship.

'Do too! Your need to be in control is obsessive. But I'm okay with it.' She raises her hands in a peace signal, but her next statement is like waving a red rag. 'I prefer men who take the reins.'

'Men?' I lower my hand to her peachy ass and slap it hard enough to make her squeal.

'I think the word you meant to use was *man*. Single. Not plural. You prefer your *man* to take the reins. And right now, I'm contemplating tying you to my bed posts with them.'

'Promises, promises, big guy.' She turns to me, grabs my shirt in both her fists and yanks me towards her mouth. 'And it's *our* bed posts, now.'

The elevator doors ping open. 'Oh my goodness!' Scarlett squeals, clutching her chest. 'I wasn't sure if James was fucking with me, but Jesus Christ you two are practically humping in the hallway.'

'Ahhhhh!' Avery's answering shriek practically deafens me, but her sheer elation at seeing her friend is worth it. 'I can't believe you're here!'

Avery drops me like a hot potato and races towards Scarlett. The two women hug like it's been years instead of weeks. In fairness, they haven't seen each other since St. Barths, and a lot has happened in that time. James steps in and slaps my bicep. I flinch. Old habits die hard.

'I would ask how you are'—his black eyes gleam—'but it's fairly fucking obvious you've never been better.' His lips stretch into a grin that is apparently contagious because I feel mine do the same.

'How long has this been going on?' Scarlett demands, her silver eyes scrutinising my woman from head to toe.

Avery shrugs, then turns to me. 'Officially, things heated up in St. Barths on a yacht. Unofficially, I've been pining after this pretty boy since the Luxor Lounge.'

'What?' Scarlett throws her hands in the air. 'Why didn't you tell me?'

'Because he's your hot broody brother-in-law who used to pretend he despised me.'

'I despised that I couldn't have you.' I shake my head. It's one thing opening up to Avery, but I don't feel like dissecting the ins and outs of my emotional awakening in my opulent hallway. 'Come through, guys. Let me get you a drink.'

Scarlett links her arm through Avery's and the two women take off towards the kitchen, talking at a million miles an hour. James falls into step beside me, glancing around at the newly acquired feminine touches in my home. 'We all fall hard in the end,' he muses.

'Not all of us. Sean has never been seen with a woman, and Rian, well, he's still dipping his dick anywhere and every-where he can.' Unfortunately for me, I have the videos to prove it. Our youngest brother has no regard for the fact that someone watches the cameras in his villa. My men are sick of the sight of Rian's cock these days.

'I often wonder about Sean.' James slides out of his suit jacket, a custom-made Italian Lora Piana cashmere-silk blend. I know, because I have several like it hanging in my own wardrobe.

'Don't. He's entitled to his privacy. We need to respect that.' I've often thought about doing a bit of digging around our mysteriously well-behaved brother, but always decided against it.

'Do you think he's gay?' James reaches into my fridge and pulls out the open champagne bottle. I grab a crystal flute for Scarlett from the cupboard.

'Does it matter if he is?' I hand it over and James fills it while I fetch him a whiskey.

'No, of course not, but I'd hate for him to think he had to hide his sexuality from us.' A frown furrows my oldest brother's forehead.

'If or when he wants us to know, he'll tell us.' I nod towards the fridge where Anabelle left an elaborate cheeseboard, overflowing with aged Comte, creamy Delice de Bourgogne triple cream, truffled Pecorino, jewel-like champagne grapes, fresh figs split and translucent ribbons of 24-month aged prosciutto di Parma, all meticulously arranged on a veined Carrara marble platter. 'Shall we?'

We cross the room to Avery and Scarlett, who are still talking at a million miles a minute, as they admire the twinkling Christmas tree. The city lights glint below and the moon hangs low over the Liffey. My heart squeezes in my chest.

I never knew it was possible to be so fucking happy. Obviously I'll be a lot happier when I catch the stalker, and even happier again when he's six-foot under, but I'm trying to live in the moment and appreciate the little wins. Spending the evening with the people I love most in the world is one of them.

James's beady eyes weigh heavily on me. 'I'm delighted for you, bro,' he whispers, not that either of our women would hear us over the sound of their own voices.

'Thanks.'

James clinks his whiskey against mine, then slaps my bicep again. This time, I don't flinch.

Chapter Thirty-Six

AVERY

Morning light pours through the floor-to-ceiling windows, catching on the silver ornaments adorning the Christmas tree. Sixteen feet of perfectly symmetrical pine, decorated in silver and blush pink—Killian had tried to draw the line at the pink, but he still can't seem to say no to me.

I sneak out of bed before Killian. I have a phone call to make before I can enjoy the day. Guilt glides through my stomach like a snake. I hate telling lies. But needs must.

I drop onto the couch and pull up my father's contact details on my phone. Taking in a deep breath, I hit dial. It rings for an eternity and just when I'm about to hang up, he answers.

'Avery? Merry Christmas, darling.'

'Merry Christmas, Dad.' Even the word 'Dad' sounds stilted. Awkward. Unnatural.

'Are you on your way over?' The sound of familiar Christmas songs from decades past travel through the phone line. A vision of him and Tessa pottering around their lavish kitchen preparing for the most talked about meal of the year pops into my head. Sebastian's probably got his nose buried in his laptop, as usual. The man is a workaholic, and I should know—I live with one. Yvonne's probably gone to mass to say a prayer for my soul.

I clear my throat, fiddling with the hem of my Agent Provocateur nightdress. 'I'm not, no.'

'What do you mean?' His voice hitches with... disappoint‐ment? Irritation? Sadly, I don't know him well enough to differentiate.

'I've come down with an awful flu. My temperature spiked during the night and I feel dreadful.' It's not a lie, I do feel dreadful—not because I'm sick, but for lying.

He harrumphs in obvious disbelief. I need to get off the phone asap. 'I'm so sorry, Dad.' That word again. Ugh.

'Tessa has gone to so much trouble. She's been preparing this meal for days. Sebastian's here already. Surely you can make it across the city for a couple of hours?'

'I wish I could.' More lies. 'I have to go. I promise I'll visit in the new year. Merry Christmas to all of you.'

I hang up. A weird sense of relief and sadness settles in my stomach as I slump back into the sofa. Killian strides in, concern etched into the fine lines of his face. He offered to make the call for me, but I figured it was the least I could do. In casual grey, low hanging sweats and a soft white t-shirt, he still looks like he could command armies or close million-euro deals.

'Is it done?' he asks, crossing the room to drop a kiss on my forehead.

'It's done.' I nod more assertively than I feel.

'Good. I know it might not seem like it, but it's the right thing. For you, and for him.' He drops onto the couch beside me, taking my hand in his.

I exhale heavily. 'I know. It's just our relationship is

already stilted and I've probably just made things a million times worse.'

'Sweetheart, the reason your relationship is stilted is because he left you and your mother for another woman.' He threads his fingers through mine and offers a reassuring squeeze. 'You are not responsible for his fuck ups, or for the fact that he's a shitty father. I refuse to let you beat yourself up about this.'

'I know, it's just...' Words fail me. I want to make an excuse for my father, but I can't. 'I think I'm at the age where it's finally sinking in that I will never have the relationship with him that I want. And it's probably time to make my peace with that.'

'No matter how long you live, or how old you are, he will always be the parent in your relationship. It's not on you to fix the past. He's a grown man. Inviting you for Christmas dinner might be his olive branch, but even if you were to go, even if you enjoyed the day, it doesn't eradicate what he put you and your mother through. He can't make up for a million missed memories with one meal. His disappointment probably stems from his own guilt.'

'And I thought I was the one with the psychology doctorate.' I force a small smile.

'You're too close to see it clearly.' He pulls me into his lap like I'm a child, holding me tightly against his chest. My shoulders automatically sag with relief. 'We'll do things so differently when we have our own kids.'

'Easy, tiger.' I place a palm on his pec. 'First all this talk of a ring, now kids—it's a good job I'm not easily spooked.'

'You will be when I flush your packet of pills down the toilet.'

My mouth drops open and he winks. Phew. He's joking—I think.

'Relax. I was just trying to lighten the mood. I'm nowhere

near ready to share you—yet.' He slides me back on to the couch like I'm weightless and stands.

'Where are you going?' I miss being in his arms already.

'To make you coffee.'

'Thank you.' I pull my legs up and cross them underneath me.

'It's Christmas Day. Our first Christmas together. You were the one who wanted it to be memorable. Let's try to enjoy it. We deserve to, given the stress of the past couple of months.'

'You're right.' And it's not over yet. There's still a lunatic out there somewhere convinced I'm destined to be with him.

I reach for Killian's hand again, bring it to my lips and kiss the back of it. 'Merry Christmas baby. Let's start the morning again.'

'Merry Christmas, sweetheart.' A trace of concern lingers in his eye, but he stalks towards the kitchen to make our drinks. I grab the remote for his inbuilt speaker system and flick until I find something festive.

Jasper strolls in from wherever he spent the night curled up. He hasn't yet clawed Killian's curtains, so that's one bonus. He hops up onto my lap and I stroke his furry head thoughtfully as he butts it against me.

Killian returns with two steaming mugs and hands one to me before scowling at Jasper.

'Oh, come on. You don't need to pretend anymore. I know you love him.'

'I love you, and unfortunately, that furry freak comes as part of the package,' he says, but with nowhere near as much disdain as he used to. 'Come on, fleabag, let's get you some breakfast.' Jasper leaps from my knee and follows Killian across the plush carpet. I warm my hands around my mug of coffee, biting back a smile. I might never have what I hoped for from my dad, but I have so much more than most—a man who adores me... and my pussy.

He returns a couple of minutes later and nods towards the pristinely arranged presents beneath the tree, wrapped in silver and pink to match the baubles.

'The presents didn't have to be perfectly aligned. The world won't end if everything isn't symmetrical.'

'Structure is important,' he replies, that smile I've grown to love touching his lips. When I first moved in, I kept a mental tally of those smiles. Now they're frequent enough that I've lost count.

Progress.

He sinks onto the sofa beside me once again, his warmth immediately enveloping me as he tugs me against his side. I kiss the underside of his jaw, feeling the slight rasp of stubble. 'Can I give you your present now or do we need to wait for a specific, strategically optimal gift-exchange time?' I tease.

He rolls his eyes. 'Presents now. Croissants after. Save room for lunch, my mother goes way overboard.'

I disentangle myself from him and fetch the small, meticulously wrapped box from under the tree. My hands tremble slightly as I pass it to him. 'I had help from Thomson. So, if you hate it, blame him.'

Killian's eyebrow arches as he unwraps the gift with surgical precision, not tearing a single piece of paper. When he opens the box, he goes completely still.

'It's a 1963 Rolex Submariner,' I explain nervously. 'The same model used by special forces back then. Thomson said it would resonate with your military background and—'

His mouth captures mine, cutting my rambling explanation short. When he pulls back, his eyes are darker, more intense. 'It's perfect,' he says, voice rough.

'You didn't see the best bit.' I prise the watch from his

fingers and turn it over so he can see the engraving. *Better late than never.*

His low chuckle slides beneath my skin and all the way to my soul. 'I promise you, sweetheart, I'll never be late for you again.'

I quite believe it with all his talk the other night about 'this time next year, you'll be wearing my ring.' I'm not sure if I'm flattered or frightened at the speed he's progressing at, but he did say he's an all-or-nothing type of guy. And I did say I'm an all-or-nothing type of girl. Looks like I might have to put my money where my mouth is, sooner rather than later.

He fastens the watch around his wrist before reaching under the tree. 'My turn.'

The box he hands me is small, wrapped in silver paper with a blush pink bow. I tear into it with none of his restraint, pieces of wrapping paper flying in every direction. Inside is a Cartier watch, its elegant face gleaming with tiny diamonds around the border. 'Oh my God,' I breathe. 'It's stunning.'

'It's a Santos,' he explains, taking it from the box and fastening it around my wrist with gentle precision. 'The original was designed for a pilot. Built to withstand pressure changes, turbulence.' His eyes meet mine, and I understand what he's not saying. He picked a watch that's both beautiful and strong, that can withstand unexpected storms. I suppose our start has been a little bumpy, but as soon as we catch the stalk—no I'm not even going to entertain that word today. He's taken up so much of my time and energy already. He's not getting Christmas Day as well.

'I love it,' I whisper, lacing my fingers through his. 'Can you believe we bought each other the same gift?'

'Great minds.' He yanks me back against him. 'I have another gift for you. But given Thomson and Sterling are lurking around here somewhere, I better give it to you in the bedroom.'

'They've seen it all before.' I remind him. Oh my god, when I think back, I can't believe he did that.

Actually—I can. I just can't believe I let him.

Who am I kidding? I'd let that man do whatever he wanted to me, whenever he wanted, wherever he wanted. Because I am head over heel, irrevocably in love with him.

'Yeah, but the fur baby wasn't there then. He's far too young to watch his daddy ravish his mammy.'

Chapter Thirty-Seven

THE WATCHER

Mother has outdone herself with the decorations this year. The spruce pine in the foyer is adorned with antique ornaments—many from my grandmother's collection that I remember examining as a child, cataloguing their fragility. Three hundred and twelve perfect glass bubbles of memory, each precisely placed.

I run my finger along the dining table, inspecting the settings. Fine bone china, Georgian silver, crystal that captures light in precisely calculated facets. The pattern is flawless: Father will sit at the head, Mother to his right, myself at his left, and directly across from me is where Avery will sit when the world operates according to its proper order.

The conversation drifts from the kitchen. Father's voice is pitched low as it always is when he speaks with Avery. Even through the closed door, his disappointment is palpable. When he emerges, his expression confirms what I already suspect.

'Sebastian,' he begins, the rehearsed neutrality in his tone betraying the effort it costs him. 'Avery won't be joining us today, after all. She's come down with the flu.'

I maintain an expression of appropriate concern. 'That's unfortunate. Did she reschedule?'

'Not exactly.' He glances at Mother. 'Hopefully in the New Year.'

The crystal wine glass shatters musically in my grip before I register squeezing it. Glass fragments splinter in every direction. The sound draws Mother's attention, concern etching across her features.

'Sebastian? What happened? Are you hurt?'

'A momentary lapse in attention,' I reply, voice modulated to project appropriate remorse. 'How careless of me.'

She fusses with a cloth, gathering fragments while I retreat to father's study, with my laptop, closing the door behind me. The room smells of leather, cedar, and failure.

Flu and fever.

The transparent lie offends me more than the cancellation itself. She couldn't even craft a plausible excuse—not for us. Not for family. The Baccarat decanter catches light from the window, the carefully prepared compound still waiting inside. All the preparations, the meticulous planning, the perfect scenario—rendered obsolete by her choice.

By him.

They've likely locked down a completely different plan—a different family gathering. The irony doesn't escape me. The symmetry of our parallel celebrations, now fundamentally unbalanced.

I open the encrypted folder on my laptop, reviewing the contingency plans. The blueprint of the Beckett estate emerges on my screen, annotated with security positions, blind spots, patrol timing. The product of weeks of observation and analysis.

My finger traces the path of least resistance—the wine cellar entrance, the staff corridor, the precise route to the main dining room. The timing would need to be immaculate. The distraction perfectly orchestrated.

But it could be done.

I open the desk drawer, removing the velvet box containing my final black lily. It was meant to be a parting gift to Beckett, after he'd succumbed to the compound.

A symbol of transition.

Now it will serve as a herald instead.

My reflection in the window shows a composed man, not the turbulent emotions beneath. The door handle turns—Father, checking on me. The facade must be maintained.

For now.

I slip the lily into my jacket pocket, alongside the precision blade that never leaves my person. Plans change, but purpose remains constant.

If Mohammed won't come to the mountain, then the mountain will come to Mohammed.

Chapter Thirty-Eight

AVERY

Two hours later, we're cruising up the seemingly endless driveway that winds through the Beckett estate. Ancient oaks and horse chestnuts line the immaculate gravel road, their bare winter branches creating a natural archway dusted with snow. The grounds stretch for acres in every direction—pristine white lawns, frozen ornamental lakes, and in the distance, the stable block where Alexander Beckett, Killian's father, keeps his prize-winning thoroughbreds.

As we round the final bend, Killian's childhood home comes into view. The house is a Georgian mansion of ridiculous proportions—honey-coloured stone and perfect symmetry. Twenty-something windows across the front facade gleam in the winter sunlight, framed by ivy that's been meticulously trained around the stonework for generations. Four enormous stone pillars frame the entrance, where a wreath the size of a small car adorns the glossy black front door. The entire place practically screams old money, power, and the kind of history that can't be bought. Anticipation melds with excitement in my stomach.

Killian pulls the Aston Martin to a stop in the circular

driveway. He finally got it back from the garage yesterday. Sterling, Thomson, Donovan and Mason travel in the SUV behind us and Killian assured me there are already sixteen other armed guards manning the perimeter. He turns to me, his expression softening in a way reserved only for when we're alone. 'Ready to face the Beckett Christmas circus?'

I swallow thickly. 'Are you sure your parents aren't horrified that you're dating a glamour model?' I run a hand over the deep green velvet Victoria Beckham dress I picked out for today. It pairs beautifully with a pair of silver Manolo Blahniks, and the gorgeous new Cartier watch decorating my wrist.

He cups my chin across the ivory leather console and angles my face to meet his unwavering stare. 'Former glamour model—not that it matters to them. And I'm not dating her. I'm in love with her. Trust me, they're going to be ecstatic with this turn of events.'

Before we can discuss it further, the front door opens. Naturally, I'm expecting a butler or a maid, given the grandeur of the place, but it's Vivienne Beckett herself. Her hair is curled around her shoulders in a professional blow-dry, but she's wearing an apron.

She waves enthusiastically from the doorway, her smile warm and genuine in a way that immediately eases some of my tension. In a simple cashmere jumper and pearls—even with that incongruous apron—she exudes elegance. The kind that comes from generations of knowing exactly who you are in the world.

Thomson appears at my door and opens it, while Sterling goes to Killian's side.

'You've got this, kid.' Thomson offers me a wink.

'Thank you.' He's my favourite out of all of Killian's men. 'And thank you so much for the help with the watch. He loved it.'

'Of course he did.' He taps the side of his nose conspiratorially. 'It's from you.'

'I'm sorry you have to work today.' I feel bad that the staff are all working overtime because I have a stupid stalker on the loose.

'Don't be. Walsh is swapping out with me in a couple of hours.' He winks again. 'Got to give the Mrs her present too, if you know what I mean.' His low laughter carries on the breeze.

'Happy wife, happy life, right?' I tease.

'Exactly.'

Killian comes round to my side and slips his arm around me. Vivienne's eyes quadruple in size as she freezes momentarily. Killian chuckles beside me.

Finally, she overcomes her initial shock, starting down the steps despite the frosty air. 'Merry Christmas! We were beginning to think you'd changed your minds.'

Killian's hand settles on the base of my spine, his thumb stroking me in reassuring circles. 'Still time to run,' he murmurs, 'Doesn't mean I won't chase you down, but you could try.'

'That could be a game for another time.' I bite back my grin and beam at Killian's mother instead.

'Avery, it's so wonderful to see you again.' Before I know it, I'm enveloped in a cloud of Coco Chanel and squished against her bosom. 'We're absolutely delighted you're joining us for Christmas. When James told me you two were...' She pauses for a second, seeming to search for the right word. 'Together, I thought he was winding me up. I mean, you two didn't exactly look like you were hitting it off at the wedding, and then boom, next thing you know, it's serious. Tell me, what happened? I want to know every single detail.'

'Trust me, you don't, Mother.' Killian offers his mother a perfunctory peck on the cheek when she finally releases me.

'Oh, don't be coy! I love a bit of romance. Tell me everything.' She waggles her finger at her son.

'Me too,' a deep voice calls gleefully from the doorway. Rian. He's clutching a large tumbler of amber coloured liquid, and from the glow in his cheeks, it's not his first of the day. 'Merry Christmas! Come on in and tell us *everything.*'

Killian growls beside me as Vivienne ushers us in through the grand entrance. Rian throws his arms around me and places a slobbery kiss on my cheek. I fight the urge to wipe it off. 'Welcome to the family, Avery,' he slurs.

It's not like him. Every time I've been in Rian's company and he's been drinking, he's held it much better than this. My eyes flick to Killian, who's staring at his youngest brother with a mix of wariness and confusion.

'Thanks. Merry Christmas.' I remove myself from his grip, before Killian does it for me, then step further inside the grand hallway, trying not to gawk like an absolute tourist at the opulence surrounding me. The entrance hall has soaring ceilings adorned with intricate plasterwork and a huge crystal chandelier. Gleaming marble floors stretch out beneath our feet, partially covered by antique Persian rugs in deep reds and blues.

To our right, a sweeping double staircase curves upward, the dark mahogany banister polished to a mirror shine. Family portraits line the wall alongside the stairs—generations of Becketts staring down with the same intense gaze Killian sometimes fixes on me. I spot him immediately in one of the larger frames—a serious-looking teenager standing ramrod straight between his brothers, not quite smiling but not quite frowning either.

'Come on through, everyone's in here.' Vivienne motions for us to follow her into what must be the main living area.

A Christmas tree dominates the space, making the one I ordered for Killian's place look positively miniature. It must be at least twenty-feet tall, decorated with what appear to be antique ornaments and twinkling lights that cast a warm glow over the surrounding furniture. Elegant sofas and armchairs in rich fabrics look so pristine I'm almost afraid to sit on them.

'You made it!' Scarlett squeals from her position on the floor, where her daughters are swinging from her like she's a climbing frame. In a red Valentino dress that skims her to just below her knee, she looks festive and fabulous. A fire crackles in a fireplace large enough to roast an entire deer, a testament to how far Scarlett has come. For years she couldn't stand the sound or heat of an open fire, but these days, it doesn't seem to affect her. Killian isn't the only one with a troubled past to overcome, but that's another story entirely.

'Welcome!' Zara, Killian's gorgeous and glamorous little sister rushes over, eyeing me like I'm a shiny rare object before flinging her arms around me.

Caelon and Ivy snuggle together in a plush velvet love seat while Caelon's children, Orla and Owen, suck on red and white striped candy canes at their feet. They rise when we enter. Surprise flickers in Caelon's eyes as they flit between Killian and me, but he welcomes us both warmly.

Ivy is positively bouncing around the place with excitement. 'I can't believe it,' she whispers into my ear. 'I thought you two were fit to kill each other at the wedding and now look at you!' Her brilliant engagement ring sparkles on her left hand.

'There was certainly a little tension, but we found other ways to work it off.' I bite my lip.

Vivienne announces she's going to fetch champagne—and her husband—from the kitchen. Rian heads towards the majestic mahogany sideboard where his brother, Sean, is pouring from a crystal decanter.

Sean is the quietest out of all the Beckett boys. I've

known him for years, first from the Luxor Lounge, and now from social gatherings with Scarlett, yet sometimes I feel like I don't know him at all. He raises his hand from across the room and offers a warm smile. 'Merry Christmas, Avery. Welcome.'

Killian shakes hands with his brothers. It's impossible to miss the way his shoulders stiffen when his sisters-in-law peck his cheek, which makes me feel thoroughly privileged that the only places he stiffens for me these days is in his trousers.

He accepts a tumbler of whiskey, then rapidly returns to my side. 'This place is stunning.' The mantelpiece is laden with Christmas cards, family photos, and tasteful festive decorations. The scent of pine mingles with something delicious wafting from the kitchen.

The Beckett mansion is grand, undeniably so, but there are surprising touches of warmth everywhere—children's artwork framed alongside priceless paintings, a dog bed by the fire, books left open on side tables. It's a home, not just a showpiece, and that realisation makes me wonder if he's right. If maybe there is something to getting married—if it means one day, we'll build a life and a home like this one.

I get that it's a shock to my family to see me with a woman, but I wish to fuck they'd stop gawping like I've got two heads. I adjust the collar of my charcoal Oxford shirt, fighting the urge to loosen another button. My brothers beckon me over to the drinks cabinet for a top up and while I'd rather remain within two feet of Avery at all times, she's engrossed in a conversation with Ivy, Zara and Scarlett about Ivy and Caelon's upcoming wedding in the spring.

Avery settles in seamlessly, unsurprisingly. Now and again, her infectious laughter carries across the room. She looks stunning in an emerald dress that brings out the aqua flecks in her eyes. The way she carries herself—confident but warm—makes her belong anywhere she chooses to be.

My brothers, on the other hand, belong in a zoo. They're behaving like absolute pricks.

'So, the ice man finally thawed.' Caelon smirks, handing me a full crystal tumbler of whiskey. 'Never thought I'd see the day you'd willingly bring a woman home for Christmas.'

'Fuck off,' I mutter, taking a deep drink from the glass.

'Language, darling,' my mother calls as she re-enters the

room with two bottles of champagne. Her superhuman hearing hasn't diminished with age.

'She's good for you,' James adds, more seriously than Caelon. 'I haven't seen you this... present... in years.'

He's not wrong, which is precisely why I don't respond. The pre-Avery version of me would have kept his emotional distance today, would have stationed himself by a window to keep watch on the grounds, would have checked in with security every thirty minutes.

I've tripled the security detail today—fifteen men on the perimeter, two by the main gate, and three more monitoring the surveillance feeds. The stalker is still out there, and this gathering of the entire Beckett family presents a tempting target. I have my earpiece in to stay connected, though I'm trying not to let Avery see my concern. Today is for her, for us. She wanted a memorable Christmas, and I'm determined she's going to have one.

The heavy door swings open again, and my father strides into the room. Alexander Beckett is six-foot-four of imposing authority, even at his age. His steel-grey hair is immaculately styled, his posture military-straight.

The room shifts subtly as he enters—everyone sitting a little taller, conversations pausing briefly before resuming. His eyes find Avery immediately, assessing her in the same calculating manner he sizes up everyone he meets. I feel my shoulders tense involuntarily. At the wedding, they'd exchanged mere pleasantries. This is different.

'So,' he says, his deep rich voice booming across the room as he approaches her. 'This is the young woman who's managed to accomplish what none of us could.'

Avery turns, her smile faltering slightly under his scrutiny. 'Sir?'

'Getting my most stubborn son to join a family gathering without having to be physically dragged here.' His face remains impassive for a beat, then cracks into a rare smile. 'Merry Christmas, my dear. So glad you could join us.'

'Merry Christmas.' Avery's cheeks colour in a rare blush.

'Alex, will you open this champagne?' My mother brandishes the bottles.

'Certainly, my love.' My father rushes to help like a knight in shining armour. It's Beckett family tradition to give the staff Christmas Day off every year. It's the one day my mother gets to fuss over us all herself and she absolutely loves it.

Avery watches as my father kisses my mother and relieves her of one of the bottles. Something like awe flashes in her eyes.

I get it. Even after forty years of marriage, it's impossible to miss the love between my parents. Growing up, it was gross. Now it's... reassuring.

Avery slopes over to me with a look in her eyes that I've seen a hundred times over the past few weeks. Her tongue darts out to wet her lower lip, and I'd bet my life she's thinking something filthy. Before I have the chance to ask, Rian pushes his way between us with a shit-eating grin plastered across his face.

'Avery,' he purrs, leaning in to kiss her cheek, his lips lingering a fraction longer than necessary. 'That dress is absolutely criminal. I thought my brother had better manners than to upstage the rest of us by bringing the most gorgeous woman in Dublin to Christmas lunch.'

My jaw clenches as he places his hand on the small of her back, invading the space that's explicitly mine. 'Did it ever occur to you to bring a woman of your own to Christmas lunch? God knows you've had enough of them—women, I mean, not lunches.'

Rian winces but recovers quickly. 'Looks like you found a sense of humour along with your other emotions.'

What's going on with him? Out of all my brothers, he

loves to party, but today, he has an edge to him. Like he's not drinking for fun, but perhaps to forget. I should know, I've done it often enough myself over the years.

'The Luxor Lounge isn't the same without you,' he continues, oblivious to—or more likely, enjoying—my darkening expression. 'We need to reschedule your guest appearance.'

'Rian,' I warn, the word coming out like a growl. He's well aware of Avery's retirement from her glamour days. Zack Kiel splashed her resignation all over the press after our conversation a few weeks ago.

Avery shoots me an amused glance over her shoulder before turning back to my youngest brother. 'I'm retired from that particular stage, but thanks for the offer.'

'Pity.' Rian sighs dramatically, reaching out to touch Avery's bicep. 'Why are all the best women taken?'

I take a deliberate step forward, inserting myself between my brother and my girlfriend.

'Touch her again,' I say quietly, for his ears only, 'and you'll need a new hand.'

His laugh is bright and entirely untroubled. 'There's the Killian we know and love.' He winks at Avery. 'I was beginning to worry he'd gone soft.'

Avery's eyes twinkle as she slips her arm through mine. 'He's not soft where it matters.'

'Boys,' Mother calls from across the room. 'Dinner's nearly ready. Behave yourselves.'

Rian saunters away. Avery stretches on her tiptoes to whisper into my ear. 'He's doing it on purpose, you know.'

I do know.

I press my lips to her temple. 'Doesn't mean I won't kill him before dessert.'

'Did you get that, by the way?' Her eyes narrow. '*All the best ones are taken.*'

I didn't get it, and I never normally miss anything, but

she's right. It explains his weird behaviour. It would seem that my littlest brother is in love with someone he can't have. But who?

Before I have time to ponder it, the twenty-foot Christmas tree blinks into darkness, thousands of twinkling lights extinguished in an instant. The subtle background music—cuts off mid-note, plunging the room into an unnatural silence. The atmosphere shifts.

James and I lock eyes. He's the only one here who understands the significance. The Beckett estate's power system has triple redundancy. The backup generator is supposed to kick in within three seconds of mains power failing. It didn't. Which means someone deliberately disabled it.

My earpiece crackles to life.

'Boss, we have a problem.' Sterling's voice rings loud and clear. 'It's Thomson. He's been taken out.'

Chapter Forty

AVERY

Killian's face transforms in an instant. The man who was smiling moments ago vanishes, replaced by someone I barely recognise—all hard edges and cold calculation. His jaw sets like granite as he touches his earpiece.

'Execute Protocol One,' he barks at whoever's listening on the other end. Then he turns to his father. 'Get everyone to the panic room. Now.'

Alexander Beckett doesn't waste time with questions. He simply nods, placing a protective arm around Vivienne's shoulders.

'What's happening?' I whisper, but Killian's already gripping my elbow, steering me toward the door.

'We need to leave.' His voice is low, controlled, but I hear the urgency beneath it. 'Right now.'

The rest of the family moves with practiced efficiency. James shepherds Scarlett and the kids toward what looks like an ordinary bookcase, while Caelon and Ivy each have Orla and Owen by the hand and are already disappearing through another doorway. Zara, Sean and Rian flank their backs, all trace of Rian's earlier joviality gone. They've drilled for this.

'But your family—' I start to protest.

'The panic room is state-of-the-art. They'll be fine. My men will close in around them. They'll be protected.' His fingers tighten around my arm. 'You're the target. And while we're here, we're putting one on them too. We need to draw him away.'

The Christmas warmth evaporates around us as Killian guides me through the grand house with military precision. No longer a family home, but a tactical environment. I catch a glimpse of the Christmas tree in darkness as we pass, presents still nestled beneath it. The watch he gave me this morning feels suddenly heavy on my wrist.

'Is it him?' I don't need to specify who 'him' is.

Killian doesn't answer, just pulls me closer as we reach what looks like a servant's corridor.

'Stay exactly two steps behind me,' he instructs, drawing a gun from somewhere inside his jacket. 'Move when I move. Stop when I stop. Don't speak unless I ask you a direct question.'

The Killian who whispered sweet nothings in my ear this morning has disappeared completely. This is the man I first met—the controlled, lethal professional who sees threats in every shadow. But as we slip through the darkened corridor, I catch the slight tremor in his hand as he reaches back to take my clammy hand in his.

We emerge through what looks like an ordinary pantry door into the crisp winter air. The contrast between the festive warmth inside and the cold reality outside makes me shiver—or maybe it's the sight that greets us.

Sterling is struggling to lift Thomson into the back of a black SUV, his hands slick with crimson blood. So much blood. It's pooled on the gravel driveway, dark and viscous against the pale stones. The champagne churns in my stomach. Thomson's face is ghostly white, his crisp white shirt soaked to a shocking shade of scarlet. The sweet, strong man who always smiles at me, who asks about my day with genuine interest, looks like a broken doll.

'Oh my God,' I whisper, my hand covering my mouth. This is all my fault.

'Get in the car,' Killian orders, but I'm frozen in place.

'Is he...?'

'Still breathing. Sterling's taking him to hospital.' Killian's voice is clipped, cold, and professional, but I hear the undercurrent of rage. 'We need to move, Avery.'

That's when I see it—something dark against the blood-stained gravel. Another black lily, its elegant curve obscenely beautiful amid the horror. But there's something else. Something glinting in the winter sunlight.

I step closer, despite Killian's warning hand.

'Avery, don't— '

But I'm already bending down, my eyes fixed on the object wrapped around the lily's stem. A ring. For a sickening moment, I think it's meant for me—some twisted proposal from my stalker. But as I look closer, recognition hits me like a physical blow.

It's my father's signet ring. The one his father gave him. The one he never, ever takes off.

'That's my dad's ring.' My voice sounds strange to my own ears. Distant. 'Killian, that's my dad's ring.'

I'm already fumbling for my phone, scrolling to my father's number with shaking fingers.

'Avery, we don't have time for this.' Killian tries to pull me away but my feet root to the spot.

The call connects, rings once, twice, three times... then his voicemail kicks in.

'He's not answering.' Panic rises, sharp and metallic in my throat. I try again. Nothing.

'We're too exposed here, Avery. Get in the car.' Killian pushes me towards a second SUV.

'How do we know the vehicle hasn't been compromised?' A vision of it blowing up with us inside plays in my mind like a 3D horror movie.

'We don't, but we're running out of time. And this, unlike the Aston, is bulletproof, and stocked with supplies, if you get my drift.' We rush toward the vehicle. He opens the door and practically shoves me in before racing around to the driver's side, tapping his earpiece. 'Secure the premises. Restore the power. Check the camera. Find this fucking bastard. Call in a fucking SWAT team if you need to, but get him.'

As we speed down the long, sweeping driveway, I try my dad again. We don't have much of a relationship, but he's my dad at the end of the day. I might not like him, or approve of the choices he's made in life, but I do love him.

No answer again.

Shit.

Out of pure desperation, I dial Tessa, even though we've barely exchanged more than ten sentences over the years. It goes straight to voicemail. The implications crash over me in waves. 'This is my fault. He's going after my family because of me.'

Killian places a hand on my thigh, his fingers digging in just shy of painful. 'This isn't your fault. It's his. All of it.' His eyes bore into mine, fierce and certain. 'We need to get you somewhere safe.'

I clutch the ring in my palm. 'We have to check on them.' My voice steadies with determination. 'Killian, it's only five minutes away from here. I have to know if they're okay.'

'Out of the question. We'll send a team. They'll be with them in thirty minutes.' His tone is final as he steers us towards the grand exit.

'I'm going. With or without you.' I reach for the door handle, even though the vehicle is moving.

'Avery—'

I hold up the ring, my hand trembling. 'If something happens to them because of this—because of me—and we could have stopped it, I'll never forgive myself.' I swallow hard. 'Please. If it was your family, you wouldn't hesitate. Five minutes to check. Then I'll go anywhere in the world with you. I promise.'

Something shifts in his expression—understanding, perhaps, or recognition of a stubbornness that matches his own.

'Fine. Five minutes,' he finally says. 'We'll drive by, but we don't stop unless it's clear.'

The ring burns cold against my palm as Killian peels out of the driveway. 'You know where the house is?'

'Obviously. Photographic memory, remember.' He taps the side of his temple.

'Thank God my mother is out of the country.'

'I'll be happier when I get you out of the country,' he grimaces.

'When will this ever end?' A sob catches in my throat.

'Soon, sweetheart. Soon. What happened there today was an escalation. He's spiralling. That's when people like him make mistakes. One of the cameras would have picked up his image. At the very least, Thomson will have seen him and will be able to help identify him.'

If he survives.

The words hang unspoken between us.

Chapter Forty-One

KILLIAN

This is a bad idea. Every bone in my body vibrates with that knowledge, yet I still can't say no to the woman I love. The chances are, Avery's father is already dead. Fuck knows what type of blood bath we're going to find in there, but at least then, she can rest in the knowledge we can do no more. I indicate off the dual carriageway to the slipway leading to her father's place.

The house he bought for him and Tessa sits at the end of Oakwood Lane, a private road that winds through mature trees and well-maintained hedgerows. Unlike the Beckett estate, with its decades of history and hundreds of acres, this is new money—comfortable, but trying too hard. The properties here are substantial executive homes that scream 'jumped up accountant' without the subtlety of old wealth.

The house stands apart from its neighbours, separated by a small copse of pine trees that provide the privacy they clearly paid a premium for. The house isn't visible from the road, requiring visitors to navigate a curving gravel driveway. Stone pillars mark the entrance, with a wrought-iron gate that stands open. The house itself is three storeys of red brick with white trim, dormer windows in the attic space, and a circular driveway with a water feature at its centre. Christmas lights outline the roofline and windows. Everything looks normal, picture-perfect even.

Too perfect?

I slow the SUV, scanning for any sign of movement, any hint of disturbance, but there's nothing. Just a quiet, affluent home waiting for Christmas dinner to be served.

'Wait in the car,' I say, knowing that hell will freeze over first, but needing to try anyway.

The glare Avery gives me confirms it. She's getting out of this vehicle whether I like it or not. I reach over and grip her hand. 'It's probably not going to be pretty, sweetheart.'

'I know.' The column of her throat bobs. 'But I need to see.'

'Stay behind me. Do exactly as I say. Understood?'

She nods, her face pale but determined.

I check my weapon once more and step out into the deceptive calm of Oakwood Lane, every sense heightened, every instinct screaming that we're walking straight into a trap.

Before I can reach the doorstep, the front door swings open with suspicious timing. Sebastian, Avery's stepbrother, stands in the doorway, his smile wide but forced, in fitting with his profile. The man is highly intelligent by all accounts, but utterly lacking in social skills. His GP suggested a referral to investigate depression as a child, but Tessa blocked it.

'What a lovely surprise, Avery.' His eyes flick briefly to me before returning to her as he runs a hand over the front of the black cashmere sweater that sculpts his lithe, athletic frame. 'Are you feeling better? Your father was quite concerned about your fever.'

Avery and I exchange a glance of confusion. Something's off. Every cell of my body is screaming at me.

'Where's Dad?' she demands, her fists clench around her father's signet ring.

'Right here,' Sebastian replies, then steps closer and winks. 'Be warned. He's already started on the brandy.'

Is the ring a copy?

Did the stalker want us to come here?

I glance around the street. Again—we're too exposed. I don't like it one fucking bit.

'Come on in.' He opens the door wider and I glimpse Avery's father, who is indeed clutching a tumbler with something that could pass for brandy and looking slightly unsteady on his feet. But he's alive. And his face lights like a beacon when he sees his daughter on his doorstep. 'Dad! Look who dropped by. And she brought a...' His eyes narrow as they shift to me again. 'Friend.'

My fingers hover near my concealed weapon as footsteps approach. Every nerve ending is firing warning signals, but we're caught between a rock and a hard place.

Fergus Williams appears behind his stepson, looking perfectly healthy and utterly delighted. No signs of distress. No indication of coercion. Nothing to justify the alarm bells clanging in my head.

'Avery!' His voice exudes genuine pleasure. 'What a wonderful surprise! How are you feeling? Come in,' he insists, stepping back. 'Tessa will be thrilled to see you. Please introduce your friend.'

'Boyfriend.' I reach out to take Fergus's hand and shake it firmly. This man is going to be my father-in-law after all, regardless of whether I think he's a watery cunt or not. What kind of a man leaves his wife and child for his PA? It's so cliché.

'Pleased to meet you,' he says, but his tone is cautious.

'We're not staying. We just dropped by to...' Avery looks at me, hesitant but relieved.

'Nonsense,' Sebastian insists, beckoning us in like we're old friends.

To refuse now would seem bizarre, suspicious. And I need to get in out of the open until I get an update from Sterling. Hopefully he's locked the stalker down. Protocol One involves locking down the entire house. If the stalker is inside, the only way he's getting out is in a body bag.

At least here she's with family. Her father might be devoid of morals when it comes to his marriage, but he won't hurt her. And Sebastian's strange but his background check came back cleaner than a sterile operating room. With hobbies like 'metal detecting' on his elaborately detailed CV, the only risk he possesses to us is death by boredom.

'Five minutes,' I concede, my voice low. 'We're just making a pitstop on the way to my parents.' I lie.

After we cross the threshold, Sebastian closes the door behind us with a click. We follow Fergus through the tiled entrance hall, past a towering Christmas tree festooned with matching silver and gold ornaments. Tessa Williams sits perched on a cream leather armchair in the family sitting room, her posture rigid despite the casual setting. She's an attractive brunette, with sharp-angled cheekbones and expensive highlights. Her smile seems slightly forced as she raises her crystal tumbler in greeting.

'What a wonderful surprise,' she says, though her tone lacks genuine warmth. No wonder Avery didn't want to come here. Her father might have a romantic notion about them all being one big happy family, but one look at Tessa tells me she doesn't share the same dream. Her heavily lined eyes flick between Avery and me curiously, but she doesn't attempt to get up to greet us.

Family photos line the mantelpiece, Sebastian featuring prominently, Avery notably absent except for one token graduation picture.

'Please, sit, sit.' Fergus gestures enthusiastically to the sofa. 'We were just having a toast. Join us!'

He retrieves an ornate crystal decanter from a side table and moves to pour drinks. I notice Sebastian watching him with unusual intensity.

'None for me, thanks.' I remain standing, positioning myself where I can see both exits. 'We can't stay long.'

'Nonsense!' Fergus insists, already filling a tumbler. 'One drink. It's Christmas Day. It's practically the law. And it's not every day I get to meet my daughter's boyfriend.'

Sebastian's silver eyes narrow as Fergus pushes the glass toward me with surprising force. 'This is quality stuff. Twenty-five years old.'

Quality stuff is what my family's distillery produces. This is horse piss in comparison, but I accept it reluctantly. With the amount of adrenaline pumping through my blood, I'll have burnt it off in seconds anyway.

Avery perches beside me, her body tense. She accepts the glass she's offered, taking a deep drink. She winces as it hits the back of her throat.

Under Fergus's persistent gaze, I relent and take the drink, figuring it might steady the slight tremor in my hand.

'To family,' Sebastian raises his glass but doesn't drink—a detail that registers but doesn't fully process as I take a cautious sip. Horse piss, as suspected, but I'm not going to get a better offer in here.

The next few minutes pass in stilted conversation. Where did we meet? The weather. Sebastian's smile never wavers, but something about his eyes—the way they fixate on Avery makes my skin crawl.

'Where's Yvonne?' Avery asks Sebastian.

'We parted ways a long time ago,' Sebastian says. Something registers then. His address is her address. If they parted ways a long time ago, why are all of his accounts, revenue details, and even his car still registered to her house?

I notice Tessa's eyes growing increasingly unfocused, her speech slightly slurred. Fergus too seems unsteady, leaning heavily against the fireplace. Neither has refilled their drinks, yet both appear increasingly intoxicated.

When Fergus offers a refill, I accept mostly to study his movements. Sebastian hovers nearby, watching with an intensity that doesn't match his casual stance. For a man that was overly welcoming at the door, he's oddly silent throughout the entire exchange.

Tessa slumps back on the couch. Her eyes are open, but there's definitely nobody home. Shit, what time did they start on the hard stuff?

'Where's your ring, Dad?' Avery's eyes drift to her father's hand as he puts down the decanter.

Fergus glances at Sebastian with what looks like pride. 'I passed it on. A Christmas gift. It was time.' His voice is slurred, his legs are wobbling beneath him. He tries to steady himself by gripping the mantlepiece—unsuccessfully. In slow motion, he slithers to the floor in a heap.

Realisation strikes like a bolt of lightning. I try to jolt forwards but for some reason I can't.

Sterling's voice suddenly crackles through my earpiece at the exact same second it occurs to me that Sebastian hasn't touched a drop of his drink.

'Boss, we've got an identity. Do you hear me?'

I don't need him to say it. I know it better than my own name. And I walked straight into the unhinged mother-fucker's lair.

I go to touch my earpiece, but my arm feels like a dead weight. My eyes land on Sebastian, a slow, cruel smile splits open his face.

'It's Avery's stepbrother. I repeat, the stalker is Avery's stepbrother, Sebastian Harrow. Do you receive—'

The weight of my limbs registers before Sterling can finish. My fingers tingle with sudden numbness. The glass feels impossibly heavy in my hand. It falls to the floor with a thud.

'Boss?'

I turn to warn Avery, but my tongue feels thick, uncooperative. Across the room, Sebastian's expression shifts, and he begins to clap, slowly.

Our eyes lock, and I see the depth of his insanity. He poisoned his own fucking parents to get what he truly believes is his.

Avery's eyes flit between Sebastian and me.

As my vision begins to blur, Sebastian crouches beside me, his face close enough that I can smell his sickly cologne. He removes the earpiece from my ear, drops it on the floor, and stamps on it.

'Plans change, but destiny doesn't,' he whispers, the same words from the note at the Luxor Lounge. 'She was always meant to be with me.'

The horror of our current situation clicks into place as my muscles fail me completely. Every black lily. Every threat. Every step ahead of my security. It was him. And he wasn't even on my radar.

He stands, prowling toward a now-slumping Avery with chilling prowess. She doesn't—clearly can't resist when he lifts her to her feet, supporting her weight as though he's done this countless times before.

'I've got you,' he murmurs to her with disturbing tenderness. 'It's time to go home, where you belong.'

I fight against the paralytic with everything I have, but my body refuses to respond. It's futile. The beast inside me roars, but I can't even open my mouth. I can only watch, as he takes the woman I love from me. And there's fuck all I can do about it.

He turns back, his eyes meeting mine with something like triumph.

'I should pleasure her right here in front of you, and make you watch, like you made me watch.' He pauses like he's contemplating it.

I'm screaming, writhing, dying inside, but utterly paralysed.

'But I have more respect for her than that. Her days of exposing herself in public are over. Every inch of her skin is purely for my pleasure now.'

The door closes behind them with a soft, final click.

Chapter Forty-Two

AVERY

My mind screams for my body to move, to fight, to run, but nothing responds. Not my fingers, not my toes—not even my eyelids obey. I'm a passenger in my own body, fully aware but utterly powerless as Sebastian carries me from the house to his car, which is parked around the back. His athletically lithe arms feel repulsive around me—an unwanted intimacy that makes my skin crawl, but I can't physically recoil.

He places me in the passenger seat with disturbing gentleness, buckling my seatbelt as if I'm precious cargo. His fingers linger at my collarbone, brushing against my skin as his sharp silver eyes drink me in.

How did I not see this?

How did I not spot the silent psychopath in my socially awkward stepbrother?

Five years in college couldn't prepare me for this twisted horror story. I pray to fuck I don't end up on a Netflix documentary—one which I'll never see because I'm six-feet under the ground.

He gets into the driver's side and pats my bare thigh where my dress has hitched up. Nausea rises within me.

'The drug will wear off in a couple of hours,' he explains as he slides into the seat. His voice has changed—no longer the awkward, erudite stepbrother I barely acknowledge at rare family gatherings. This voice is confident, possessive. 'If you're a good girl and cooperate, I won't have to dose you again. I don't want to, Avery. I want you awake. Present. With me. That's where you belong. But if it takes months of keeping you docile like this, then I'll do it.'

I try to scream, to lift a finger, to do anything. Nothing happens. Panic claws at my chest, but I can do nothing except watch and try to work out where the fuck he's taking me. He starts the car, leaving his hand on my bare skin as we drive into the distance. His thumb traces small circles and the urge to vomit consumes me.

'Our parents thought they found true love. The real love story in this family is ours.' His thumb inches higher. Why didn't I wear trousers today? I feel horrifically violated, and he's barely even begun.

Sebastian continues, one hand on the wheel. 'Remember the first time we met? You were sixteen. Your father— brought you to our house to introduce us before he proposed to my mother.'

I do remember, vaguely. A forgettable meeting with the awkward, skinny son of the woman my father ran off with. I'd barely looked at him, too angry with all of them to care.

'You were wearing a sundress with calla lilies printed on it. Black ones, against white fabric.' His voice softens with the memory. 'You were so stunning, even then. Young, but stunning. I knew then. I knew we were meant to be together. It made it easier overhearing your father grunt and pant on top of my mother every night, knowing that I would have the last laugh. That his daughter would be in my arms, in my bed, and her body would be mine.'

He's even more deranged than I can comprehend. I try to

move again, but nothing. My mind wanders to Killian. He had more of the brandy—or whatever it was—than me. If anything happens to him, so help me, I will bide my time and kill this twisted motherfucker in his sleep.

'I was at college then, of course. You were too young. I knew I needed to wait, to give you time to grow up, to become the woman you were meant to be.' He speaks as if reading from a love story, not describing years of stalking. 'I promised myself I'd build a life worthy of you. That I'd earn enough to give you everything you deserve. And I have, my darling. Wait until you see the tower I've built for you.'

Oh my god. If Killian doesn't find me, I might have to fling myself from it. There's no way I can stay with this delusional bastard.

'You pretended not to notice me, of course. At our parents' wedding. It would have been inappropriate. I brought Yvonne so no one would suspect my feelings for you. She was merely the means to an end. I loved you from the second I saw you. I know you felt it too.' A hint of bitterness creeps into Sebastian's voice. 'But then you started parading yourself around at that disgusting club. You lost your way.'

He exhales heavily, snatches his hand from my thigh and grips the steering wheel so tightly his fingers turn white. Fear floods my stomach. The silence is almost worse than the deranged love story he crafted.

We drive through the city, then onto smaller roads, then winding coastal lanes. My paralysed body slides slightly with each turn, and Sebastian reaches over to adjust me. I count each touch, each violation, storing them away as fuel for when I can finally move again.

Through the windscreen, it's clear we're heading up the coast, away from Dublin, away from Killian. Oh God, Killian. Please, please, please, find me.

'When you weren't unnerved by the first few lilies, I knew

that you understood the significance of them, that somewhere deep in your subconscious, you remembered the sundress and the day we met. I booked that trip to St. Barths to surprise you. To propose to you. Then Beckett bulldozed in and tried to take you from me. Tried to ruin everything I'd ever worked for.'

The car turns onto a narrow, bumpy track that jostles my limp body. Sebastian steadies me, his hand on my thigh again. I'm going to be sick. And I can't even move to vomit, which means I'll probably choke on it and die. Fuck. Fuck. Fuck.

'I watched you, though. I watched you finish college. I was so proud when you got your psychology doctorate. I was so sure you'd finish at that hellhole club. And then you went on to betray me again, baring what's mine to the world.' He tuts in disgust.

The sea comes into view, grey-blue and angry in the winter light. And there, standing stark against the horizon, is a lighthouse. Old, stone, isolated on a rocky outcrop that's barely connected to the mainland.

'It's okay, though, princess. You can spend the rest of your life making it up to me. Your body is for my eyes only now. For my pleasure alone, and for yours. We're going to be so happy together.'

I stare straight ahead as he drives silently for another forty minutes. Finally, we slow to a stop outside the abandoned lighthouse. It looms above us, tall and imposing—and utterly remote. No other structures in sight. No neighbours. No witnesses.

'Home sweet home,' Sebastian says, a note of pride in his voice. 'I've spent years preparing it for us. You'll love it once you see it properly.'

He exits the car and comes around to my side, lifting me into his arms again.

'I know it seems extreme,' he continues as he carries me

up a winding stone path. 'But Beckett left me no choice. The way he touched you, the way he looked at you... The way he violated you in front of his men... He doesn't deserve you, Avery. He doesn't know you like I do.'

The door creaks open, and warm air rushes out. Inside, the lighthouse is nothing like I expected. It's been entirely renovated, transformed into a modern home. Plush rugs over polished wood floors. Expensive furniture. There's even a Christmas tree decorated in silver and white standing in the circular main room. My eyes drift to the walls, and my blood turns to ice. Dozens of framed photographs line the space— family portraits, vacation snapshots, wedding pictures—all featuring Sebastian and me together. Except we were never together. He's meticulously photoshopped himself into moments of my life with disturbing precision—standing beside me at my graduation, arm around my waist, at my birthday dinner last year in Paris, even at Scarlett's wedding on the beach at St. Barths. The images are so perfectly edited that at first glance, they look genuine—a curated history of a relationship that never existed. The physical manifestation of his delusion hangs on the wall like a shrine. It's beyond unsettling.

'Surprise,' Sebastian whispers against my hair as he carries me inside. 'I've thought of everything. And we have an off-grid power system. Satellite internet. Enough supplies to last months if needed. No one will ever find us here.'

He lays me carefully on a sofa, positioning me so I can see the room. My eyes dart frantically, taking in potential weapons, exits, anything that might help when I can move again.

'I know what you're thinking,' he says, kneeling beside me, stroking the smooth hand across my cheek. I can't even flinch. 'You're wondering if Beckett will find you. He won't.'

No one knows about this place. I bought it through a shell corporation years ago. On paper, it doesn't even exist.'

He leans closer, his face inches from mine. 'Plans change, but destiny doesn't, Avery. We were always meant to be together. And soon, you'll see it too.'

The certainty in his voice sends ice through my veins. As he moves away to adjust the lighting, my mind races to Killian. Please be okay. Please find me. Please.

Because the way Sebastian is looking at me makes me certain of one thing: he has no intention of ever letting me go.

Chapter Forty-Three

KILLIAN

The grandfather clock in the corner ticks with maddening precision. Each second stretches into eternity as I sit frozen, a prisoner in my own body. One hour, four minutes, and seventeen seconds since that bastard walked out with Avery.

One hour, four minutes, and eighteen seconds of wondering what he's doing to her.

The rage builds with nowhere to go, no muscle to tense, no fist to clench. It burns through me, molten and useless. Sebastian. The fucking stalker was Sebastian. Right under my nose the entire time. A million signs I should have seen flash through my mind—his technical background, his family connection giving him access to her entire history.

One hour. Twelve minutes. Nine seconds.

Fergus Williams remains slumped against the wall where he collapsed, his eyes wide and aware, tracking the same clock I am. Silent tears stream down his face. Tessa sits rigid in her armchair, her hands clutching the armrests, fingers white with the strain of trying to move. Drugged by her own son. This must be a proud moment for her. Avery wanted a memorable Christmas. This is one none of us will ever forget.

The acrid smell of burning meat begins to permeate the room. The turkey left unattended in the oven. The smell grows stronger with each passing minute. Smoke will follow. Then flames. If there's any justice in the world, someone installed smoke detectors. But given Sebastian's meticulous planning, perhaps he disabled them to destroy the evidence—us.

One hour. Sixteen minutes. Twenty-two seconds.

I focus everything on moving my pinky finger. Nothing happens. I'm still a spectator in my own body while Avery is God knows where with a fucking psychopath.

Sterling should have realised something was wrong by now. But I know why he hasn't. The attack at the Beckett estate wasn't random—it was calculated. Thomson was just collateral damage, a way to spread my security team thin. Sterling will be coordinating protection for my entire family, believing I'm safe with Avery. He has no reason to think I'm in danger because he didn't know about Avery's father's ring, or that we would be stupid enough to drive straight here to check on him.

One hour. Sixteen minutes. Forty-five seconds.

A tingling sensation begins in my extremities. So faint I might be imagining it, but it's there. The drug is finally wearing off. I try again to move my finger. Nothing visible happens, but I feel the attempt now, the ghost of a response.

One hour. Twenty-four minutes. Eighteen seconds.

The burning smell grows stronger. Smoke begins to curl from under the kitchen door. No alarm sounds. Of course not. Sebastian wouldn't leave that to chance.

One hour. Thirty-six minutes. Nine seconds.

I can finally twitch my fingers. The movement is minuscule, but it's there. My jaw remains locked, my vocal cords frozen. I can't warn Fergus or Tessa that feeling will return. I can only watch the clock and wait.

One hour. Forty-six minutes. Thirty-one seconds.

My hand lifts an inch off the armrest. Progress, but not enough. The smoke is thickening, forming a layer near the ceiling. Tessa's pupils are wide with panic. Fergus is still weeping silently. I knew he was a watery prick.

The tingling intensifies, becoming pins and needles, then burning pain as circulation returns. I welcome it. Pain means recovery. Recovery means I can find her.

My earpiece lies crushed on the floor, I can't hear anything through it but it still has its own emergency system. The second I can reach it, I press the crown three times, sending an SOS signal to Sterling and activating the GPS tracker.

Two hours. Four minutes. Fifty-two seconds since Sebastian took Avery.

I force myself to stand on trembling legs that feel like they belong to someone else. Every movement is agony, but I push through it, staggering toward Fergus first. His eyes plead with me as I haul him to his feet, his body a deadweight against mine.

'Going to get you out,' I manage, my voice a hoarse whisper. 'Then I'm going to find your daughter and kill your stepson.'

Fergus can't respond, but the look in his eyes tells me he wouldn't object to the latter.

I half-drag, half-carry him toward the front door and out onto the neatly manicured lawn, then go back for Tessa. The smoke is getting thicker, the heat from the kitchen more intense. I manage to get her outside and place her on the ground beside her husband.

My phone buzzes in my pocket. Sterling. The text is simple: 'Coordinates received. Team en route. 3 minutes.'

I wait until Sterling's SUV comes into view to dial the emergency services. I was never here.

I need to get to Avery.

Thank fuck for the tiny, carefully concealed GPS tracker inside the diamond Cartier. I made some almighty fucking errors along the way, but her Christmas gift wasn't one of them.

Sterling screeches to a stop ten feet away, staring at Avery's father and stepmother with confusion. I'm going to tear Sebastian Williams apart with my bare hands. I've had a change of heart regarding my feelings on torture. A sick psycho stealing my girlfriend has brought out the sadist in me. If he's so much as laid a finger on her, he's going to lose every single one of them—slowly.

Chapter Forty-Four

AVERY

The feeling returns to my limbs with agonising slowness—pins and needles giving way to dull, throbbing circulation. Sebastian has loosely tied my wrists to the arms of an antique chair, 'a precaution' he called it, as if this entire situation isn't five thousand shades of fucked up. The restraints are silken cords, carefully padded where they touch my skin. His planning and consideration make things infinitely more terrifying.

I scan the lighthouse's main floor, searching once again for potential weapons, exits, anything that might help. It's a circular room. There's one main door. A spiral staircase leading up. The windows are too small to climb through. There's a kitchen area with knives visible on a magnetic strip, tantalisingly out of reach.

'You have such beautiful hair,' Sebastian murmurs from his position behind me. I'm doing my best to block out the fact he's drawing a silver-handled brush through my long blonde strands with disturbing gentleness. 'I used to watch you brushing it before bed. You always do exactly one hundred strokes.'

My stomach turns. How many nights has he watched me

through my bedroom window? How did I never notice? How did it never even occur to me that my stalker was my highly intelligent, ridiculously affluent, socially awkward step-brother? My father even bragged about his diving qualification. I could kick myself for not paying more attention.

'That's better,' he says, placing the brush on a nearby table. 'Now let's get this muck off your face. You don't need make up, Avery. I prefer you in your natural state.'

My stomach churns as he kneels before me brandishing a cotton pad soaked in cleanser. He reaches for my cheek. I jerk my head away, but his other hand grips my chin firmly.

'Fighting me is futile,' he insists, methodically removing my makeup. 'Everything I've done has been in service of a greater purpose—our future together.'

His touch makes my skin crawl, but I force myself to remain still. Antagonising him seems unwise until I have a plan. The restraints aren't tight—he clearly wants me compliant, not uncomfortable. If I can gain his trust, maybe he'll loosen them further.

'Hungry?' He moves to the kitchen area, returning with a bowl of mint chocolate chip ice cream—my favourite flavour. Another detail he shouldn't know. 'You need to keep your strength up for later.'

The implication in those words sends a fresh wave of horror over my spine. I press my lips together as he tries to feed me a spoonful, turning my head away.

'Avery,' he sighs, disappointed. 'Don't be difficult. We both know it's your favourite.'

'What do you want from me, Sebastian?' I finally ask, my voice steadier than I feel.

He sets the bowl aside, cupping my face with both hands. 'Everything. I want everything you gave to him. And so much more.'

The reference to Killian sends a fresh wave of panic through me. Is he alive? Did he survive the drug?

'You gave yourself to him so easily,' Sebastian continues, his fingers tightening slightly. 'You *will* give yourself to me. I'll cleanse you of every one of his touches until you can't remember any of them. I'll eradicate him from your memories. It'll be like he never existed.'

'Even if you keep me here for a hundred years, I'll never forget him.' Rage replaces the panic in a hot burst of fury. 'Killian is a better man than you'll ever be,' I snap.

His face darkens. 'He's an uneducated thug. A murderer. A man who destroys everything he touches.'

'I love him, and he loves me.' The words are both a declaration and a weapon. 'And I loved every moment he touched me.'

Sebastian's hand strikes the arm of the chair, inches from my bound wrist. His silver irises burn with fury. 'Don't say that! He's loved you for weeks. I've loved you for years.' For the first time, his carefully controlled façade cracks. 'You barely know him. You don't know what he's done.'

'I know everything.' I lean forward as much as the restraints allow. 'And I know I will never, ever give myself to you.'

'You will give yourself to me, or die. The choice is yours.' His expression shifts from rage to something almost pitying. 'You truly believe he loves you? Do you have any idea what he did to the last woman he claimed to love?'

'What do you know about it?' My curiosity piques despite the situation.

'Did he tell you how she died—Sarah, that is.' He prowls around the chair, circling me like a shark. 'Did he tell you who killed her?'

My stomach bottoms out. The accusation in his tone is

obvious. He thinks Killian killed the only other woman he'd been in love with.

But he's wrong.

Killian would never do that. I know what he's capable of and it's not that.

Before he can continue, the door explodes inward with a deafening crash.

Killian stands in the doorway, his face a mask of cold fury unlike anything I've ever seen. Behind him, Sterling, Walsh, Mason, Lynch, and Donovan fan out, weapons raised—six guns trained unwaveringly on Sebastian.

Thank fuck.

'Don't shoot,' the words are out of my mouth before I can stop them. As deranged as my stepbrother is, I don't wish to witness his demise, and I don't wish to wear his blood, literally and figuratively.

Confusion darts through Killian's eyes, but he holds his fire. I scan him from head to toe, searching for any sign of injury, but he's fine. And I'm going to be fine now he's here.

'You're surrounded. There are fifteen more armed soldiers outside.'

Sweet relief floods my bloodstream.

Sebastian has no way out.

It's over.

He freezes, genuine shock spreading across his features. 'Impossible,' he whispers almost to himself. 'This place doesn't exist on paper. No one knows—'

His eyes narrow to slits and drop to my wrist, to the Cartier watch Killian gave me this morning. Understanding dawns, followed by something like admiration. 'The watch. Of course. A tracking device disguised as a Christmas gift.' He laughs bitterly. 'In my excitement at being reunited with Avery, I missed that. Clever, Beckett. Very clever.'

'Get away from her.' Killian's voice is low and cold.

Sebastian doesn't move, his stance relaxed despite the six weapons aimed at him. 'Quite the cavalry you've brought,' he observes coolly. 'Though I expected nothing less from a man with your particular... background.'

His right hand drifts casually toward his pocket, the movement so natural it almost goes unnoticed.

'Hands where I can see them,' Killian orders, taking a careful step forward, gun steady.

In one fluid motion, Sebastian's hand emerges from his pocket. Light catches on polished steel—a tactical folding knife. The blade flicks open with a soft, menacing click. Before anyone can react, he's behind my chair, the knife positioned precisely against my carotid artery.

Why didn't I let Killian shoot the bastard when he had the chance?

Fuck. Adrenaline courses through my bloodstream. My eyelids close. I can't watch. I can barely breathe.

You will give yourself to me or die.

Killian freezes mid-step, horror flashing across his face. Six guns remain trained on Sebastian, but no one fires—not with the knife's edge pressing against my skin.

I silently will Killian to fire at Sebastian. There's no way he's going to let me live, so Killian has to at least try to take him out, before he snaps and slices me open anyway.

'How's Thomson?' Sebastian goads.

Killian's nostrils flare. 'He'll live. Which is more than I can say for you.'

The knife presses slightly harder, not enough to break skin but enough to make me acutely aware of my mortality. The armed men at the door shift imperceptibly, weapons steady, gazes calculating angles and risks. The tension in the room is unbearable. Six fingers on six triggers, Killian's gaze never leaves Sebastian.

Sebastian's lips curve into a smile that doesn't quite reach his eyes. 'You know, Avery and I were just having a little chat before you so rudely interrupted us,' his tone is calm and conversational. 'About Sarah, actually.'

A muscle ticks in Killian's jaw. 'Don't.'

'I believe in informed consent, Beckett,' Sebastian replies smoothly. 'Avery should have all the relevant information before making life-altering decisions. Such as, for instance, whether the man she trusts with her safety has a history of executing women he claims to love.'

No.

It can't be right.

But the horror in in Killian's expression confirms it is.

Bile rises in my chest.

I get a flashback of the department store in San Francisco. Specifically of the way he grabbed that man's wrist. The way that in a single split second, he transformed into someone lethal—someone I didn't recognise.

'Tell her, Beckett.' Sebastian's voice is cool like steel. 'Tell her how the last woman you loved ended up. Tell her how you put a bullet in her head without hesitation.'

There has to be an explanation.

There has to be.

Otherwise, I don't know the man I'm in love with at all.

The world seems to stop. I look at Killian, searching his face. His expression is stone, but his eyes—his eyes are full of a pain so raw it takes my breath away.

The memory of that day in the department store continues to play out in my head. *He cups my chin, angling my face to meet his stare. 'Never be scared of me, baby. I'd kill for you. I'd die for you. But I'd never ever hurt you.'*

I believed him then.

And I believe him now.

There *is* an explanation.

But in order for him to get the chance to give it to me, he

has to end this now. End Sebastian. I was foolish to think there was any other option.

'Cat got your tongue?' Sebastian taunts.

Killian's focus shifts back to me. To the blade on my neck, then back to meet my silent stare. His eyes convey one question.

Can I kill him now?

I give the subtlest of nods, then all hell breaks loose.

Chapter Forty-Five

KILLIAN

The moment Avery gives that almost imperceptible nod, the world narrows to a series of tactical calculations.

Distance to target: 3.2 meters.

Knife position: Carotid artery, left side.

Sebastian's focus: Split between me and Avery.

Probability of success: Acceptable.

I move.

Not toward Sebastian—that's what he expects. Instead, I drop to one knee, creating two simultaneous distractions: changing my silhouette and drawing his eye downward. In the millisecond his focus shifts, Sterling fires from my right. The shot is precise—through Sebastian's right shoulder, exactly as planned in the three-second eye contact we exchanged earlier.

Sebastian jerks backward, the knife falling away from Avery's throat as his arm goes momentarily limp. I'm already crossing the distance between us, moving on instinct honed through years of combat. Before he can recover, I'm on him, driving him to the ground with controlled force.

The knife clatters across the wooden floor. Sebastian

writhes beneath me, his face contorted with pain and fury, but I pin his arms with well-honed precision. Blood soaks through his cashmere sweater. The wound is painful, but non-lethal. Exactly as intended. I haven't ruled out torturing the psychotic bastard yet.

'It's over,' I tell him, my voice steady despite the rage still coursing through me.

'It will never be over,' he spits, eyes wild as Walsh and Mason secure his wrists with zip ties. 'She knows what you are now. She knows I'm the better man.'

He's even more delusional than he looks. I ignore him, turning to Avery. She's standing, rubbing her wrists where the silken restraints had been, her face pale but composed. The relief that floods through me is so intense it's almost painful.

'Are you hurt?' I reach for her hands, scanning her for any injuries.

'I'm fine.' Her voice is remarkably steady. She squeezes my hands and our eyes lock. Hers are full of questions.

'Get him out of here,' I order my men. 'And call in his injury. I want him treated, then directly to holding.'

Sebastian laughs, a hollow sound as they haul him upright. 'Treated? How civilised of you, Beckett. Does it make you feel better? Less like a killer?'

'Move him,' I say, without breaking eye contact with Avery.

As they drag Sebastian toward the door, he yells manically at Avery. 'Ask him about the hostages, Avery. Ask him how many children died because of his mistake!'

The door closes behind them, leaving Avery and me alone in the suddenly quiet lighthouse. For a moment, neither of us speaks. I look around at the 'home' this mad cunt created for them. Thank fuck for the Cartier watch. A day earlier and I wouldn't have found her half as fast. The adrenaline begins to ebb, leaving in its wake the awareness of how close I came to losing her.

'Are you sure you're okay?' I pull her against my torso, cautious, uncertain if she wants my touch after what Sebastian revealed. She doesn't pull away, nor does she flinch when I carefully examine the slight red mark on her neck where the knife had pressed.

'Did he hurt you? Did he...' I can barely bring myself to say the words. I squeeze my eyelids shut and open them again. 'Did he touch you?'

'I'm okay. He didn't...' She swallows hard. 'Killian—'

'When he took you, and I could do nothing but watch— fuck it was the worst moment of my entire existence. I should have seen it,' the guilt rising like bile. 'I ran rigorous background checks on everyone close to you, but he looked boringly clean, and he was your brother. I missed the signs.'

'So did I,' she says softly. 'He's my stepbrother. I've known him for years, and I never suspected. Never dreamed he felt that way about me.' She shudders.

'I'll never forgive myself.'

'You will. Because I refuse to be another woman you spend your life hating yourself over.' She leads me to the sofa, sitting beside me, close enough that our shoulders touch. Outside, I can hear my team securing the perimeter, calling in medical support for Sebastian's wound. Inside, the ticking of a clock on the mantel marks the seconds of silence between us.

'Sarah,' she finally says, not a question but an opening.

I owe her the truth.

All of it.

I stare at my hands, remembering the weight of the gun. 'I killed her.'

'Tell me,' Avery says simply.

I've never told anyone the full story. Not my family, not

even my brothers in arms who were there. But Avery deserves to know exactly what kind of man she's with.

'We were stationed in Mali. Peacekeeping mission. Sarah was military intelligence, or so I thought.' The words come easier than I expected. 'We were together for six months when I discovered she was working for arms traffickers. She used information I gave her—information I shouldn't have shared—to set up an ambush.'

Avery takes my hand, her fingers intertwining with mine. The scent of her familiar peony perfume is like a balm to my shattered soul.

'Thirty-two hostages,' I continue. 'Including four children. She made me watch as they began to execute them, one by one.' The memory surfaces, sharp and clear despite the years. 'When I managed to break free, I saved as many as I could—but I was too late for most of them.'

'And Sarah?'

'She tried to escape. I had orders to bring her in alive, if possible. She pulled a weapon.' I can still see her face, the hatred in her eyes replacing what I thought had been love. 'I didn't hesitate. One shot.'

Avery is silent for a long moment. I wait as she processes.

Finally, she speaks. 'You did what you had to do. You said it yourself; you never killed anyone who didn't deserve it.'

Relief floods my bloodstream.

We're going to get through this—all of it. No matter how fucked up it is.

'Sebastian was right about one thing,' I say, finally meeting her eyes. 'Those deaths are on me. I trusted the wrong person. I let my guard down, and innocents paid the price.'

'It wasn't your fault. She used you. Played you. Abused your trust. Is that why you built those walls?' she places her hand on my chest, directly over my heart. 'Why you kept everyone at a distance?'

'Partly. Deep down, after everything, I thought I didn't deserve to be happy. Or to forget.'

'Until me.'

'Until you.' I reach up to touch her face, half-expecting her to pull away. She doesn't. 'I swore I'd never make that mistake again. Never trust, never feel, never let anyone close enough to matter. Then you crashed into my life with your bubbly, extrovert ways, demanding my attention. I didn't want to let you in, but I didn't stand a chance.'

'Your past doesn't scare me. Not now I understand.'

'It should,' I murmur.

'Maybe. But it doesn't.' She pulls back just enough to meet my eyes. 'For what it's worth, I would have made the same choice.'

For the first time since Mali, the weight I've carried feels lighter. Not gone—it will never be gone completely—but bearable. Shared.

A ghost of a smile touches her lips. 'I've said it before, and I'll say it again; you *are* a good man, Killian. Let's leave the horrors of the past where they belong so we can concentrate on a future.'

'I want to but...'

'But what?'

'I'm terrified,' I admit.

'Of what?'

'Of losing you. Of fucking this up.'

Her free hand comes up to cover mine against her cheek. 'You won't. I only met your parents briefly earlier, but I glimpsed why you're so set on the whole marriage and big family thing. Life is short. Unless it's spent in close proximity with Psycho Sebastian.'

I growl. I'm going to find out what his worst nightmare is and make him relive it over and over again, the way I had to relive mine—him taking the woman I loved while I could only sit there and watch.

'Life *is* short.' I agree.

'I told you once before, the most reckless thing we can do is waste it.'

Despite everything—the fear, the rage, the guilt—hope flares in my chest. My lips curve into a smile. 'Does that mean you're going to wear my ring?'

'One day.' She leans forward, resting her forehead against mine. 'As long as it's embarrassingly big and beautiful. But not yet. I need a little time. I promise I won't take too long.'

I pull her gently into my arms, careful of the bruises forming on her wrists, the slight redness on her neck. She comes willingly, fitting against me where she belongs.

'You wanted a memorable Christmas.' I shake my head in disbelief at the sheer madness of the day.

'Next year, I want a memorably different one please.' She snuggles in closer.

We sit in silence as the lighthouse fills with the subdued sounds of my team securing the scene. Tomorrow there will be a hundred loose ends to tie up. But for now, in this moment, there is only this. Avery safe in my arms. The walls I built crumbling to dust. And the unexpected discovery that I can't control everything, but maybe I don't have to.

Maybe that sick fuck was right about one thing. *Plans change but destiny doesn't.*

I never believed in destiny before, but Avery's too fucking perfect for me not to be mine.

'Take me home,' she whispers against my shoulder.

I press my lips to her hair. 'With pleasure.'

Chapter Forty-Six

AVERY

Two months later.

The ELEGANCE magazine sits on Killian's kitchen counter—my kitchen counter now, I suppose, since I officially sold my house earlier this month. The glossy cover stares back at me, my own face looking more elegant and sophisticated than I ever thought possible. 'Beauty and Brains: The Model Breaking All the Rules.'

No seductive lingerie on display.

No suggestive pose.

Just me in a perfectly tailored cream suit, staring directly into the camera with an unwavering elegance (pun intended). That particular edition sold more copies than any other ever published, which is why they offered me a regular feature that utilises my psychology doctorate—"Mind & Style," a monthly column exploring the cognitive and emotional connections between identity, appearance, and confidence.

The column examines everything from the psychological impact of power dressing to the neuroscience behind retail therapy, giving readers substance beneath the glossy surface. My first piece on the psychology of transformative dressing—

how changing our outward appearance can genuinely alter our internal mindset—apparently resonated with women who'd been told for years that caring about fashion was somehow shallow or frivolous.

Turns out having a legitimately educated voice explaining why self-presentation matters on a psychological level makes people feel less guilty about splurging on that designer bag they've been eyeing. Who knew?

For next month's issue, I'm crafting a thoughtful exploration examining how women's sexual autonomy and desire can be acknowledged as natural aspects of human experience rather than subjects of societal judgment or shame. The piece aims to deconstruct lingering puritanical attitudes that disproportionately stigmatise women's sexual expression while advocating for a more balanced discourse that recognises sexual wellness as an integral component of overall well-being, regardless of gender. I've found my niche. The balance between fashion, femininity and doing something meaningful —and I am in my element.

'Still staring at it?' Killian's arms slide around my waist from behind, his chin resting on my shoulder. 'It's been a week. I think the words have probably remained the same.'

'Shut up.' I lean back into his solid, muscular warmth. 'I'm allowed to take a few minutes to be proud.'

'You are.' He presses his lips to the spot just below my ear. 'I'm proud of you too.'

The Killian Beckett who now shares his coffee, his bed, and his life with me is almost unrecognisable from the rigid, controlled man I first met. He still does perimeter checks before bed. Still keeps his gun within reach. Still wakes occasionally in the night, reaching for me as if to confirm I haven't been taken from him again. But the walls that once surrounded him have crumbled, replaced by a quiet certainty that makes my heart ache in the best possible way.

'Did you see the email that came in from Mandy this morning?' I ask, nodding toward my laptop. 'She hasn't given up on the idea of getting both of us on the cover of ELEGANCE yet.'

'Hmm.' His arms tighten slightly. 'Still looking to wear those white dresses you were so keen on last year?'

'Maybe.'

'That's the only way you'll get me on the cover of that magazine. So you just let me know when you're ready.' His dark eyes gleam. He's made no secret of the fact he wants to spend the rest of his life with me, but unlike my deranged stepbrother, he's leaving the details of if and when to me. Must be hard for a control freak like him, but still he manages to rein it, even though I'm sure it's killing him inside.

'Are you serious?'

'Am I ever not serious?'

True.

Looks like Mandy will be getting her exposure before the year is out. Marriage always seemed like a risk that wasn't worth taking—not after witnessing my parents' collapse. Yet lately, I find myself yearning to take the vows I once doubted, increasingly certain this love is worth the leap.

Who knew my moody, broody billionaire bodyguard would turn out to be the man of my dreams? And I plan on making those dreams—both his and mine—a reality very soon.

My heart stutters. 'Are you asking me to marry you while I'm wearing your t-shirt and bed hair?'

His lips quirk into that smile that still makes my stomach flip. 'Absolutely not. When I propose, you'll know it.' He steps closer, tugging me against him. 'I'm just gathering intelligence.'

'Is that what the security experts call it?' I wind my arms around his neck.

'Strategic reconnaissance,' he confirms, his eyes darkening as his hands slip under my—his—t-shirt.

As his lips find mine, I can't help but marvel at how we got here. From reluctant protector and unwilling protectee to this—a love that survived a stalker, family secrets, and enough emotional baggage to fill the cargo hold of a 747. We haven't been to therapy, but we talk openly about all that happened to us, at the light house and long before.

The magazine on the counter represents more than just a career milestone. It's tangible proof that life continues, evolves, improves, even after trauma. That sometimes the worst moments lead to the best ones.

Killian finally drags his lips from mine. 'Let's go back to bed.' The domesticity of these moments still catches me off guard sometimes. The notorious Killian Beckett, wearing low-slung grey sweatpants and nothing else, making me coffee in our kitchen on a Sunday morning.

Jasper slinks in and circles Killian's ankles. 'Furry fucking cockblock,' he tuts affectionately. These days he doesn't even pretend to dislike him. He scoops him up against his broad bare chest and my ovaries explode.

'Have you decided what to do about your father's invitation?' he asks, scratching Jasper's head before placing him down on the floor again.

The question brings a familiar knot of tension. My father and Tessa have been trying to rebuild their lives since Christmas. They call more regularly, invite me to dinner, make tentative efforts to reconnect. It's complicated by the fact that Tessa's son—my stepbrother—now resides in a high-security psychiatric facility outside Dublin. Killian wanted to torture him. Confining a mind like Sebastian's is crueller than any physical pain, or any prison sentence could have been. The worst punishment for a man of his intelligence is to be trapped not just physically, but intellectually. Killing him would have been a mercy.

'Not yet.' I take a sip of coffee, buying time. 'Part of me wants to go, but...'

'But you're not ready.'

'Is that terrible?'

Killian shakes his head. 'I'm sure they understand.'

Sebastian doesn't understand, according to the doctors. The official diagnosis was Erotomania coupled with Narcissistic Personality Disorder—a particularly dangerous combination. The man who stalked me for years, who left black lilies as tokens of his twisted affection, who drugged his own mother and nearly killed my father, now spends his days in a supervised ward, writing me letters I've asked not to receive.

'Where did you go?' Killian asks softly, tapping my forehead.

'Nowhere important.' I force myself back to the present. 'Now, are we going back to bed, or are you going to take me on the island, where anyone could walk in?'

'Which would you prefer?'

'What do you think? You're the one who calls me reckless.'

He hoists me up on to the counter and I squeal as my ass lands on the cold composite.

Everything else is forgotten. This is what healing really looks like—for both of us. Not the absence of scars, but the presence of joy despite them.

EPILOGUE
Killian

Four months later...

From my vantage point on the mezzanine of Caelon's new flagship hotel, I have a perfect view of Dublin's elite as they mingle beneath crystal chandeliers and gold leaf ceilings. Beckett's Bliss Dublin is officially the most expensive hotel ever built in Ireland—five hundred million euros of luxury that my brother insisted was 'an investment in the future.' Looking at the crowd fighting to be seen here tonight, perhaps he was right.

The grand ballroom glitters with wealth and privilege. Women draped in couture and diamonds, men in bespoke tuxedos trying to look like they're not impressed by the thirty-foot waterfall feature cascading down black marble. A five-piece acoustic band with soulful vocals occupies the elevated stage at the far end of the ballroom, their contemporary pop covers elegantly understated yet powerful enough to fill the vast space without overwhelming conversation.

Paparazzi line the red carpet outside, desperate for a glimpse of the Becketts and their illustrious guests. If they so much as think about taking an inappropriate photo of Avery, they'll end up like the last man who did.

'All clear on the south entrance,' Thomson's voice comes through my earpiece. Fully recovered from his Christmas ordeal, he's back to his efficient, interfering self. He persistently asks when Avery and I are going to tie the knot.

My answer?

The second she's ready.

'Copy that,' I respond automatically, my eyes finding Sterling across the room. He gives me a subtle nod. Since I allowed him to invest in Beckett Security last month, he's taken even more ownership of these events, which gives me more free time to spend with the woman I love, and finally put a smile on his sullen face.

My attention shifts to my family scattered throughout the crowd. Caelon stands proudly by the main entrance with Ivy, her gold gown draped elegantly over her baby bump. Beside them, James has his arm protectively around Scarlett, who looks radiant carrying their third child. My mother moves gracefully between guests, her hair swept into an elegant chignon, while my father watches her with the same admiration he's shown for forty years.

But it's Avery who holds my attention, as always. Some things will never change. In a backless black gown that hugs every curve, diamonds at her throat and wrist—including the Cartier watch, which she never takes off—she outshines every woman in the room. Not just because of the dress or the jewels, but because of the confidence she carries. The magazine column, the wedding dress shoots she finally secured, the charity foundation she's established for victims of stalking—she's become a force entirely her own.

I watch as she laughs with her mother, who's brought her latest boy toy—a Spanish artist fifteen years her junior, but still the longest relationship she's maintained since Avery's father abandoned them. The Spanish artist is besotted with her, following her around like an eager puppy. His background checks came back clean thankfully, or he'd be somewhere in the Wicklow mountains already.

'You're doing that thing again,' Rian remarks, appearing at my side with two whiskeys.

'What thing?' I accept the drink, not taking my eyes off Avery.

'That thing where you drool over Avery and stare at her like she's the centre of the universe.' He smirks.

'She's the centre of *my* universe.'

His eyebrows skyrocket at my blatant admission. 'What happened to my cold, emotionless brother?'

'He fell in love.' I shrug, unembarrassed. 'Speaking of which, who's your target tonight?'

Rian's gaze drifts to a blonde actress by the bar. 'She's in town filming some historical drama. Thought I might show her some real Dublin drama, starting with the inside of my pants.'

'You ever think about settling down?'

'I've thought about it.' A wistful look mists his eyes.

His remark from Christmas stuck in my mind. *All the good ones are taken.*

He downs his whiskey before disappearing back into the crowd.

I scan the room again out of habit; cataloguing exits, security personnel, potential issues. All clear, yet something nags at me.

Sean.

He's not here yet. It's not like him to be late. Especially not for a family event of this magnitude. I'm about to check in with his security detail when Avery appears beside me, sliding her slim arms around my waist.

'Stop working,' she chides gently. 'The world won't implode if you take a night off.'

'Force of habit.' I kiss her temple, breathing in the scent of her peony perfume.

The band starts a new song, its familiar chord emblazoned on to my heart, a cover of James Arthur's 'Say You Won't Let Go', the first song Avery and I ever danced to. We glance at each other, the memory bouncing between us. 'This has got to be our wedding song,' she sighs, leaning into me. 'Better buck up with that ring so I can start planning.'

'I have the ring. I'm just waiting for confirmation you're ready.' I keep my tone light, but we both know how much it means to me.

Her eyes meet mine with the directness that first captivated me. 'I'm ready.'

I cradle her face in my hands. 'Better late than never.'

Laughter bursts from her mouth. 'But make it good, Beckett. I only plan on being proposed to once, so it needs to be epic.'

'Epic.' I repeat. I'm going to need Thomson's interference after all, the romantic bastard that he is.

'And I want the best photographer in Dublin to capture every second of it.'

'You want that micro penis sporting weirdo to photograph me proposing to you?'

'No, but I want a proper engagement shoot afterwards.'

It's a battle to not roll my eyes. 'Is there any other option?'

She twists her lips coyly, 'Well, there is one I suppose.'

'What is it?' Truthfully, it doesn't matter, because months later, I still can't say no to her. She'll get whatever she wants, because the only thing I want is for her to be happy.

'Remember Mandy suggesting you could be involved in an

article for ELEGANCE? I know they'd love to do a feature on us together.'

I sigh in resignation. 'Fine.'

'Yay! I love you so much,' she says, her tone earnest, her eyes softening.

'And I love you.' My lips catch hers and for a second, the entire world fades to nothing.

She pulls away all too soon. 'You're ruining my lingerie.'

'Let's get out of here so you can show me.'

A sudden hush falls over the crowd near the entrance. I look up, instantly alert, to see my brother Sean standing in the doorway.

And he's not alone.

'Holy shit,' Avery whispers beside me. 'That's—'

'Princess Layla Sinclair, third daughter of the King of England.' And she's hanging off my brother's arm in a way that would suggest they know each other–intimately.

In a deep red gown, she looks utterly regal. But it's the way she looks at my quiet, intensely private brother that catches my attention. Like he's her entire world.

'She hasn't been seen in months!'

'I guess now we know why.'

'Did you know about this?' Avery squeals, gripping my arm.

'Nope.'

The crowd parts as Sean guides the princess through the ballroom. My parents' faces are a study in shock. Caelon nearly drops his champagne. Even James looks stunned, which takes some doing. Rian is back to grinning like a madman.

Avery turns to me, her eyes as wide as dinner plates. 'A fucking princess, Killian. An actual royal princess. And not any princess—my favourite royal out of the whole damn lot.'

She shakes her head in disbelief. 'How did Sean even...? It's always the quiet ones, isn't it?'

'You thought I was quiet once,' I remind her, enjoying her expression.

'Yes, and you turned out to be a filthy depraved nympho.' She nudges my torso.

'Says the woman who just admitted to ruining her lingerie,' I remind her, smoothing my hand over the curve of her ass as I watch Sean and the princess, noting the subtle security detail that surrounds them, and the way my brother's hand never leaves the small of her back.

'There's a story there,' I murmur into Avery's ear.

'Damn right there is.' She grins and rubs her hands together. 'And I, for one, can't wait to hear it. Let's go introduce ourselves.'

As the night unfolds around us, I hold Avery against me, finally at peace with my past and unexpectedly eager for our future. Whatever it holds, we'll face it together.

Some men spend their lives building walls. I spent mine constructing the perfect fortress—until a blue-eyed blonde with a smart mouth and a stubborn streak found her way in and taught me that the real strength isn't in the walls we build, but in knowing when to tear them down.

THE END...

Not ready to say goodbye to Killian & Avery? Click here for a bonus epilogue ⬇️

https://dl.bookfunnel.com/hhwz57shc8

. . .

The Beckett Brothers Series continues with Sean and Layla's super-sexy BDSM romance... click here to preorder REVEAL ME

And here's a sneak peek of the blurb...

REVEAL ME
LAYLA:

My life is a prison of protocols and paparazzi—an occupational hazard of being a princess of England.

When I publicly refuse the "perfectly suitable" – and painfully boring match my parents are pushing on me, I'm banished to our family's remote Irish estate until I come to my senses...

Unfortunately for my pearl-clutching mother, I'm exposed to a whole different type of senses when I accidentally stumble upon Reveal, Ireland's most exclusive "club"...and straight into the hands of its darkly devastating owner...

Our meet-cute is far from a fairytale.

But it allows me to live out my darkest fantasies.

When duty calls, will I have the strength to walk away...

or the courage to defy a crown?

SEAN:

I've kept my secret life hidden for years—so well that even my brothers have no clue who I really am. And I intend to keep it that way... until one mistake with a masked princess threatens everything I've built in the shadows.

She knows my name.

She knows my family.

And now, she's blackmailing me for access to my club.

I should despise her for it. But watching her surrender to me is a decadence I can't resist.

She's playing a dangerous game.

But I'm the one with everything to lose now she has the power to reveal me...

🩶BDSM Club
 🩶Billionaire Dom MMC
 🩶Royal FMC
 🩶Forbidden Romance
 🩶Blush-inducing steam
 🩶Standalone with interlinking characters from a wider series

ALSO BY L A GALLAGHER

WRECK ME

SCARLETT:

Pole dancing at the most exclusive 'Gentlemen's Club' in the country is lucrative, though the men are anything but gentle. They're all desperate to take the only significant possession I have—my virginity.

I've spent five years hiding in plain sight, burying my head in my books, courtesy of a scholarship at Dublin's most prestigious college. But now, for the first time in my life, I feel seen. Wanted. Desired. And I've awakened a need I never knew I had.

Enter James Beckett, a billionaire bachelor with a reputation as famous as his family's whiskey empire, and he wants *me* to be his fake girlfriend until he conquers the next part of his empire.

He'll even tutor me through my final exams... and anything else I require tuition in...

Our arrangement will either secure my future, or shatter my world...

JAMES:

Yet another sex scandal means I'm heartbeat away from being fired as CEO from my own family's whiskey distillery, unless I can prove to my father and The Board that I've shed my playboy reputation.

The last thing I want is a showpiece society wife.

Especially when I'm obsessed with The Luxor Lounge's newest pole dancer.

At only twenty-three, Scarlett radiates an innocence that drives me wild. Turns out, my little dancer is a virgin.

Fooling around with my fake girlfriend was *always* part of my plan.

Falling for her *wasn't*.

She's everything I crave, but everything my father forbids.

Even if I can convince him that Scarlett is the one for me, she's been keeping a secret.

One that could wreck me...

Get WRECK ME here...

REDEEM ME

IVY:

I'm the queen of handling tiny tyrants—I've been nannying since the era of bedtime bribery. But there's no guidebook for living with Dublin's most notorious grump and widower—my brother's brooding best friend.

Mr. Tall, Dark, and Tortured isn't just a challenge; he's a full-blown occupational hazard.

Under his icy shell, a fierce fire burns. Every fleeting touch ignites an attraction so intense it's impossible to fight.

He's broken.

And I'm compelled to fix him.

But who will fix me afterward?

Because if my brother discovers our forbidden fling, it won't just be fireworks—it'll be an inferno the size of hell.

And that's before Caelon's shadowy past comes bulldozing back into our lives...

CAELON:

I live for two things: my kids and a relentless pursuit of revenge for the love of my life.

Tragically, I'm failing at both.

Then Ivy Winters, my best friend's sassy little sister, blazes into my world in search of a job and a fresh start. And while she's babysitting my children, I'm stuck with a promise to her brother to keep an eye on her.

But Ivy defies my rules.

Challenges me at every turn.

And somehow, she manages to ignite a spark that threatens to melt the ice surrounding my heart.

But just as I start to see the possibility of a life beyond my pain, the past comes knocking, demanding its due.

Now, I'm faced with the ultimate choice: revenge or redemption...

🩶 Brother's best friend

🩶 Single dad trope

🩶 Forbidden romance

🩶 She's the nanny

🩶 Grumpy/sunshine

🩶 Forced proximity

🩶 Billionaire possessive hero

🩶 Dating the boss

🩶 Opposites attract

🩶 Touch her and d*e vibes

🩶 Blush-inducing steam

🩶 10 year age gap

🩶 Set in Dublin

Get it here... REDEEM ME

REVEAL ME

LAYLA:

My life is a prison of protocols and paparazzi—an occupational hazard of being a princess of England.

When I publicly refuse the "perfectly suitable" – and painfully boring match my parents are pushing on me, I'm banished to our family's remote Irish estate until I come to my senses...

Unfortunately for my pearl-clutching mother, I'm exposed to a whole different type of senses when I accidentally stumble upon Reveal, Ireland's most exclusive "club"...and straight into the hands of its darkly devastating owner...

Our meet-cute is far from a fairytale.

But it allows me to live out my darkest fantasies.

When duty calls, will I have the strength to walk away...

or the courage to defy a crown?

SEAN:

I've kept my secret life hidden for years—so well that even my brothers have no clue who I really am. And I intend to keep it that way... until one mistake with a masked princess threatens everything I've built in the shadows.

She knows my name.

She knows my family.

And now, she's blackmailing me for access to my club.

I should despise her for it. But watching her surrender to me is a decadence I can't resist.

She's playing a dangerous game.

But I'm the one with everything to lose now she has the power to reveal me...

💚BDSM Club

💚Billionaire Dom MMC

🤍Royal FMC

🤍Forbidden Romance

🤍Blush-inducing steam

🤍Standalone with interlinking characters from a wider series

Click here to learn more... REVEAL ME

RELEASE ME

RIAN:

What's worse than falling for my best friend's sister?

Falling for his wife...

One deep, stolen conversation at their engagement party, and my heart was ripped from my chest.

Years of craving. Aching. Burning.

I've lost myself in hundreds of women trying to forget her, but every time I close my eyes, it's her face that haunts my darkest fantasies.

Now she's in my club every weekend, her husband's latest betrayal written all over her face.

Watching my best friend destroy the only woman I've ever loved is a special kind of torture.

I'm running out of reasons to keep my distance...

But taking what I want could start a war—and fighting an enemy is one thing, but betraying my best friend is another...

REBEKKA:

I married the devil's prodigy to save my family's business—but my husband's true talents lie in sabotaging everything he touches—including me.

When he flaunts his latest conquest through his best friend's club, it's the final straw.

I'm done playing the perfect corporate wife.

Done playing by the rules.

Done fighting the heat in Rian Beckett's eyes each time they devour me.

My body aches for his touch, and there's only so much pain I can take.

It was supposed to be a fling.

But somehow, Rian became my everything.

Which is terrifying because no matter what I do, or where I go... my husband will never release me...

💟 Best friend's wife

💟 Forbidden romance

💟 Billionaire playboy

💟 Reverse age gap

💟 Pining

💟 Forced proximity

💟 Who did this to you?

💟 Touch her and d*e vibes

💟 Blush-inducing steam

Learn more here.... **RELEASE ME**

LA Gallagher also writes super hot steamy romance under Lyndsey Gallagher... be sure to check out:

Falling For The Rockstar At Christmas

THE COLDEST HOLIDAY OF THE YEAR IS ABOUT TO GET BLISTERINGLY HOT...

SASHA

Ten years ago, I inherited our family castle and sole care of my youngest sister. More Cinderella, than Sleeping Beauty, at the mere age of twenty-eight I have a teenager to raise and a hotel to run. If the hotel is to survive past Christmas, I need a lottery win, a miracle, or Prince Charming himself to sweep in with a humongous... wad of cash.

When my super successful middle sister announces she's coming home for the holiday season, I'm determined to put my problems aside and make this the most fabulous Christmas ever. Especially as it might just be the last one in our family home.

I didn't factor in the return of my first love, Ryan Cooper. Back then he was the boy next door. Now, he's a world famous singer/song writer. We were supposed to go the States together. He left without me. Now he's back. Rumour is he has writers block. Apparently this is a last-ditch attempt to find inspiration before his record label pulls the plug permanently.

And guess where he wants to stay? You have it in one- the most inspiring castle hotel in Dublin's fair city.

Every woman in the city wants to pull this Hollywood Christmas cracker. Except me.I'm going to avoid him at all costs.

Easier said than done when he's parading around under my roof, with enough heat exuding from his molten eyes to melt every square inch of snow from the peaks of the Dublin mountains...

Falling For The Rock Star At Christmas is an OPEN DOOR steamy, love conquers all, stand alone romance, with no cliff hanger- and a guaranteed happy ever after.

Get FALLING FOR THE ROCKSTAR AT CHRISTMAS here...

Falling For My Forbidden Fling

WHAT GOES ON TOUR STAYS ON TOUR, RIGHT?

CHLOE

Even the name **Jayden Cooper** sends a hot flush of irritation through my veins. His rockstar brother might be about to marry my darling sister, but that does *NOT* make us family.

Thankfully, there's a continent separating me from his ridiculously attractive but super-smug face. And his arrogant tongue.

I'm rapidly carving my name in the glittering world of celebrity event management... and what better event to manage than the final farewell tour of my sister's fiancé, Ryan Cooper.

It's the biggest gig of my career.

Eight cities.

Eight concerts.

Eight opportunities to propel my business to a global level.

I couldn't turn it down if I wanted to.

The catch?

It involves working with closely with Ryan's agent- his brother, Jayden-Super-Smug-Cooper.

Going on tour with Jayden is almost as inconvenient as the hate-fuelled lust that steals the air straight from my lungs every time he's near.

Someone somewhere is testing me, but I've survived worse. And I'll survive him.

As long as I don't melt under the intensity of his smug but admittedly smouldering stare ...or fall foul of the talents of the aforementioned arrogant tongue...

Especially when technically...like it or not, we're about to be related.

JAYDEN

I've been through hell to get to where I am today.

I'm *the* best agent in Hollywood's cut-throat industry because I clawed and dragged myself there inch by excruciating inch.

Which is why I refuse to be bossed around by a pushy, Prada-wearing princess when it comes to organising my Rockstar brother's farewell tour. I've got bigger fish to fry, starting with upholding a promise I made a lifetime ago...

But Chloe is about to find out the hard way, what goes on tour stays on tour.

Get FALLING FOR MY FORBIDDEN FLING here...

Falling For My Bodyguard

I'M TRYING TO PROTECT HER. SHE'S TRYING TO KILL ME- ONE INDECENT LITTLE BLACK DRESS AT A TIME.

VICTORIA

As a student doctor, I deal with bullet wounds on a regular basis, but one teeny nightclub shooting is all it takes for my sister and her rock star husband to send me a new bodyguard/ babysitter.

The last person I expect to turn up is Archie "can't-bear-to-look-you-in-the-eye" Mason.

Now we're roommates until graduation. I can't turn around without tripping over him. If only I could trip underneath him. Because he is every bit as alluring as he was five years ago. And equally as unavailable.

But when my night terrors result in us sharing the same bed, our situation sparks a brand new danger.

One that could hurt both of us irreparably...

ARCHIE

I've been *obsessed* with Victoria Sexton for years.

If my boss and friend, Ryan Cooper, had any idea how bad I have it for his wife's little sister, he'd sack me on the spot.

Living with her is testing every inch of willpower I possess.

How can I watch her back when I can't stop imagining her on it?

Falling For My Bodyguard

DATING IN THE DEEP END

Savannah:

When He-Who-Has-Never-Been-Named knocked me up and ceremoniously knocked me down with the revelation, "I'm actually married," I fled back to Dublin. There, I dusted off my big girl (maternity) pants and launched my blog, chronicling my life as "Single Sav."

Fast forward six years, and I've built a lucrative empire on that premise, which is precisely why I haven't so much as looked at the opposite sex for over half a decade.

Well, apart from slyly perving on my twin daughters' swimming coach, Ronan Rivers, a former Olympic gold medalist.

The man is ridiculously easy on the eyes. He's also a complete manwh*re who lives to torment me with his filthy mouth and decadent innuendos.

When Coral Chic, Ireland's hottest new swimwear brand, offers me a million euros to represent their new swimwear range, it's impossible to turn down. Becoming the face and body of that campaign has the potential to take my Single Sav brand global.

But there's one tiny problem... I can't swim and the photo shoots are in the sea.

When Ronan offers to give me a crash course in the deep end, the only thing I'm drowning in is his mesmerising baby blues.

I've built my entire brand on being single.

The one man who can save me is also the same man who can sink me...

Ronan:

I've been obsessed with Savannah Kingsley since she crashed into my Aston Martin two years ago, but Single Sav is the one woman I can never have.

Which is precisely why I spend Saturday mornings tormenting her with my tongue, and Saturday nights wishing I could tease her with it, instead of embarking on yet another meaningless, lackluster liaison.

When fate forces us together in the form of one-to-one swimming lessons, her skimpy yellow bikini betrays the extent of her body's baser needs and no amount of water can dampen the sizzling attraction between us.

But while she's floundering in the shallows, I'm already in deep.

Can I turn the tide and persuade her to shed her single status?

Click here for Dating In The Deep End

Dating In The Deep End: A hot, single parent romcom! (Dating In Dublin)

DATING THE DELINQUENT

Being with a bad boy never felt so good...

Ashley:

I've always played by the book. As the principal of a prestigious all-girls Catholic school, my life is as orderly as the plaid on my students' skirts. My future was perfectly planned—until a humiliating public proposal ended my decade-long relationship.

It turns out, playing it safe was the riskiest move of all...

Now it's time to let loose.

Which is precisely why I've decided to swap my notions of a ring for an orgasm-fueled fling...

Enter Damien, my younger, intoxicatingly handsome new mechanic. With his rough, oil-covered hands and dirty mouth, he's the perfect distraction—to the point he's ALL I can think about.

Our nights together are explosive, but the days we spend together are what could truly burn my future to the ground.

Because it turns out, Damien is even badder than I could have ever imagined...and it's not just my heart that's on the line—it's my entire world.

It's time to choose between my good girl reputation and the bad boy who's hijacked my heart...

Damien:

Falling for a saint was never in the cards for this sinner...

Life's taught me that sometimes you have to take the fall to protect what's important. I paid a price in the shadows for reasons only I know. Now, I keep to myself, avoiding complications—until Ashley walks into my garage with an overheating motor and an urgent pressure issue—in her panties...

She's everything I'm not—polished, composed, and completely out of my league. But her eyes tell me she's looking for an escape, and I'm reckless enough to offer her one.

But with each day that passes, the weight of my past grows heavier, threatening to pull us both under.

She thinks I'm just a bad boy, but if she knew the truth, it could unravel everything.

Now, I'm faced with the hardest choice: keep hiding the darkness within or let it come to light, risking the only connection that feels real...

My Book

Dating The Delinquent: A hot reverse-age-gap, opposites-attract romance. (Dating In Dublin)

DATING FOR DECEMBER

Ava:

My perpetually single status hardly serves as a shining advertisement for HeartSync, the dating agency I own. Nor is it likely to convince my incredibly successful movie star brother, Nate, to invest in my business. Which is precisely why I agree to fake-date Cillian "can't-crack-a-smile" Callaghan for the month of December.

Sure, his role as a stoically single father and a notoriously grumpy divorce lawyer is far from ideal, but his silver eyes, sculptured shoulders and sharp tongue tick all the right boxes.

Even boxes that are supposed to remain, ahem, unticked...

One mistletoe kiss sparks a lust that could melt Lapland, and frosty fake dates blaze into something feverishly real...

Cillian:

I'm the country's most successful divorce lawyer. It doesn't take a genius to figure out why I don't date. Add in the fact that I'm a full-time single dad, even if I had the inclination, I don't have the time. But when my cheating ex blows back into town, the only way I can convince her it's over for good is by fake-dating someone else...

Enter Ava Jackson, with her infectious laugh, long legs, and luscious lips.

Throughout December, her witty one-liners and effortless bond with my daughter thaw my every defence.

She's everything I never knew I needed.

I'm an expert at breakups... but perhaps this Christmas, it's time to master a love that lasts...

Click here for Dating For December

ABOUT THE AUTHOR

L A Gallagher writes swoon-worth contemporary romance featuring billionaire bad-boys, blush-inducing steam, and copious amounts of glamour. She lives in the west of Ireland with her own book boyfriend (that accent–swoon!), two crazy kids, and an even crazier fur baby.

Come hang out at her Facebook reader group Lyndsey's Book Lushes to find out more! https://www.facebook.com/groups/530398645913222

Or check out her Lyndsey Gallagher books here...
https://www.amazon.com/Kindle-Store-Lyndsey-Gallagher/s?rh=n%3A133140011%2Cp_27%3ALyndsey+Gallagher

ACKNOWLEDGMENTS

Thank you so much for reading Ruin Me. Without you, dear readers, I wouldn't be able to dream up walking red flags and call it work! I'm beyond grateful to all of you that read my words. I hope you enjoyed Killian & Avery's story as much as I enjoyed writing it.

I need to say a massive thank you to my beta readers. I really appreciate you!! 🤍 And to my exceptionally patient friend and helper, Lona McCombie!

Thanks to all the lovely members of my Facebook reader group, *Lyndsey's Book Lushes*. I appreciate your friendship and support, and I love our daily check-ins, the inappropriate memes, and just hanging out with you all.

If you'd like to hang out with us too, we'd love to have you. https://www.facebook.com/groups/530398645913222

A massive thank you to my bookish besties, Sara Madderson and Margaret Amatt. I don't know what I'd do without both of you.

Last but not least, thank you to my endlessly patient husband who listens to my ideas, supports my dreams, and helps with my research! 😉

If you enjoyed Ruin Me, please consider leaving review on Amazon, Goodreads & Book Bub.

Printed in Great Britain
by Amazon